"I care ab...
You...

He'd always cared, but she didn't know *that*. These past few weeks, that old passion of his had been rejuvenated. He'd dared to dream that she might return some of his feelings. She seemed to enjoy his company. And he didn't think he'd imagined the sexual energy between them all evening. Not judging by the conspiratorial wink he'd gotten from a friend as he was going out the door.

Perhaps Miranda's feelings for him just weren't strong enough yet....

No, that really wasn't the problem. She was still holding on. To Chad. To the losses of her past. And he had no idea how to make her let go.

"Warren, you're not upset with me, are you?"

"Absolutely not." He wasn't going to push her. That would be the dumbest mistake he could make. "I don't want you to think I planned for anything to happen between us. Though I won't deny I hoped it would...."

She hugged him. "You're a wonderful guy, Warren. I'm going to be very jealous when some lucky woman captures your heart and I've lost you forever."

Dear Reader,

Several years ago, when I wrote A *Daughter's Place*, I knew I would one day write more books set in the mostly fictional town of Chatsworth, Saskatchewan. And indeed, when I decided I wanted to tell the story of a woman who just can't get over the first guy she fell in love with—a guy who married another woman, and is *still* married to that woman—Chatsworth seemed the perfect setting.

It is the kind of place where it's hard to keep a secret. Your neighbors always know, and if they don't, they *think* they know. You can't hide your past in a place like Chatsworth. People remember which kid was the brain, the athlete, the loner, which girl was most popular and which high school sweethearts were destined to stay together.

Of course, people grow after high school. They change. And that's what has happened to the class of 1990. As circumstances conspire to bring five of the original eleven graduating students together, they'll have an opportunity to examine who they really are...and whom they really love.

Hope you enjoy the story and that you are able to spend your Christmas with the ones you love.

Happy holidays!

C.J. *Carmichael*

P.S. I'd love to hear from you. Please send mail to the following Canadian address: #1754 - 246 Stewart Green S.W., Calgary, Alberta, T3H 3C8, Canada. Or e-mail me at cj@cjcarmichael.com.

Together by Christmas
C.J. Carmichael

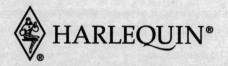

HARLEQUIN®

TORONTO • NEW YORK • LONDON
AMSTERDAM • PARIS • SYDNEY • HAMBURG
STOCKHOLM • ATHENS • TOKYO • MILAN • MADRID
PRAGUE • WARSAW • BUDAPEST • AUCKLAND

ISBN 0-373-71095-X

TOGETHER BY CHRISTMAS

This edition published by arrangement with Harlequin Books S.A.

® and TM are trademarks of the publisher. Trademarks indicated with ® are registered in the United States Patent and Trademark Office, the Canadian Trade Marks Office and in other countries.

Visit us at www.eHarlequin.com

Printed in U.S.A.

CHAPTER ONE

MIRANDA JAMES PUSHED aside the wicker basket of crusty rolls at the center of the table and replaced it with her high school yearbook, open to the page with photos of her graduating class.

"I knew you wouldn't believe me. But we really did go to school together. Grades one through twelve. See?" She pointed to Warren's picture first, then her own.

Catherine Cox, producer at the Canadian Broadcasting Corporation, peered through dark-framed glasses at the caption beneath the photo. "'Warren Addison,'" she read, squinting at the small print. "'Favorite subject: anything to do with books. Nickname: Warty.'"

She shifted her attention to Miranda. "Warty? Warren Addison had warts?"

"No. A pet frog in grade eight." Miranda tapped her pen against the saltshaker, impatient to move on. But Catherine was scrutinizing the yearbook again, holding it close to the window, where the light was better.

"Trust you to be gorgeous even in high school. Let's see what they wrote about you...."

"Oh, no, you don't." Miranda reached for the book, but Catherine shifted it just beyond her grasp.

"'Miranda James,'" she began, quoting the couplet beneath the photo, "'Most beautiful and the boys' favorite pick. If she wasn't so nice, she'd make us sick.'"

"Give that here!"

Catherine relinquished the book, laughing. The husky sound caught the attention of two men lunching at a nearby table. Their glances flickered over Catherine and settled on Miranda.

"Okay, you went to school with Warren Addison," Catherine conceded. "But what makes you think he'll be onside for a video biography? I've spoken to the publicist at his publishing house and he's notoriously uncooperative when it comes to promoting his own work. Everyone but *him* is talking about *Where It Began.* He wouldn't even return Oprah's call when she asked him to appear on her show."

"We grew up together, Catherine. I heard him read the first story he ever wrote to the class."

Well, she probably had, she just couldn't remember.

"Don't worry about me not being able to deliver," she continued. "The challenge will be editing all the material down to a reasonable length."

Catherine opened her briefcase. "I suppose if anyone can do this, it's you. Here. I had Accounting cut you a check."

Thrilled, Miranda accepted the check before Catherine could change her mind. None of her other projects had ever been accepted this easily.

"I'd love to chat longer, but I have another meeting." Catherine laid a fifty on the table to cover lunch. "Would you mind saving a copy of the bill for me? I need to run, but there's no reason you shouldn't stay and enjoy dessert and coffee."

"Thanks, Catherine." *For everything,* she wanted to add. But the svelte producer was already hustling out of the restaurant. The two men at the next table noticed her departure, too. One of them tried to catch Miranda's eye, but she gazed deliberately down at the yearbook still in her hands.

"Can I get you anything else?" The server was back, whisking away the used wineglasses and salad plates.

"Mmm..." She glanced up from the yearbook. "An espresso, please?"

"Certainly."

She hadn't looked at this book for years... probably not since her mother, in one of her housecleaning frenzies, had boxed it with a collection of other childhood mementos and shipped it to Toronto. She flipped through the glossy pages, finally returning to the photos of the 1990 graduation class.

A sweet ache lodged behind her ribs. She recognized the feeling as nostalgia, but cynically, she had to wonder. Did she yearn for what had been? Or for what never could be?

She focused on the picture of Chad English. With his smooth blond hair, tanned skin and even features he didn't need his killer smile to stand out from the crowd. Still, he had it. As well as eyes born to flirt. She felt he was watching her from the yearbook page, about to include her in a fabulous secret.

Ah, Chad.

If she'd been the most popular girl in that small-town class of eleven students, he'd definitely been the most popular guy. Was she the only one who had seen them as the perfect couple? It seemed she'd dated just about all the guys in her grade and the one above it at one time or another. Except Chad. And Warren, of course, but he didn't count, because as far as she knew, he'd never asked *any* of the girls out.

Maybe he was gay. Mentally filing the idea for future consideration, she refocused on Chad.

Why had he never asked her out? She'd always wondered. They'd been good friends since grade seven—still were good friends. But while he'd flirted plenty, he'd never taken their relationship that one crucial step further.

Of course, after his marriage to Bernie, Miranda had filed her feelings for him away as inappropriate. They'd continued their friendship, but she'd been cautious not to overstep the bounds of appro-priateness.

Despite her circumspection, she knew Bernie didn't like her. Actually, the other woman never had. Miranda picked out the photo of the petite girl with the light brown hair. Cute, bordering on pretty, but not a woman to turn a man's head. Yet she'd turned Chad's, when Miranda never had.

Oh, don't start feeling sorry for yourself. This is ancient history.... The person she was *supposed* to be interested in right now had had nothing to do with all of that.

She studied Warren's photo again. His dark hair was unruly, curling around his ears and down to his collar. In his long, thin face, his nose stood out prominently.

A different emotion stirred inside her now. Uncomfortable, unsettling. Warren had always had that effect, she remembered.

He hadn't been an attractive kid. Especially compared with... Miranda's gaze slid to Chad's photo, then back to Warren's. His recent success couldn't help but have an impact on her assessment. Those dark-gray eyes she'd once found disconcerting now gleamed with intelligence and wit. The smile she'd thought of as crooked sported an ironic twist.

She stared a few minutes longer, but the photograph refused to yield anything more. She snapped the book shut and returned it to her briefcase, frustrated that of all her classmates, Warren was the one she'd known the least.

"Your espresso, miss."

She smiled her thanks to the unobtrusive server before taking a sip.

Yes, Warren had been the most enigmatic of her classmates, and yet, he would be the subject of her next video biography. The check from the CBC, which she now carefully stowed in a zipper compartment of her purse, made it official, even though the idea had come to her only a week ago, during her Sunday phone call to her mother.

Annie James, who still lived in the small town in Saskatchewan where Miranda had grown up, had asked, "You remember Warren Addison?"

"Sure I do, Mom."

"He's back in Chatsworth. They say that book he wrote is a real blockbuster. They say there's a producer who wants to make it into a movie."

"I know. *Where It Began* is topping the bestseller lists all over North America." She'd read the novel and loved it, found it absolutely magical.

"Well, he's living on his parents' farm, in that old clapboard the Addisons abandoned when they retired to Victoria."

According to the dust jacket of his book—which, frustratingly, had included no photo of the author— Warren had a master's in English from the University of Toronto and now resided and worked in New York City. That he would choose to return to a backwater prairie town remained incomprehensible to Miranda.

"Whatever for?"

"Lucky says he's working on his second book. The press wouldn't give him any peace in New York."

Good old Lucky. The gray-haired proprietor of Chatsworth's tiny grocery store could always be counted on to hand out more than change and a receipt at the till.

After the call ended, Miranda had thought over her mother's news. Between projects at the moment, she'd been on the hunt for a challenge. And this struck her as the perfect opportunity. She could do a video biography on Warren Addison *and* spend some time with her mother.

Annie hadn't been the same since a heart attack last June. The specialist in Regina had diagnosed only minimal damage, but the scare had raised a specter of worry in the fifty-eight-year-old and had caused her to curtail her lifestyle as well as to revamp her diet.

Miranda was guiltily aware that she hadn't seen her mother since that week in Regina when Annie had undergone a battery of medical tests. She'd known her mother was waiting for an invitation to Toronto, but she'd been afraid that Annie might end up staying permanently, and so she'd stalled.

Miranda traveling to Chatsworth, rather than Annie visiting Toronto, was definitely safer.

Mind made up to pursue this project, Miranda had begun her research. Typing ''Warren Addison Author'' into the Internet had yielded no official Web site. Likewise, the library had had little biographical information.

Which was perfect, from Miranda's point of view. Apparently Warren was as much of an unknown to his fans as he was to her. A situation she fully intended to rectify.

Now, sipping her espresso, Miranda basked in anticipation of her upcoming project.

Of course, Warren could turn out to be a boring man with no layers to explore. Having read his book, however, she doubted that. What a wonderful coup for her career if she could reveal this man's creative heart and soul to the world.

But what if Warren didn't cooperate with her?

She pushed that uncertainty aside. They'd grown up together in the same small town. Of course he would.

A separate, larger anxiety gnawed at her. She hadn't spent much time in Chatsworth since high school graduation. What would it be like? Chad and Bernie still lived in the small town. So did Adrienne Jenson, who'd also been in their class. Counting Warren and herself, that made five of the original eleven graduating students.

It would feel like stepping back in time. Not that such a thing was possible, of course. But if it was...

Miranda set down her empty cup. Cramming the receipt into her purse for Catherine, she once again ignored the smiles and raised eyebrows from the men at the table beside her as she strode through the busy restaurant.

Outside, a gust of wind whipped her skirt against her calves. She glanced up at the little section of sky that peeked out amid Toronto's skyscrapers and saw rain clouds.

Unbidden, it came back to her—the way it had felt to be eighteen and in love with someone who didn't love her back. The old longing hit her, a heavy weight in her chest.

The pattern of her life had been set during those years in Chatsworth. And the choices she'd made then had led her to this point: working in Toronto, living alone, pursuing happiness while trying to pretend to everyone around her that she'd already found it.

What if she *could* change the past?

For a moment she could smell chalk dust and musty old textbooks in the swirling city air. She was in math class and Warren Addison was sitting in the aisle next to hers. A loner, he'd rarely spoken in class. But when he had—here it was, her first distinct memory of him—he hadn't bothered to raise his hand first.

The teachers had never let the rest of them get away with that. But they had him. Funny thing for her to remember.

The wind died and the rain started. Holding her briefcase over her head, Miranda beckoned to a passing cab. She had to get home. Had to start packing.

FROM THE METROPOLIS of Toronto, Ontario, Miranda had to travel west, more than twelve hundred miles, to reach Chatsworth, Saskatchewan. The sleepy prairie town lay just past the Manitoba border. The drive, through stark November landscape, promised to be long and exhausting, but Miranda couldn't fly because she would definitely need her car once she arrived.

She set out on Wednesday with a suitcase of clothes, a bag of gifts she'd purchased early for Christmas and her equipment: a Canon XL1, extra lenses, wireless microphones, tripod, her portable Mac for editing.

Hopefully, she hadn't forgotten anything, because if she had, she'd have to drive an extra two and a half hours southwest to Regina for replacements. Chatsworth's isolation was one of the main reasons—other than her mother's prodding for her to become a model or actress—that Miranda had left. Indeed, many of the young people raised there relocated after graduation. Now the prospect of spending two months in the small community brought on a claustrophobic anxiety she tried to ignore.

Her mother was waiting supper when she arrived at her destination on Friday night after several long days behind the wheel.

"You made it! I've been so worried. The weather reports say it's snowing in Winnipeg." Lovely as ever in a hand-knit sweater and stretch black jeans, Annie James offered her daughter a fragile hug and a peck on the cheek.

"Must have been after I passed through. I saw a few wispy clouds, but that was it." She lugged her bags down the hall. "Same room?" she asked over her shoulder.

"Of course."

"Same room" being a shrine to white French-provincial furniture, the best you could order from the Sears catalog. At least her mother had removed the canopy. Cleaning that thing year after year must have been hell.

Miranda settled her bags at the foot of the bed, then put her purse on the dresser, next to the phone her parents had given her for her thirteenth birthday. How many hours had she spent on that thing? Mostly talking to Chad....

She went to the washroom, and when she emerged, Annie was removing her green-bean casserole from the oven.

"You haven't cooked this big meal for just the two of us?" A lentil casserole sat steaming on the table, next to the beans, a green salad and cauliflower.

"This is a special occasion. I even made brownies for dessert—low fat, unfortunately, thanks to my diet."

"Sticking to it, are you? That's great." They discussed Annie's health for a while, then moved on to Miranda's work. Annie wasn't very interested in the video on the Canadian artist Harry Palmer, which Miranda had just finished collaborating on with his son and the CBC. But Annie did have some input to offer on the upcoming project.

"You realize Warren's book is going to be made into a movie?"

"You mentioned the possibility on the phone."

"Well, I've been wondering. There might be a role for you." Her mother's eyes sparkled. "After we spoke, I took the book out of the library and read it.

I could see you in the lead, playing Olena. You're the right age and the description is you to a tee!''

"Oh, Mom." Annie had never recovered from her disappointment when Miranda dropped modeling to study film at Concordia University in Montreal. While she'd accepted that Miranda was now too old for modeling, she frequently reminded her daughter it wasn't too late for acting. In her opinion, her beautiful daughter belonged in front of a camera, not behind it.

"What's the matter?"

"I talked to Warren's agent about the film rights. Yes, they've been sold, but the screenplay hasn't even been written yet. Warren insists that he wants to do it himself, and first he has to finish his current book."

"All the better. You need to get your name in early. Just mention the idea to Warren when you interview him for that video of yours."

"I have no acting experience."

"You've taken several classes. And you did that commercial."

"Right." She ought to command about a million for a picture, based on those qualifications.

Her mother smiled, assuming that one word meant Miranda had agreed with everything she'd just said.

"So when are you planning to meet with Warren?"

"Tomorrow. You'll have to help me figure out how to get to his farm." Miranda had only an idea of the general direction.

"I'll draw you a map. It's not that hard, but it is far. About twelve miles from town, and at least two miles from the closest neighbors, the Brownings. Frankly, I can't understand why any sane person with a choice would want to live on his own in such an isolated place.

"In fact," Annie continued, "I'm not at all sure you should be going out to his farm to conduct your interviews. Couldn't he drive into town?"

Miranda dug deep for patience. Something she suspected she was going to need a lot of this next little while.

"Mom, this video isn't something I can accomplish in a couple of short interviews. I need to hang around him, see how he lives, how he works."

Discovering what made Warren Addison tick would take time. But she had two months, and she'd succeed. The completed video would be her Christmas present to herself.

Vegetables were silently passed back and forth; Miranda topped up her mother's wine from one of the bottles she'd stashed in the trunk of her Volkswagen.

"The Brownings had a baby boy last year," Annie said finally. "Did I tell you?"

"Yes." Miranda was glad for Gibson and Libby. They both had daughters from previous relationships. According to Chad, they wouldn't necessarily stop at three, either.

"I don't suppose you've heard about poor Chad and Bernie English."

The piece of cauliflower in her mouth suddenly felt like a cork stuck in her throat. Miranda coughed, reached for her wineglass.

"Are you okay?"

Miranda waved a hand dismissively. "What about Chad and Bernie?"

"Oh, it's just terrible. His poor mother is so upset. You know Dorothy belongs to my bridge group."

"Mother. What happened?"

"Why, Bernie booted Chad out of the house." Annie James looked as if Miranda was a little slow not to have figured this out on her own. "After Dorothy left last Wednesday, one of the ladies said she'd heard Chad had been cheating on Bernie."

"Cheating?"

"No one knows who the woman is. At least not yet. I'm sure the truth will come out eventually."

Miranda set down her fork, trying to absorb this news. Something major must have happened for Bernie to have kicked out Chad. But an affair? The very idea made Miranda sick. She could only imagine how much worse Bernie would feel.

And how could any of this be true? She'd e-mailed Chad the night before she'd left Toronto and had had a reply from him the following morning.

He hadn't mentioned a word about any troubles with Bernie. Her mother had to have gotten this wrong. The bridge ladies must have been doing too much raising and doubling—and not with cards, either.

"That's very hard to believe, Mom. Bernie and Chad have been married for *years*."

"You think that's any guarantee?" Her mother's tone was sharp as she glanced at the sideboard, where they'd once kept their only family photograph.

"I suppose not. But—" *Bernie and Chad?* "Where's he staying, then?"

"Chad? Not at his mother's—you can be sure of that. Dorothy is furious with him."

"But Chad is her son." And she'd always doted on him over his two older sisters.

"Dorothy's granddaughter's well-being is at stake here, too," Annie reminded her.

"Yes, of course. But if Chad isn't staying with his mother…"

"He's shacked up at the clubhouse on his golf course. According to Dorothy, he was spending most of his time there, anyway. Probably that's where he and this other woman have their rendezvous…."

Miranda held back the temptation to roll her eyes at her mother's leap in logic.

"He's a grown man, Mom. Besides, do you have any proof that he's been unfaithful?"

"Proof? This isn't a court case, Miranda."

Just as she'd thought. The rumors were baseless. If anything untoward was going on, Miranda would have picked it up in her regular e-mails with Chad, or heard something different in his voice during their more occasional phone calls.

Her mother raised her wineglass with a flourish. "My dear, you've been doing biographies long enough now. You should have a better grasp of human nature. When marriages break up for no apparent reason, you can be sure one of the parties has a replacement waiting in the wings.''

For a moment Miranda felt a flicker of doubt. But this was *Chad* they were talking about. ''Yes, often... But I'm sure there are times when a couple realize their marriage was just not meant to be.''

''*Meant to be?* Dear, I had no idea you were so romantic. Perhaps that's why you're still single. If you're waiting for Mr. Perfect—''

Miranda began to clear the dishes from the table. ''Your idea of my perfect match would be a movie director. He'd cast me in his next film and we'd move to Los Angeles and I'd buy you a big house with a pool and a maid.''

''Please don't tease, Miranda. It isn't very funny.''

Annie was right on that score. Miranda let the topic drop. ''Why don't we get the dishes done, then have your brownies in the living room.''

''Would you prefer tea or coffee, dear?''

Knowing how weak Annie made her coffee, Miranda chose tea. What she really wanted, of course, was to find Chad and ask him about the rumors from her mother's bridge club. That Chad's own mother had been present should have been validation enough, she supposed.

But she wouldn't believe a word of it until she'd heard the news directly from Chad.

CHAPTER TWO

WITH TEMPERATURES SETTLED well below zero and a hazy light reflecting off the sprinkling of snow that dusted the harvested fields, Miranda set out for the Addison farm the next morning, following the directions her mother had written out for her over breakfast.

Already the air between the two of them was a little clouded. And they hadn't been under the same roof for twenty-four hours yet. Maybe staying at home wasn't such a good idea after all, but she couldn't see any choice. Annie would be mortified if she moved to a friend's, or the local hotel.

Miranda turned her car onto the graveled road leading north of Chatsworth. Her cute yellow Volkswagen Beetle jostled on the dried ruts, and the tires crunched over the exposed gravel. So far, not much snow had fallen, and the roads were dry. Miranda dreaded dealing with this route after a heavy snowfall. Especially in her little car. Something with allwheel drive would definitely be better.

But for now—once she got used to the bouncing—she had to admit that driving here was certainly less stressful than negotiating Toronto's freeways. She turned on the radio, but paid no attention to the Bach cello concerto playing.

She was thinking of Chad. So far she hadn't managed to get in touch with him. She'd tried calling the golf course this morning, but no one had answered. She hadn't left a message, since she couldn't be sure who would retrieve it and she didn't want anyone drawing the wrong conclusion from her call. As her mother would say, people would talk. And for once, Miranda saw the benefits of being circumspect.

That didn't stop her from worrying. Why hadn't he told her about his problems with Bernie? If others were surmising, like the ladies in her mother's bridge club, that somehow Chad was responsible for the breakup, then Chad was probably feeling pretty lonesome about now.

Unless there really was another woman…?

No, no, no. That couldn't be it….

A mailbox caught her eye. She was here. Thoughts of Chad vanished as Miranda contemplated the barely standing box at the side of the road—left over from the days when mail had been delivered rather than picked up at a post office box in town. Stenciled in fading black paint was the name "Addison." She glanced down the long lane. The road curved gently to the right, then disappeared in a second curve to the left. A stand of poplars, naked without their leaves, huddled on either side of the dirt road. They'd provided enough cover, however, to preserve a thin dusting of snow.

Later in the season this private access would be unpassable unless Warren had it plowed. Oh, well, she could always leave her car on the main road.

Optimistic thoughts for someone who hasn't even talked Warren into the project yet, she reminded herself. She'd decided early on her chances of success were highest with a face-to-face meeting. Unfortunately, she hadn't developed her strategy beyond that. Now she felt edgy and nervous. She'd put up such a brave front for others. And she'd deposited Catherine's check. No way could she fail now that she was here.

She nosed her vehicle along the lane. Her initial glimpse of the Addison farmhouse wasn't reassuring. The old two-story clapboard desperately needed paint. The utilitarian structure sat unconnected to the surrounding land. No cozy porch or veranda. No flower gardens or shrub borders.

A truck parked by the front door and wisps of smoke drifting from the chimney indicated Warren was home. He must have heard her drive up, but so far he hadn't made an appearance.

Realizing she was working herself into a genuine case of nerves, Miranda turned off the ignition and jumped out of her car. She couldn't stand around or she'd lose her courage entirely. Avoiding the front door, which was boarded shut, she went round to the back, where she opened the screen to knock on the wooden door.

Just at the moment her knuckles were about to

connect with the wood, the door gave way and she found herself staring at a plaid shirt. Lifting her gaze, she saw a face she never would have recognized—masculine, compelling, mature. No trace of the yearbook boy remained.

Except those eyes. And that funny, twisting smile.

"Warren?"

WARREN ADDISON FELT THE COLD wind blasting in and therefore knew he wasn't hallucinating. But the improbability of the sight stole his words for several long, awkward seconds. Finally, he regained articulation.

"Miranda James."

God, but she was still so beautiful. Her blond hair was short, bluntly cut and curly. It framed her exquisite face perfectly. She stood taller than he remembered, slim in her boyish jeans, her upper body bundled into a fleece jacket, with a down vest over top.

"None other," she agreed cheerfully. "Um, mind if I come in? I may track in a little snow, but other than that my boots are clean. I bought them before I came here—never needed snow boots like this in Toronto—we don't get much snow there. Slush falls from the sky directly."

Her words overwhelmed him. He hadn't heard so many in weeks. At last a basic meaning penetrated. "I'm sorry. Of course, come in." He took a few backward steps to make room. "And don't worry about snow—or slush, for that matter. As you'll soon see, I don't fuss much about things like that.''

But the place wasn't *dirty,* he reassured himself, trying to imagine how the old farm kitchen must look in her eyes. At least he wasn't one to stack dishes between meals or leave food out on the counters. He couldn't. The mice would make an all-night diner of the place.

"Is that a wood-burning stove?"

"Yeah. Mom wouldn't part with it. We do have running water and electricity, however."

He'd meant it as a joke, but she nodded seriously.

"Oh, and an *espresso* machine!"

"A city comfort I couldn't imagine doing without. Would you like a cup?"

"Oh, would I." She brushed the snow off her boots, then sat in one of the wooden kitchen chairs. "Did you bring any other goodies from New York with you?"

"A bag of bagels, frozen in the fridge. I'd offer you one, but I have no microwave." He shrugged in apology. "Other than that, I packed a few changes of clothing, my books and my computer, of course."

He measured beans for grinding, still not able to believe that the gorgeous Miranda James was sitting in his kitchen. If she knew how often he'd fantasized about her when they were teenagers...

But hell. That didn't make him different from any of the other guys who'd gone to Chatsworth High.

"I've seen some of your biographies on TV," he told her. Actually, *all* of them. "I especially enjoyed the one on prairie musicians. Jack Semple has always been a favorite of mine.''

''Wow, you've seen my stuff? In New York?''

''Well, I do get cable.'' He noticed her glancing around. ''Not here, though. Mom and Dad took the TV with them to Victoria.''

''What do you *do* with yourself? Isn't it awfully lonely?''

''I spend a lot of time walking around the property. And I read, play Age of Empires on the computer....'' He placed a small pitcher under the espresso spout, then turned on the motor. ''And of course I write.''

''Do you ever. Warren, I read your book. Frankly, I was blown away. You deserve all your success.''

He shrugged. Talking about *Where It Began* was difficult. He was glad, naturally, that the book had done so well. But success had definitely come at a cost.

''You know, back in Toronto, I checked the Internet *and* the library. I found very little material about you. Not even a photograph.''

Her eyes ran over him, marking the changes, he supposed. Foolishly, he hoped she liked what she saw. He sure liked what he saw. But then, he always had.

''Sugar?'' he asked, passing her the froth-covered cup.

''No, thanks.'' She hooked the handle with her finger, and as she raised the mug to her mouth he noticed her fragile wrist, with its jangle of silver bracelets.

"I came here to escape notoriety," he said, referring to the lack of information about him.

"Well, you've done a good job."

"So far," he acknowledged. "But what about you? Why are you in Chatsworth?" And more particularly, here with him? Not that he didn't welcome her company, but face it—twenty years ago she wouldn't have crossed the school yard to speak to him, let alone driven twelve miles of backcountry roads.

No, that wasn't altogether fair. Miranda had never been a snob. She always gave the impression that she liked *everyone,* that she would be your very best friend, if only she had more time.

And it wasn't an act. After twelve years in the same classroom, he'd have sensed it. Miranda was one of those rare people born without an ounce of meanness, or spite, or cruelty. Not that she'd been a goody-goody. Miranda knew, had always known, how to have fun.

That she wasn't already married was a miracle. Unless there'd been some late developments in that area…no, she had rings on many of her fingers—and even on one thumb—but nothing adorned that all-important fourth finger of the left hand.

"Actually, Warren, I'm here because of *you.*"

He felt a crazy, scary rhythm in his heart, absent since adolescence. Then reality set in. She didn't mean *that* way. He pulled in a breath of air as he took his own espresso to the table and settled himself, too aware of her quiet observation.

And then it hit him. God, he was such an idiot. She filmed biographies for a living. That comment about the paltry information available about him. Of course. That had to be it.

He couldn't believe how disappointed he felt. Dreamy Miranda wasn't here to see Warren Addison, her old schoolmate, but Warren Addison, the famous author.

Crap.

"You don't look pleased. I'm guessing you don't want to be the subject of my next video."

"I think my books should stand on their own. Who I am, and whether I write in the night or in the morning, whether I work from an outline or just create, shouldn't figure into the equation."

"But isn't it human nature to wonder about the author of a book you've loved? When Mrs. MacIntire read us *Huckleberry Finn,* weren't you curious about Samuel Clemens?"

"Mark Twain was a literary icon. I've written one book."

"Warren, your book will oversell the Harry Potter books. A movie's in the works...."

"But we're still talking only one novel. And who knows how the next one will be received. If I ever finish writing it..."

"Trust me, Warren. All artists worry that their next work may not be as good as their last—even us lowly video biographers. So you aren't alone in that.

Even if you never publish another story, the success of *Where It Began* will make you immortal. Think of Margaret Mitchell. And Harper Lee.''

''I appreciate your faith. But selling lots of copies doesn't guarantee anyone will remember who I am twenty years from now.''

''Yes, but your reviews...''

''Reviewers can be flawed, too.''

''Oh, Warren!''

She laughed, and the clear, musical sound made his heart feel strange again. Her presence in the large kitchen was clear and bright, like a vase of yellow daffodils on the table. He had to admit it would be wonderful to have her around while she worked on that video. But would the cost to his soul be worth the benefit?

''I need quiet to write. That's why I'm here. If you did that video, my cover would be shot.''

''Warren, persistent journalists will find you eventually. It's not like where you grew up is a secret.''

''Miranda, surely you've got better prospects.''

''Not a one.'' Miranda leaned over the table and grasped his hand. Her cool, silky touch was unlike any woman's he'd ever known.

''I'll be as unobtrusive as possible. I'll work around your schedule. Warren, I can be very flexible.''

Oh, he just bet she could. With that slender, willowy body...

''Hell, Miranda. Has anyone ever been able to say no to you?''

CHAPTER THREE

ACTUALLY, TWO PEOPLE had said no to her, Miranda reflected, on the drive back to Chatsworth. Her mother had honed that talent to an art long ago. The other—well, he hadn't truly said no. He'd just never said yes.

Chad. She'd promised her mom she'd pick up a few groceries for dinner tonight, but after that she was going to drive to the golf course to see him. She simply couldn't wait any longer. If anyone asked, she'd say she was inquiring about cross-country ski lessons.

Too bad there wasn't much snow.

There would be soon, though. On her car radio, after Beethoven's "Hammerklavier" piano sonata had concluded, had come storm warnings for the southeastern corner of Saskatchewan. Heavy snowfalls and driving winds were expected within hours. Already a few flakes were falling from the gray, depthless sky.

It had taken only the hour she'd spent at Warren's for the weather to change. Now she wondered what the roads would be like tomorrow when she drove out again to begin work on the video. She dismissed the faint worry. One thing Saskatchewan had lots of was snowplows.

She picked up her cell and dialed Catherine with the good news that Warren had agreed to work with her on the video. After leaving a message, she thought about Warren. He hadn't exactly brimmed over with enthusiasm for the project. She couldn't take his cooperation for granted. She'd have to tread cautiously.

But at least she'd received a chance. Something she was very relieved about, because after meeting Warren again, her enthusiasm for doing his biography had increased exponentially.

Physically, he'd changed so much from his youth. He could have matured into a skinny, prematurely balding man who wore cardigans and smoked American cigarettes—didn't most novelists smoke?

But she'd smelled no trace of tobacco in his house and observed no ashtrays or matches. His dark, unruly hair was still thick and he'd grown into his strong facial features. As for his physique, while he remained lanky, his height had been balanced by a broadening of his shoulders. He still wasn't handsome, but maturity had definitely given him an edge. She'd bet money the camera would love his face. And sex appeal was never something to ignore in the TV business.

She liked the way he moved, too, and was eager to capture that masculine grace with her camera. She'd enjoyed watching him operate the espresso machine. His long, slender fingers were so fluid she'd immediately imagined filming him at the keyboard. Smiling, she tapped her fingers against the steering wheel. Working on Warren was going to be such divine fun.

As for the possibility he was gay… No. Definitely not. She couldn't pinpoint the reason for her certainty. She just knew. Not that he'd flirted or acted attracted to her at all. In fact, it might have been nice if he'd done either, just a little. Still, there'd been something in his eyes when he'd looked at her. And he'd done a lot of that.

Had Warren dated anyone during their school years? She couldn't remember that he had, but she'd have to make sure. She'd compile a list of people in Chatsworth she should talk to. Not just about his social life, of course, but all sorts of things. How he'd done at school, if he'd participated in any extracurricular activities, and whether anything in his childhood might have affected his destiny to write.

She was already at the road turning into Chatsworth. A quick stop at Lucky's grocery store extended fifteen minutes when she ran into some familiar faces. Back in the car, her bag of groceries on the passenger seat next to her, she headed for Willow Road. The graveled lane provided the only access to the Chatsworth Golf Club. Built when she was a kid, the eighteen-hole course had proved extremely popular. Many of the members traveled from surrounding towns such as Bredenbury and Churchbridge…even Yorkton, twenty-six miles away on the Yellowhead highway.

Years ago, Chad's father had purchased a good chunk of lakefront footage, transformed the surrounding acres of wood and cleared land into a top-quality resort. Besides golf, his club offered clay tennis courts and an outdoor pool in the summer, supplementing the public beach just down the road.

In the winter, they groomed the course for cross-country skiing. This had been Chad's innovation, as well as the idea of adding a minigym so people would have something to do during what was, after all, Saskatchewan's longest season. Since his father's death several years ago, Chad had run the entire operation on his own.

Miranda switched on the wipers. The snowflakes fell faster now, and grew thicker and heavier. She passed through the main gates to the clubhouse. A lone truck sat parked at the front door. She had no idea if it belonged to Chad, but likely it did.

She pulled down the visor, then used the mirror as she reapplied her lipstick. The lip-liner went on crooked and she had to start over. God, she was nervous! How long had it been since she and Chad had actually *seen* each other? Sure, they e-mailed once or twice a week and spoke to each other on the phone every now and then. But neither was the same as a face-to-face meeting.

If he was here. Please let him be here.

Her new boots etched treaded prints all the way

from her car to the double front doors of the club-house. She looked back at them. Already fresh snow had begun to fill them in. It was really dumping now, although she was protected under the overhang from the roof.

She tried the door. It wasn't locked. Knowing Chad slept here, though, she didn't feel right entering without warning. So she knocked, then pushed the door inward a few inches.

"Anybody home?"

At the faraway sound of a male talking, she opened the door farther and stepped inside. She couldn't see Chad. He wasn't at the reception desk, or by the racks of sporting equipment lined up to take advantage of the ill-prepared sportsman. She passed through a doorway to the cafeteria. During the summer, staff prepared casual meals on-site and served from a long buffet that ran along the kitchen wall. Now the only sustenance offered sat in vending machines.

She passed through the room into a short hall. On the right were change rooms; to the left, an office. Chad was just hanging up the telephone. Seeing her, he smiled, revealing a mixture of surprise and pleasure.

"I don't believe it. Miranda James, in person. I wasn't sure whether to take your e-mail seriously."

Chad was always teasing her about being a city girl, too important to waste her time visiting old friends. But Miranda hadn't consciously avoided

Chatsworth. Her mother honestly preferred to fly to Toronto for their visits and avail herself of the city's theater, shopping, fine restaurants.

"I can't quite believe I'm here, either," she admitted.

She found it hard to take her gaze off Chad. Even unshaven, he looked gorgeous. His blond hair had probably only been finger-combed, but it shone clean and bright. His green polo shirt brought out the color of his eyes, and his jeans showed off powerful quads.

"Ah, honey, it's so good to see you." He captured her in a hug that swamped her senses like the snow-storm outside. God, his smell, she remembered his smell. The strength of his arms, the firmness of his chest, though—they were new.

"You've been working out?" She pressed on one bicep.

"I've got the time, don't I?" He let her go to check her out. She tilted her head and dared him to find a flaw. He just grinned. "Gorgeous as ever, hon. Toronto must agree with you."

You agree with me. Just to see him again, hear his voice without the aid of human technology, felt so good.

"How are you, Chad?"

"Oh, fine."

She regarded him steadily, until finally he dropped his gaze.

"You've heard."

"Yes."

He sank onto the sofa across from his desk and she followed, leaving one square cushion between the two of them.

"Shit," he said.

Miranda let him sit quietly for a while, stewing in his obvious unhappiness. Finally she had to ask. "Tell me what happened."

"What's to tell? She kicked me out."

"You're talking about Bernie."

"Yeah, I'm talking about Bernie. My goddamn wife of twelve years. Not that she seems to care how long we've been together or even that we have a daughter and a house and a *life* invested in each other."

"Would you mind backtracking a minute here? I had no idea you and Bernie were having problems. What's been going on?"

"*Nothing's* been going on," Chad said, his words heartfelt. "I don't know what's gotten into her. She never used to be so emotional. She says I'm not giving her enough attention—well, how is kicking me out of the house going to solve that?"

"Oh, Chad…"

"She says I'm spending all my time at work or with my buddies. But she never complained before. It's not as if she doesn't have friends…not to mention the nicest house in town and a luxury car. I've provided *well* for that woman. Last birthday I bought her one of those bracelets with the diamonds all around—"

"A *tennis* bracelet?"

"Yeah, that's what the salesperson called it. But I might as well have bought her a bloody blender for all the points it earned me."

She'd had no idea Chad and Bernie's marriage was so precarious. From occasional comments of Chad's, Miranda had surmised they weren't the closest of couples. But they'd muddled through the years.

On reflection, she wasn't that surprised they'd hit a snag. They'd married out of high school and Bernie had been pregnant at the time. Not the ideal prescription for wedded bliss.

Not that she was one to judge. After all, at thirty-two she still had no experience with marriage.

Glancing around, she noticed an open suitcase by the window. Some dirty dishes on the coffee table. On the floor, beside the sofa, lay a pillow and some blankets.

"So you've been staying here."

"Hey, I have a pullout sofa bed, and a big-screen TV and a vending machine in the main room—all the comforts of home." He managed a smile. A weak one.

She supposed he *could* camp out here as long as necessary. The convenient sofa bed reminded her of the bridge club talk.

"You haven't done anything stupid, have you?"

He took a moment to digest her question, then protested. "Like sleep with someone else? Come on,

Randy. You should know me better than that. 'Course I haven't.''

But he'd probably had opportunities. Women were *always* interested in Chad. He hadn't lost any of the looks or charm that had made him so popular in high school.

"There has to be *something*. Wives don't kick their husbands out for no reason." Another wild thought. "Bernie hasn't found someone else?"

"God, no. I'm telling you, it isn't anything like that—her falling in love with another guy or me crawling into bed with some woman. And don't tell me it could be happening without me knowing, because in a town of five hundred people these things get around."

Miranda believed him. Since about grade seven, when the girls had first starting taking note of the boys, Bernie had been devoted to Chad.

"This is awful, Chad. I wish I could help...."

"Having someone to talk to helps. You've always been that person for me, hey, Randy? Such a good pal. Too bad you and me weren't the ones who fell in love back in grade twelve."

Who says I didn't fall in love with you, Chad?
"Yeah, well, that's probably why we're still such good friends."

"Right."

She reached over to lay a hand on his shoulder, then noticed a framed collage on the wall next to him. The photographs, taken from years ago, included a snapshot of her and Chad on the night of their high school graduation. Not that they'd been dates. No, they'd each gone with someone else. She couldn't remember either of the names at the moment.

On his desk stood more recent photos. One of Bernie, Chad and a cute little girl with a gap-toothed smile. Vicky was almost a teenager now.

"How's your daughter taking this?"

"Oh, she's a real trouper." Chad straightened his back. "Bernie explained the situation to her. Married couples needing a little downtime, stuff like that."

"Is that what this is, Chad? A little downtime?"

"I don't know, Randy. Christ, I don't know." He sniffed, closer to tears than she'd ever seen him. "I don't want my daughter to become another statistic. The victim of a broken home...."

"Surely it won't come to that."

He took a deep breath. Plucked at a loose thread in the cushion that separated them. "Bernie's got me on a schedule. I see Vicky every other weekend, and Wednesdays I pick her up from piano lessons, then take her out for dinner. To the café."

"She's twelve now, right?"

"Yeah, she's grown up fast. Just wait till you see her."

"I *have* seen her. Ten minutes ago at Lucky's. She's lovely, Chad. But what about Bernie? Have you been talking to her?"

"Hardly. Just a minute here and there in passing."

He dropped his head into his hands, and Miranda patted his back sympathetically.

"Have you thought of marriage counseling?"

Incredulous, Chad stiffened and turned to her. "You're kidding, right? Do you know what the guys would say when they found out? Hell, all Vicky's friends would tease her at school...."

"Everyone knows you and Bernie aren't living together, Chad. If you went to counseling, at least they could see that you're trying to work things out. More important, *Bernie* would know you were serious about fixing things."

"But that's just the point. Nothing's broken, so what is there to fix?"

Miranda struggled for patience. "Chad, don't be a fool. You know damn well your marriage is in trouble."

"Okay," he admitted. "But counseling won't help. Bernie's made up her mind."

Miranda felt as if her heart had stopped beating. "She wants a divorce?"

"No..." Chad waved a hand impatiently. "She's got a list of three things she wants changed. She won't let me move back in until I agree to all of them."

"Three things. That doesn't sound too bad. Why don't you just concede the points and go home?"

Chad gave her a half smile, then shrugged. "Randy, one of them is that I have to stop being friends with you."

CHAPTER FOUR

"OUR FRIENDSHIP'S ALWAYS been completely above-board." Miranda jumped up from the sofa. She hadn't realized Bernie was aware she and Chad kept in touch. Not that it had been a secret or anything. She merely found it more convenient to send e-mails and make phone calls to Chad at his office.

"My wife knows that, Randy," Chad assured her. "She's just being unreasonable, trying to keep me on a short leash. But she's always been jealous of you."

The one-sided competition hadn't been fostered by Miranda. Still, she'd been conscious—how could she not be—that Bernie had constantly compared the two of them. Miranda's better marks at school had annoyed her. In sports, Bernie had always aimed to beat Miranda.

The rivalry had been strongest when it came to boys. Miranda hadn't needed to do much to attract their interest. Her mother didn't allow her to date until she was sixteen. Once she'd reached that milestone age, she rarely had a free weekend.

From Bernie's mean-spirited teasing, Miranda had known she was jealous. But Miranda could never understand why. After all, the best guy of the lot, the only one Miranda was truly interested in, belonged to Bernie.

And Bernie had the nerve to be jealous of *her?*

"What do we do, Chad?"

"Nothing. Sit down. Relax." He pulled her to the cushion right next to him. With their thighs touching, he kept hold of one hand. "I shouldn't have said anything. I didn't expect you to be so upset."

She could feel the heat of his leg next to her leg, his fingers cupping hers. The intense sensitivity of her nerves was not, she realized, an appropriate reaction to a man who was married to another woman. The good thing about their long-distance friendship was that she rarely had to worry about how to behave when she was with Chad. Now she eased over—creating space between them. She slipped her hand out of his on the pretext of smoothing out a wrinkle in her jeans.

"I'm not that upset," she said. "Just—surprised."

"We don't have anything to feel guilty about. And I refuse to act like a kid when I'm a grown man. I guess I can pick my own friends. Give in on this, and next thing Bernie will start expecting me to cut out my annual fly-in fishing trip to Pelican Narrows."

"She wouldn't!"

"Oh, sure, you can laugh. Imagine if someone tried to keep you from going to that artsy-fartsy Toronto Film Festival next fall."

"As if."

"So you get my point."

"Yeah, but maybe I'm the wrong one to be talking to about this. I've never been married. I suppose you have to make compromises...." On some things. But surely someone who loved you wouldn't want you to give up those pastimes that meant the most to you...or friends you'd had almost your entire life.

"Chad, what were the other items on Bernie's list?" He'd said there were three.

This time Chad was the one to separate himself from her. He got up from the sofa, went to the window to glance at the snow, then shuffled a few papers around on his desk.

"She wanted me to give up one of my curling nights with the guys and rejoin the mixed league with her."

"How many nights do you curl with the guys?"

"Three right now." He gave a bashful grin. "Not counting bonspiels."

"Well, giving up one of those nights to play with your wife sounds reasonable. What's the last thing?"

Chad turned back to the window, but not before she saw his neck and ears redden. She waited, but he didn't say anything.

"Aren't you going to tell me?"

"Her third request is kind of...personal."

No kidding. Wasn't this entire conversation? But obviously some problems between a husband and wife you didn't feel comfortable discussing even with your best friend.

"Not another woman?"

His back went rigid. "I already told you no."

Yes, he had. But what else could be making him so embarrassed? Something about their sex life? Did Bernie want more? Or less?

Or better?

Hmm… Tempted to tease Chad a little, Miranda just kept her mouth shut. Chad had never liked being made fun of. And over the years Miranda had figured out if there was one subject men were especially sensitive about it was their technique in bed. Politics and religion were safer topics by far.

"I should be heading home. I've got the groceries for supper." And her mother liked to have the meal on the table for six o'clock sharp. As did most of the families in Chatsworth. "Say, do they still ring the town bell at noon and six?"

Chad laughed. "Honey, you *have* been away for a long time, haven't you?"

He walked back over to the sofa, slung an arm around her shoulders and led her to the front door. Miranda was pleased that his mood had lightened. Still, she hesitated to leave him.

"Are you okay out here on your own?"

"Thank you for being concerned. You may be the only person in town who doesn't hate me right now. Even my mother wouldn't let me move back in with her."

"Yeah, I heard. What's going on there?"

"She has this crazy idea that the split is all my fault. Anyway, it's not that bad out here. Especially when I get pretty visitors. How did a hick town like Chatsworth ever produce a glamorous creature like you?" He stepped back and stared at her. Smiled and shook his head.

Her thoughts were still spinning with all he'd told her. "Chad, why didn't you let me know sooner about all this?"

"I kept thinking Bernie would change her mind. I had no idea she could be this stubborn. Randy, I never pictured my life this way. I don't want a divorce."

"Bernie loves you, Chad. I'm sure that's not what she wants, either."

"Well, that's not the way she's acting."

"Maybe not right now. But she'll come round. You'll see." Miranda sought for something to say to cheer him up. "I'll bet the two of you are together again by Christmas."

"Christmas, huh? That's less than two months away."

"Bernie has always loved you. And people who love each other belong together at Christmas."

"Can I hold you to that, Randy?"

"Money-back guarantee."

BERNIE ENGLISH SAT IN the bow-window nook of her beautiful new kitchen, writing in her journal. She'd started it the day she kicked Chad out, and already had about a quarter of the pages filled. She'd hoped it would only take a few nights sleeping on the couch in his office for Chad to come to his senses and realize he couldn't live without her.

But two weeks had passed and she was beginning to fear she'd totally miscalculated. Maybe even played into his hands.

Perhaps Chad had wanted out for a long time now but had been too afraid to tell her. He'd always hated unpleasant scenes. Telling your wife you no longer loved her would certainly count as unpleasant.

Especially if he never had loved her. She'd always wondered about that. If she hadn't been pregnant, would he still have asked her to marry him? Probably not, at least not so young. But as naive as they'd been, they'd been terribly happy, too. At least, she had.

Vicky had been an angel of a baby, and Chad had adored her from the start, even before *she* had. The birth had been hard and long and she'd been so tired. When the nurse tried to put that wrinkled, red child on her chest, she'd said no, thanks. But Chad had held out his hands and cradled the wee thing. As she'd watched him, tenderness had bloomed in her, too.

Bernie grabbed another tissue as her eyes began to water again. Was she going crazy? Sometimes it felt like it. Two weeks ago she'd had everything. A beautiful daughter, a good job, this house, friends...and Chad. Maybe he wasn't perfect, but he slept in her bed every night and that was something, wasn't it? Even after twelve years, it was still something.

The front door slammed and Bernie jumped. Quickly she slipped her journal under the tea towels in a kitchen drawer, swept the pile of sodden tissues into the trash, then went to the sink to splash water over her face.

She needn't have worried about her appearance. Vicky ignored her as she beelined for the fridge. "What's to eat?"

"An apple? A cheese stick? I hope you remembered to put your boots away."

"Great." Vicky ignored the comment about her boots as she dug food from the clear plastic bin. "What else can I eat?"

Wasn't that enough? Apparently not, when you were twelve and growing. "How about some crackers?" Bernie dug out a box of Wheat Thins, dumped them into a small bowl and put them on the table.

"Did you enjoy your sleepover?"

"Sure."

"What time did the two of you fall asleep?"

Vicky shrugged. She was wearing a top Bernie recognized as belonging to Karen. Trading clothes again. The two girls had done makeovers on each other, as well. Vicky's hair, almost white, the way Chad's had been at that age, was pulled off her face with about a dozen pastel clips, and her nails were painted in matching shades of polish. Probably they'd done their faces, too, but Vicky had been smart enough to wash everything off before coming home.

"Say, Mom, guess who we saw at Lucky's this afternoon."

A blizzard had started late this morning, so not likely one of Vicky's out-of-town classmates. Maybe Chad… Bernie picked up the dishcloth and cleaned the sink. "Who?"

"Her name's Miranda James. She says she used to go to school with you and Dad."

Bernie's skin flamed as if it was being scrubbed instead of the stainless-steel faucet. "You were talking to Randy?"

"Yeah, she figured I was your daughter. Said I looked a lot like you."

Here Vicky scowled, undoubtedly annoyed at the resemblance. After a moment she got over it, too impressed with Miranda James to stop talking about her.

"I've never seen anyone that pretty in real life. And she's totally awesome to talk to. Was she that cool when you guys were in school?"

"At least," Bernie said, trying not to sound as if she were choking on a mouthful of sour grapes.

"I love her hair. Should I cut mine short like that?"

She had no idea what Randy's hair looked like, but still resented the idea that Vicky would want to imitate her. "You just finished growing out your bangs," she reminded her.

Vicky pulled at a strand of hair that had escaped the row of clips. "How about if I just got some streaks put in? Miranda does that, even though her hair is naturally blond. It's so funky, Mom, and you should see her clothes. Can I get a black vest? Miranda says they're so versatile everyone should have one."

Miranda says. Bernie bit back on the desire to ask if Randy had mentioned anything about Chad. Putting ideas in Vicky's head wouldn't do, although the kid wasn't blind. If she ever saw Randy and her father together, she'd soon get enough ideas of her own.

"She lives in Toronto, Mom, and makes video biographies for a living. Right now she's doing one on Warren Addison. Isn't that awesome?"

"Totally." Bernie rinsed the soap from the dishcloth. She stared out the window into the bleak winter day. Snow continued to fall relentlessly. At least four inches sat on top of the railing that spanned the back deck.

Chad had built that deck three summers ago. When he'd finished, they'd had a barbecue to celebrate. They'd been happy then, hadn't they? When had everything started falling apart?

"And you should see her car, Mom. It's a yellow punch-buggy."

"What?"

"You know, those cars like the old-fashioned Volkswagen bugs that Dad likes so much."

Great. So the perfect girl with the perfect clothes and the perfect hair also had the perfect car. Judging from the expression on Vicky's face and the excitement in her voice, Randy had won over Bernie's daughter, as well as her husband.

In a moment of cold fear, Bernie realized that if Chad and Randy ended up together, Vicky would probably be thrilled. She might even choose to live with *them* rather than her. Just contemplating the possibility made Bernie's stomach squeeze in on itself.

Oh, God, she was going to start crying again. But she couldn't. Vicky still sat at the table, chowing down on the crackers. She'd already finished the apple and cheese. Vicky was so skinny in her jeans and tight top. Bernie had been that thin once, too. Was that why Chad's interest in her had diminished over the years? Because she'd put on too many pounds?

"Is something wrong, Mom?"

Bernie stiffened. Had Vicky noticed the wetness in her eyes? She had to pull herself together. "I'm fine." She dried her damp hands on a towel. "Why?"

Vicky shrugged. "Just wondering why you hadn't started supper. Can we have pizza?"

"Sure. I have one in the freezer. I'll just warm up the oven—"

Without another word, Vicky slipped out of
the room.

Bernie set the dial on the stove, then retrieved her
journal and sank back into her cushioned chair.

Talk in the staff room at school yesterday was
that Miranda James is in town to do a video
biography on Warren Addison.
  Bull.

In her outrage, Bernie's pen flew across the clean
page she'd just turned to.

Miranda never paid a moment's attention to
Warren when we were kids. It was always Chad
for her. They were best friends, but I knew she
wanted more. It made me proud, knowing that
the sexiest guy in the school preferred me to her.
Blond, beautiful, perfect Miranda could have
had any guy she wanted.
  But not Chad.

Bernie paused to pull a pizza from her freezer. She
removed the wrappings, then set it on the counter,
waiting for the oven to reach four hundred degrees.
Back at her journal, the words continued to flow.

I've never dared think this before—writing
down the words is even scarier. But is it possible Chad has secretly loved Miranda all along?

Why else would he have stayed such close friends with her for so many years?

She knew they communicated regularly by e-mail. On the occasions when she dropped in at the golf course, she usually found an excuse to slip into Chad's office and check his electronic in-box. Almost always she found *something* from Miranda in there. She'd never actually read the messages. Maybe she should have.

What is happening to me? I'm turning into one of those desperate women who would do anything to keep her man. What about my dignity? My self-respect?

Perhaps those qualities were overrated. They'd landed her in this mess in the first place. Spurred by comments from her friend Adrienne, when Chad had marched into the house, late as usual, demanding his supper.

"You shouldn't let him treat you that way," Adrienne had said. It was the first time she'd ever spoken the least bit negatively about Chad. Pressed, however, she'd spewed out more.

"Does he ever take you out, just the two of you? Between work and golf in the summer and work and curling in the winter, you never see him!"

True, and the trend had worsened over the years. Just this fall he'd opted out of the mixed curling league with her so he could play in Yorkton with another group of men.

Bernie loved her sports. Curling and cross-country skiing in the winter, golf in the summer. And she liked playing them with her husband. Having Chad withdraw from the mixed curling league had *hurt.*

''That man needs a wake-up call,'' Adrienne had said.

Problem was, Bernie had called, but Chad hadn't woken up.

And now Randy was in town. Bernie went on writing.

What can I do to protect my marriage? I know she'll be full of sympathy for Chad—and I can guess where *that* will lead. Meanwhile, what about me? Am I supposed to sit back and let her move in on my husband?

No! Of course not. But what were her options? She was the one who'd kicked Chad out of the house. She'd listed three requirements before he could move back in. If she went back on her demands, she'd look like a fool.

She also had no illusions about how she would look next to Randy James. No ordinary woman could compete with *her.*

Of course, I haven't seen Randy in years. Maybe she's gained a pile of weight or aged prematurely.

Not likely when her mother, Annie James, in her late fifties, was *still* the most attractive woman in town.

I won't allow myself to be dragged into a competition. It's ridiculous. I'll hold my head high and act like I couldn't care less about Randy James. No one will guess my true feelings.

Bernie stared at the words on the page. At first reading they sounded good, but now… Well, holding her head high just seemed so awfully passive. She wasn't the type to sit back and wait. Her marriage was in trouble and she had to *do* something.

Chad was *her* husband. That made Miranda James the enemy. This was a war.

And she needed a battle plan.

CHAPTER FIVE

MIRANDA SHOULDN'T have felt nervous driving out to the Addison farm this second time. She'd convinced him, hadn't she? The elusive, reclusive Warren Addison would be the subject of the next Miranda James video biography. And she hadn't even needed to promise her firstborn for the privilege.

So why did she feel like a kid facing university finals—unable to recall a single fact she'd memorized the night before, stomach queasy, palms perspiring.

Everyone thought success came so easily to her. No one in her life had ever guessed just how untrue this was. The things she didn't care about—yes, those came easily. Like those two men at the restaurant when she'd had lunch with Catherine. They'd practically drooled over their plates watching her. But they were strangers. She had no interest in them.

The men she'd really wanted in her life she'd never been able to keep.

And the work she truly loved—filming video biographies—scared her to death half the time. At the beginning of each project she was so afraid of failure. And this time the stakes were even higher than usual.

Everyone in Chatsworth knew what she'd come here to do. What if she did such a lousy job the CBC refused to air the finished project? She'd look like a fool. Everyone would consider her a fraud.

A pretty face and nothing more.

She'd feel more assured if she had more memories from her past to guide her. But no matter how hard she tried, she couldn't picture Warren playing with any of the other kids in their class when they were younger. In the high school years, he hadn't attended any of the parties with her and her friends. As far as she knew, he hadn't dated any of the girls.

Yet he'd never been teased or treated like an outcast. Warren had too much natural dignity about him. She cast her mind back and realized that while she'd never really known him, she'd always kind of admired him. He didn't care what others thought. He spoke his mind without obsessing how people might react to what he said. He had a confidence most adults never attained.

Reflecting on their meeting the other day, she acknowledged that he hadn't lost an ounce of that self-assurance.

The long red barn of a prosperous dairy farm appeared to the right, signaling an upcoming turn. Miranda eased off the gas, glad that the roads had been plowed this morning. Still, a thin layer of packed snow made them treacherously icy.

Three miles after the dairy farm, two more houses came into view, one on either side of the road. A large, shaggy mutt raced out from one spruce-lined driveway. He barked at her frantically as she passed by.

"My car is probably the most exciting thing you've seen all day...hey, boy?"

Saskatchewan was well known for being flat and treeless. In truth, this small corner of the province was neither. Admittedly, the hills were gentle contours at best, and the trees were mostly scrub poplars and willows, but Miranda found the land beautiful nonetheless. It didn't hurt that the sky was clear and blue this morning and that sparkling frost coated every surface from tree branch to fence post. The forecast was for more snow and soon, though right now that seemed highly unlikely.

Before she knew it, Miranda was driving past the turnoff to the Browning and Bateson farms. Since Libby's and Gibson's marriage, the two properties had been run as one operation, with the help of Libby's father.

Miranda didn't know Libby all that well, but she remembered Gibson, all right. He and his best friend, Libby's brother Chris, had dominated the dreams of every girl in school. She had been thrilled when Chris, two years her senior, had asked her out when she was in grade ten. Of course, her mother had nixed those plans. Probably wisely, Miranda had to admit with hindsight. At the time she'd been furious. Chris had been such a hunk. How tragic that he'd died so young in a car crash with his mother....

Half an hour after leaving Chatsworth, Miranda pulled into the Addison lane. Deep snow covered the small stretch of private road. Worried about her car getting stuck, Miranda parked off to the side of the main road and walked in, carrying her camera case in one hand and her duffel bag in the other.

Her new boots squeaked in the fresh snow; the cool breeze bit at her cheeks and the tip of her nose. On foot, she noticed the poplar trees lining the driveway appeared much larger. She could hear a flock of sparrows chattering on the branches of one of them.

She stopped twenty yards from the house and took out her camera. ''A typical Saskatchewan farmhouse,'' she said, recording her voice along with the images. ''Two stories, built from wood. Small, double-hung windows.''

Swinging the camera to the right, she centered first the barns in her viewfinder, then an equipment shed. The paint on all these buildings was in even worse shape than the paint on the house.

She turned off the power to the camera and slipped it back in its case. Smoke filtered out the plain metal chimney of the house. Peeking in one of the double-hung windows, she saw only frost. But Warren had to be in there, working, since no fresh tracks led from out his back door.

Wouldn't it be lovely to sneak inside and get a candid shot of him at his computer?

She didn't dare.

After again bypassing the boarded front entry, she

knocked at the back. Warren had the door open in a flash. He wore jeans and bare feet. He had long toes, she noted, before lifting her head to smile.

"Right on time." He closed out the frosty air with a firm shove on the slightly warped door.

Her professional eye approved the dark turtleneck he was wearing—the style suited his long, narrow face, and the color coordinated perfectly with his hair and thick eyelashes.

"It's nice and warm in here. Smells yummy, too."

"I had oatmeal and cinnamon for breakfast."

No sign of the meal remained in the tidy kitchen. "Were you working?"

"I was."

"Can I see?"

He shrugged. "This way."

She dropped the duffel bag on the worn Arborite table and shrugged her jacket onto a kitchen chair. Warren led her through an arched entry into the next room. Papers covered the polished dining room table. A laptop computer hummed gently in one corner, while a violin concerto played softly from a radio on the matching buffet table against the far wall.

As Warren hung back, Miranda moved in for a closer inspection. The seemingly chaotic piles of papers were actually organized into specific areas of research, chapter outlines, character profiles. On the computer screen were lines of typing, ending with an unfinished sentence. Her arrival had definitely interrupted him.

"Just think." She placed a hand gently on the computer. "This will be a book. Millions of people will read it."

"*If* it gets published."

"How can you doubt that? Your first novel was a phenomenon. Surely your publisher is desperate for the follow-up."

"If by 'follow-up' you mean the next in the series, then you're right. But I never intended *Where It Began* to be part of a trilogy or anything like that."

"Still, you had several unanswered questions at the end."

"The main theme was resolved. As for the dangling threads, I thought they were best left to the reader's conjecture."

"So we'll never find out whether Olena leaves her husband?"

"Whether she leaves or stays isn't really that interesting."

"Only a man could say something like that." Miranda let her fingers trace the keyboard. Warren had crossed his hands over his chest. Defensive about his work? Or just a usual distancing maneuver? "I think it would very much matter to your readers what Olena decides. It matters to *me*."

"Why? Olena and her lover face an all-too-familiar dilemma. End their affair or end their marriages. We've seen both scenarios acted out so many times in real life we know what will happen in either case."

"If you find the situation so commonplace, why write about it in the first place?"

"What interested me was how a moral, intelligent woman like Olena could end up in such a predicament."

"I see. And what about the new book? Does it take place in your fictional town of Runnymeade, too?"

"Yes, but in a later period."

"So there will be no connection to the characters in the first book."

Warren smiled. "I didn't say that."

"Ah, you're trying to torment me, aren't you?" She moved away from the computer, but not before noticing he was on page 467 of his document. "Would you sit down for a moment? Let me get some footage of you at work?" She pulled out her camera.

"I'm sorry, Miranda. I can't pose. I won't."

"But—"

"If you catch me at the computer sometime, I give you permission to film me while I'm writing. But I won't fake it. Not even for you."

Miranda wasn't sure she understood, but she was hardly in a position to argue. She was here on his grace, after all. Eating up time that he'd undoubtedly prefer to spend on his book. Besides, he'd just granted a greater gift than he'd denied. To get a shot of him when he didn't realize she was there would be a marvelous coup.

"Want to go for a walk? It's snowing."

"Already?" She put a hand to the cold window-sill. The morning's blue sky had vanished. The forecast storm had arrived.

"We can stay inside if you'd rather."

"Oh, no. I'm game. Can I bring my camera?"

"I guess I'd better say yes, since it seems permanently affixed to your arm."

Miranda bundled herself back into her outerwear. Warren offered her an extra scarf, then slipped into a thick sheepskin coat and heavy-duty Gore-Tex boots.

"Since I work at a desk, I try to make sure I get my exercise. Don't want to turn into a blob."

Now, that was something she couldn't imagine. Warren had always been thin. She'd noticed, though, he now had a definite muscularity. "You go to the gym, too?"

"When I'm in New York."

He held open the back door and Miranda stepped out into swirling ice crystals.

"What about you, Miranda? What do you do to stay in shape?"

"I like walking, too." Although she preferred graveled trails to plowing through eighteen-inch snowdrifts. She squinted against the driving snow and clutched her camera protectively.

"Here." Warren took her free arm and tucked it next to his body.

He led the way to a path that he'd obviously

walked before. A wooden gate stood open, and they passed through into an open field.

"My parents rent this land to the Hodges now. I believe they grew canola last summer."

Miranda was adjusting to the cold. And to the wind. She didn't mind walking close to Warren, either. It made it easier to hear when he spoke to her.

"Why did you decide to be a writer, Warren?"

"Because that's what I am. I've had other jobs, though. I worked on this farm every summer when I was a boy. If my parents had had their way, I'd still be working here."

"Aren't they proud of what you've accomplished? A bestselling novel and critical acclaim...."

"It doesn't mean that much to them, I'm afraid. Last visit I overheard Mom say to one of her neighbors, 'His marks were always so good he could have been anything. Even a lawyer.'"

Miranda laughed. "You're kidding."

"No, I'm not. It's too bad I was an only child. They might have had more success with other offspring."

"Gosh, don't I know that feeling. My mother has dreams of me on stage or in movies. In her mind I'm the perfect person to play Olena in the film version of your book. By the way, I'm supposed to be angling for an audition."

"Would you like the part?" he surprised her by asking.

"You're speaking hypothetically, of course. The

answer is no. I've never cared for acting—I feel too silly trying to pretend I'm someone other than myself. My mother's sure I failed at being an actress on purpose, to spite her.''

"You need to care about what she wants less. *I* think what you do is fascinating. Present project excluded.''

Compliments rarely flustered Miranda. For some reason, this one did. "Speaking of my present project, did you try any other jobs besides helping out on the farm?''

"I also worked at the potash mine in Esterhazy for a few months. God, that was an experience—clearing out debris from thousands of feet underground.''

Miranda shuddered sympathetically.

"And I've taught. I still do, from time to time.''

He was a frequent guest lecturer. Yes, she'd read that somewhere.

"But I'm most content when I'm writing. Growing up here probably had something to do with it.'' He waved a hand to indicate the white, barren landscape. "With no brothers or sisters or nearby neighbors, I had to rely on my imagination and books for entertainment.''

"No TV?''

"A little.'' He grinned. *"Star Trek.''*

"'Aye, aye, Captain.''' She pulled off a mitten—cold be damned—and turned on her camera. Good, she managed to catch the dancing amusement in his eyes before he looked away.

"Any other early influences? Besides *Star Trek?*" She held her focus on him, relying on his arm to prevent her from stumbling as they continued to walk.

"Tolkien, of course. And the Russians. I especially loved Tolstoy and later, Solzhenitsyn."

"You always had your nose in a book at school."

"I'm surprised you noticed."

Was that a dig? She could see no rancor in his expression and assumed he felt none. "Well, we did share the same classroom from grades one through twelve. I do wish now, though, that I'd been more observant."

"Ah. More fodder for your biography?"

Partly, yes. But also she wondered… "I think we might have been friends. You're so easy to talk to. I didn't expect that at the outset of this project."

He sighed, and she wondered if she'd said the wrong thing. Eager to get the conversation flowing again, she asked another question. "Would you say your childhood was happy?"

He glanced into the camera as if it were an annoying insect. "This is beginning to feel like a therapy session. Were *you* happy as a kid?"

"Yeah. Generally speaking. But the video isn't about me."

"I don't care. I can't handle all these one-sided confessions. Let's make a deal." He stopped and took the camera out of her hand. After a moment, he figured out how to switch it off. Then he passed it back to her.

"What deal?"

"Any question you ask me, I get to turn around on you. If I want."

"That's very sneaky, Warren Addison."

"Did you know all the boys in our class had a crush on you?"

Not true. Chad hadn't. And probably not Warren, either.

"You're exaggerating."

"Maybe a little," he admitted. "But pretty damn close."

"That's ridiculous."

"You're embarrassed." He seemed amused by the discovery.

"We aren't meant to be discussing *my* love life," she pointed out. "Why don't you tell me something about *yours?*"

"What did you want to ask?"

"Is there a woman in your life right now?"

"Right now?" He stared into the distance, then glanced back at her. "No."

"Well, what about the women in your past, then?"

"What about them?"

He wasn't making this easy. "Warren, this is a subject we'll have to cover. Eventually. I'd like to meet some of them, if I could. I'd like to meet with all the people who've been important to you. Have you ever been married?"

"No. Haven't even lived with anyone. I'm a private guy, Miranda."

But there had been women. And some of them had mattered. She knew these things with total certainty, although she couldn't say how.

"Was there ever anyone special? Someone you never managed to forget...?"

Knowing Warren had been a loner, knowing how private he was, she didn't really expect him to answer.

He surprised her, though, when he said slowly, "There was this girl...."

After giving him a few seconds to finish his sentence, she was forced to prod. "What was her name, Warren? Was she in our class?"

With the force of a magnetic attraction, her gaze was drawn to the gray of his eyes.

"Just a girl," he said. "I don't think you ever really knew her."

WARREN REALIZED his answer was evasive. It was also true. At thirty-two Miranda was as oblivious to her extraordinary qualities as she'd been at eighteen. She allowed her obvious natural beauty to define her, even as she tried to discount its value—to herself and to others.

Miranda's kindness, her sense of fun, her intelligence. Those were the qualities that drew her friends. That drew him.

But they didn't totally explain her appeal to the

opposite sex. Since their meeting the other day, he'd given this subject some thought. And he realized that what made Miranda so utterly irresistible was that she just didn't care about the impression she was making. That kind of laid-back attitude was bound to trigger any man's competitive instincts. It had triggered his.

Way back when.

And now.

"What about you, Miranda? Are you seeing anyone right now? Have you ever been married?"

"No and no." She slipped her camera back inside its case. "Why do you refuse to do promotion for your book?"

He sighed. He'd have to add *tenacious* to the list of qualities this woman possessed. Summoning patience, he tried to be brief. "Book signings are difficult. People meet you…they think they know you because they've read your book. But the fact remains that they're strangers."

"Well, what about interviews?"

"I dislike the narcissism. Why should anyone be that interested in me? Also, most journalists are pretty predictable. Interviews get dull after a while."

"Oh. So today has been—"

"No. Today was different." He stopped in front of the gate. They'd circled back to where they'd begun.

"The tip of your nose is turning white. How about we go back to the house and I'll make you an espresso?"

CHAPTER SIX

SIPPING ESPRESSO in a warm farm kitchen was just the thing on a cold winter afternoon, Miranda decided. Warren had made her cup first, then frothed his own cappuccino. Now he sat in one of the vinyl-covered chairs and stretched out his legs until his feet almost touched the heat-spewing woodstove.

He wore thick wool socks, the kind you'd team with a sturdy pair of leather work boots. Miranda found herself remembering how his feet had looked bare, those long, slender toes with squarely cut nails. Her imagination traveled upward, picturing long, toned legs, narrow hips, a tight butt—

Better stop there.

"Warren, why did the teachers never get mad at you for not raising your hand?"

"What are you talking about?"

"At school. When you had something to say."

"Miranda, did I make your coffee too strong?"

"Come on. It's a valid question. We all had to raise our hands and wait for the teacher to call on us before daring to talk. Why didn't the same rules apply to you?"

His expression remained puzzled, and finally she waved a hand dismissively.

"Oh, never mind. I already know the answer."

"And what would that be?"

"The teachers forgot about the rules because they were so eager to hear what you had to say. We all were," she added, remembering how the air had seemed to clear a little when Warren started to speak.

"You didn't talk in class much, but when you did, you said such interesting things."

"Interesting?"

"Even bizarre sometimes." And yet, his ideas had made people think.

"Suddenly I'm very nervous about how you're going to portray me in this video of yours."

"Just keep making me these lovely espressos and I'll be very kind," she promised.

"Are you happy with how things went today?"

"Yes, I think so. A slow start in some ways, but that's better than beginning too intensely."

"Yes."

He gave her one of those odd looks, his old unsettling gaze that penetrated barriers like skin and bones. She supposed she'd have to get used to this strange, off-balance feeling. They would be spending a lot of time together these next few months.

"At least we laid the ground rules," he said. "Anything you ask me, I get to ask you."

"I'm not sure how you talked me into that. I hope I don't live to regret my lenience."

"You may." He raised his eyebrows, hinting at mischievous thoughts. "For instance, you asked me if there was one special, unforgettable person in my past. What would you say, I wonder, if I asked the same question of you?"

She thought instantly of Chad. With her muscles tense and her throat dry, she was surprised she could keep her reply casual. "I would say 'no comment.' Which is essentially what you said to me," she reminded him.

"Fair enough."

Humor lurked in his voice, and the knowing glint in his eyes increased her nervousness. She felt quite sure then that he'd known about her crush on Chad. That he'd asked this question to test her.

Just what had her response told him?

"I see I'll have to watch my step around you." She finished her coffee and set down the cup.

"Likewise," he replied.

AFTER HER LONG DAY with Warren, Miranda had resolved to drive straight back to her mother's. Once in Chatsworth, however, she found herself taking the turns that led to Willow Road and the golf clubhouse. Chad's truck was parked in its usual spot.

Stopping in for a few minutes couldn't hurt. She got out of the car, trying to block that last ten minutes at Warren's house from her mind.

She'd always taken great pains to keep her feelings for Chad private. How had Warren guessed? And why bring it up now? Had he suspected where she would be heading after their interview?

Not that she had reason to feel guilty about visiting Chad. They were good friends, nothing more. Sure, she still found him attractive—she thought about that moment when their legs had touched as they'd sat on the sofa in his office.

But she wasn't still in love with him. She was here because she was concerned about him. Marriage problems were stressful. Friends needed to support each other.

"Miranda!"

Chad must have been right by the door. He looked smashing in a Nordic sweater and tight black ski pants.

"I should've called...."

"You wouldn't have reached me, anyway. I just got in from grooming the track. Can you believe all this snow? I was afraid it would keep you from visiting. Come on." He put a hand to her shoulder and pulled her forward. "Let me spring for hot chocolate."

"It's the weather for it," she agreed. The spacious clubhouse was cool compared with Warren's snug farm kitchen and its old-fashioned, wood-burning stove. As for the paper cup of watery brown cocoa, it couldn't match the rich espresso Warren had brewed for her.

But Chad didn't seem bothered by his situation. He pulled up chairs at one of the tables by the buffet line and smiled at her broadly. "Did you start work on that video today?"

"I've been at the Addison farm since ten this morning." The day had flown by. She couldn't remember the last time she'd been so captivated. If Warren hadn't needed to get back to his writing, she might not have left for several more hours.

"Weird that he decided to set himself up in his parents' old farmhouse for the winter. With all those books he's sold, you'd think he could afford a condo on the beach in the Caribbean or a ski chalet in the Rockies. But then, Warren always was different."

"Do you remember much about him?" She propped her feet on a nearby chair and sipped at the sweet cocoa mixture. Ugh, it really was disgusting. Maybe she'd just use the cup to keep her hands warm.

"What do you want to know? He wasn't into sports much."

Chad had been a wizard in the hockey arena. And he'd had a more-than-decent golf game since he was sixteen.

"He won a lot of ribbons at the track-and-field meets, though," Chad conceded.

"But who were his friends?" Surely *someone* from their circle in Chatsworth had known him better than the two of them did.

"You could ask Adrienne at the hair salon. Warren used to hang out with her sister. More than just hang out, actually, if the rumors were true." He winked.

There was this girl. You wouldn't know her....

Miranda had been more than a little intrigued by that comment of Warren's. She wanted to know which girl he'd been referring to.

Adrienne, in the same grade as her and Chad and Bernie and Warren and all the rest of them, had two sisters. Miranda concentrated on remembering their names.

"You mean the younger one...Tammy?"

"Nah. The *older* one." Chad raised his eyebrows suggestively and added in a deep voice, *"Bronwyn."*

"But she was—" Miranda counted the grades in her head "—three years older than us." Not much of an age gap for an adult. But for young teenagers it was pretty darn significant.

"Exactly. And an early bloomer, to boot. But then, Warren always did go for older women."

He did? Where did Chad get this stuff? "You're making this up. You hardly knew the guy."

"Believe me, information like this gets around. I can't believe you never heard the rumors."

"What rumors?"

Chad shook his head. "Forget it. I already said too much. We guys gotta stick together."

Miranda rolled her eyes at the small-town credo. Chad didn't really mean any of this; he was just teasing her. "Come on, this is important. It's my *job* to get the scoop on Warren Addison."

"Exactly. It's your job. You're going to make a video that people all around the country will watch. I'm not passing on stories I'm not even sure are true. Like I said, talk to Adrienne. She'll know better than me."

"You're really not going to tell me."

"Don't look at me like that. I'm on your side, but right now there's a lot of gossip being spread around town about me. I'm not going to do the same to some other poor fellow."

Immediately she felt ashamed. "You're right. I can't use secondhand information, anyway." She could talk to Adrienne. She'd make an appointment at the salon tomorrow. In the meantime, Chad had his own worries.

What were the townspeople saying about him? The same story making the rounds at her mother's bridge club sessions—that a third party was somehow involved in Chad and Bernie's marriage breakdown? She was tempted to quiz him again, but realized he would view further questioning as an insult.

She'd already asked Chad if he'd had an affair and he'd said no. She believed him. It wouldn't be the first time the biddies in town got their facts all wrong.

Chad left his chair, heading for the vending machine. "You want more?"

She set her lukewarm cup on the table. "No, thanks. Chad, are you sure you're doing okay out here?" If he could stomach two servings of this stuff, he had to be in more trouble than he let on.

"Oh, it's a pain, all right," he admitted. "Gotta take my laundry into town, and I'm getting pretty sick of the café menu. Wouldn't mind my own bed and my favorite recliner chair, either."

Interesting that he'd skirted the more difficult, emotional issues and headed his list with the comforts of home. "What about Bernie? You must miss her. And Vicky…"

"Sure." Chad gulped at the cocoa. A trace of brown liquid remained at the corners of his mouth. She removed a napkin from the dispenser at the center of the table and cleaned him up.

Chad's gaze dropped to her fingers, then shifted to her eyes, *her* mouth.

"Have I got a cocoa mustache, too?"

He shook his head and Miranda swallowed. For a second there it had almost seemed that…he'd wanted to kiss her. Or was she just projecting her childhood passion onto him?

There'd been so many moments like this between them when they were teenagers. And not once had Chad made even the smallest move on her. He hadn't been interested then. She was only imagining he would be interested now.

Besides, his marriage might be in trouble, but he still had a wife. A wife he cared about. Or maybe not, if what he truly missed most was having his shirts laundered and his meals on the table.

"I want to help, Chad." If he could open up to anyone, surely it would be her. They'd never had trouble communicating in the past, although Bernie had been a subject rarely broached.

"Really? That would be great. Any idea how to wash these sweaters?" He ran a hand over the one he was wearing. "I have a couple of them and the labels all read Hand Wash Only. How do you do that?"

He couldn't be serious. He was! Boy, Bernie had really spoiled him. "Cold water, mild soap and lots of rinsing. Don't wring, either. Lay the sweater flat on a towel to dry."

"I don't suppose…"

He raised his eyebrows, put on his fakest, most beautiful smile.

"Don't tell me women fall for that routine?"

"Usually." He wasn't at all abashed.

"Oh, Lord…" She wasn't going to cave in, was she? Maybe. Just this once. "Fine. Give me the sweaters. I'll wash them for you."

"I was hoping you'd offer."

No kidding. "I'd invite you over for a lesson. But I don't think my mother's bridge club would approve." To put it *mildly*.

"I'll pay you back," Chad promised. "How about free ski rentals? The track is looking pretty good and I'll bet you didn't bring your boards with you."

She hadn't even considered packing her cross-country ski gear. She'd forgotten all about the trail that ran through the rolling fields of the golf course, then along the frozen lake. "Sounds like fun." Between walks with Warren and skiing with Chad, she would definitely get her exercise.

"Come by tomorrow around noon. That's the best time, really. We'll add some color to those city-white cheeks of yours."

Miranda put a hand to her face. City-white?

"Let me get those sweaters."

He came back with three. Two she hadn't seen before and the one he'd been wearing. He'd stripped it off, leaving a white turtleneck that emphasized the healthy color of his face. For a moment, she drank in the sight of him. His smooth, defined features, blond tousled hair, bright eyes...

"So we're on for tomorrow?" He passed the balled-up sweaters into her hands.

"These won't be dry by then. But sure, we can go for a ski."

"I'll look forward to it."

And so would she.

AT FIVE O'CLOCK Bernie had still not taken a shower, brushed her hair or even put on her wristwatch. Vicky would be home from her friend's in an hour and she'd expect dinner. They always had pot roast on Sunday.

Not this Sunday, though.

Bernie stood in front of the almost-empty freezer. She hadn't been herself these past few weeks. She'd let many of her household routines slide, including cooking and shopping. Unless Vicky would be satisfied with a meal of frozen peas and blanched almonds, she had nothing in the house to throw together for a meal.

She *had* to go shopping. And she had to hurry. Lucky's opened at noon and closed at five-thirty on Sundays.

After slipping her down-filled coat over her sweatsuit, Bernie ran her fingers through her limp hair. At the mirror by the side door to the garage, she averted her eyes. No sense bothering with lipstick. She wouldn't see anyone, anyway. Who shopped thirty minutes before dinnertime in Chatsworth?

Reaching for a box of fresh-scented Tide five minutes later, she found out who. A tall, slender woman breezed up from behind her. Bernie caught the subtle, delicate scent of her perfume, and admired the cute blond haircut briefly, before her throat closed over in shock.

Miranda James! Oh, Lord, no. Not Miranda James, here in Lucky's grocery store, looking like a perky model, in her cashmere coat and red turtleneck sweater. In comparison, Bernie felt like a scarecrow.

Bending low, she pretended to search for something on the bottom shelf, hiding her face behind the screen of her unstyled hair.

Above her she saw a slender, long-boned hand with buffed nails and lots of silver jewelry pick out a bottle of Ivory detergent. Then liquid Fleecy.

Was she done?

Please, God, make her go away. Don't let her glance down. Don't let her recognize—

"Bernie? Bernie English?"

Miranda's voice was as polished as her appearance.

Shit. Bernie wouldn't stand. No way was she letting Miranda see the gaping hole in her sweatpants. Hand firmly clasped over the offending kneecap, she nodded. "Heard you were in town visiting your mom. How are you doing, Miranda? You look well."

Well? She looked gorgeous. Bernie could see the surprise—face it, barely veiled shock—in Miranda's face as she duly noted every last detail about Bernie's appearance. Greasy limp hair, cheap unflattering clothes, wan skin and dry lips.

Damn it to hell, why was this happening to her? Was it Dump on Bernie English Year? Would nothing go right in her life ever again?

"I'm staying until Christmas," Miranda said.

Bernie prayed she would move on, but she kept standing there. Staring…

She knew what Miranda was thinking. *God, is she ever unattractive. No wonder Chad doesn't love her.*

"You've caught me in my lazing-around clothes. I'm afraid I didn't have time—" Bernie bit her lip to stop the drivel. Why was she apologizing? She was only drawing attention to how awful she looked.

But Miranda smiled warmly. "Isn't it just the way. If you'd bothered to change and put on makeup, you wouldn't have seen a person you knew."

"Exactly." Acting on reflex, Bernie straightened. Then felt cool air from the store's ventilation system shoot straight at the bare spot on her knee. Miranda's gaze dropped to the very place Bernie hadn't wanted her to notice, and she smiled again.

"I have sweatpants just like those. Comfy, aren't they? I don't care if they wear out to threads—I'm never throwing them away."

Jeez, now Bernie remembered another thing she'd always hated about Miranda. She was so damn *nice.* And she was walking forward slowly, as if she expected Bernie to come join her at the checkout.

Bernie shoved the box of detergent back on the shelf. "You know, I'm not going to bother with laundry tonight, after all." And to hell with dinner, as well. She'd order in Chinese from the café.

With a swift goodbye, she exited the store, certain her cheeks were brighter than good old Rudolph's nose, painted on the front window of the store. Lucky's idea of festive decorating. At the row of angle parking, she spotted Miranda's bright-yellow VW. The car Vicky had thought was so wonderful. Passing it on the way to her own sedate Buick, Bernie glanced into the interior. The steering wheel was covered in a wild, furry leopard print. Oh, please!

No fast-food wrappers, tissues or empty coffee containers littered Miranda's vehicle. Though there was a duffel bag and a black carrying case on the passenger-side floor. And something tossed on the back seat.

Bernie did a double take, unwilling to believe her own eyesight. But there could be no doubt. Those were Chad's Nordic sweaters. She'd bet money on it.

Suddenly the scene in the grocery store took on new significance. Miranda had been buying soap and fabric softener for delicate items.

And she'd been so pleasant and friendly! Did she think Bernie wouldn't guess? That she wouldn't put two and two together?

That woman was washing Chad's laundry. And she'd only been in town three days!

MIRANDA PHONED ADRIENNE'S Hair Salon Monday morning, hoping for an appointment any time that week. She was told to come over at eleven and she'd be done by noon.

"Wow, that was easy." In Toronto she booked her appointments six weeks in advance to make sure she got the day and time of her preference.

Adrienne ran her business in the basement of her two-toned bungalow at the corner of Mallard and Main. Miranda parked on the street, then ran down a half flight of stairs and paused at a door with a square glass insert at the top. The hand-painted sign on the inside of the window read Adrienne's Is Open. Come On In.

Bells chimed as Miranda stepped onto a floral welcome mat. She closed the door firmly behind her to keep out the winter chill. The snow had stopped and the sky was blue once more, but the temperature had dipped to twenty below last night and didn't seem in any hurry to climb upward.

"Miranda! Long time no see!" A curvy woman, just over five feet in her black platform shoes, waved at her from a room at the back.

Miranda passed by a white Kenmore washer-dryer set tucked under the stairs leading to the main floor and entered the "salon." Painted a bright raspberry, with black-and-white photos on one long wall and a bank of mirrors opposite, it had a certain funky style.

"Interesting." She paused to take in a wild, abstract mural on the wall above the sink for washing hair, then turned to Adrienne.

They hadn't seen each other since high school graduation, she was sure. Except for her hair, Adrienne looked the same—pretty and petite.

Once an insipid blonde, she had upgraded to the most unnatural shade of red Miranda had ever seen. And her formerly straight locks now frizzed in every direction. A perm gone bad? Or was this the look that Adrienne had been after?

Miranda suddenly felt nervous about her appointment. Perhaps she should have just suggested they meet for a coffee.

"Yeah, it's pretty cool." Adrienne ran her painted nails down one smooth wall. "Ernie—that's my husband—almost gagged when he opened the paint can and saw the color I wanted. He still doesn't like it. But hey, if it's good enough for my hair, it ought to be good enough for the walls." She winked, then eyed Miranda's short hair speculatively. "So. What can I do for you today? A little trim?"

Let Adrienne near her with a pair of scissors? "Oh, I just thought a shampoo and style would be a fun treat."

"Do you want to take off your sweater?"

She'd worn a turtleneck and wool pullover for skiing later. "No, just put a smock over top and I'll roll down the neck."

"Sure thing." Adrienne opened a drawer and selected a pink vinyl cape, which she draped over Miranda's outfit.

Although her short cut looked simple, getting it just right was actually a bit of a trick. With some trepidation, Miranda sank into the chair Adrienne indicated and leaned back.

"Relax." Adrienne cupped Miranda's head with one hand, and adjusted the water temperature with the other. "This is going to be fun, and we've got lots of time. Mrs. Pearce isn't due until twelve-thirty."

"Is that the Mrs. Pearce who taught us grade five?" Miranda had a perfect view up Adrienne's armpit as the hairdresser squirted a generous amount of shampoo into her hair and began to work up a lather. She closed her eyes.

"None other. She's retired now, of course. Comes in every Monday for a set and blow-dry."

Adrienne was still scrubbing. Clearly, she gave good value in the shampooing department. During the final rinse she said, "Heard you were doing a biography film on Warren Addison."

Just the opening Miranda had been waiting for.

"That's true. He was in our grade. Do you remember much about him?"

"Nice guy, I always thought. I had a bit of a crush for a while, but…"

A crush! Miranda tried to picture tiny Adrienne with six-foot Warren. No dice. "You two ever date?"

"No." Adrienne sounded quite regretful. "Actually, he was more interested in my sister, Bronwyn."

So Chad had been right. "Isn't Bronwyn your oldest sister?"

"Yeah, by three years. She's married now and lives in Calgary. They have their own graphic design company. We're all artists in our family. My youngest sister has a certificate in floral design. She lives in Calgary, too."

Abruptly the room went silent as Adrienne simultaneously stopped talking and turned off the water. She wrapped Miranda's head in a rather stiff towel. "Okay, move over to my chair. Now the real fun starts. Want some temporary highlights? A little purple, maybe a streak of pink?"

"Um…no, thanks." Miranda caught her reflection in the mirror, and automatically shifted her gaze to the woman who was now combing through the knots she'd created at the washing sink.

"Three years is quite an age gap…."

"Huh? Oh, you're talking about Warren and Bronwyn again. I suppose it is."

"When did their relationship start?"

"Bronwyn was in grade twelve—we were in grade nine. I was so glad when she left home to go to university. I thought I'd have my big chance then, but of course you know who Warren got involved with then.''

Another girlfriend? And she'd thought he was a loner. ''Actually, no, I didn't hear.''

''Well, you had a busy social calendar yourself in those days, didn't you?'' she said without rancor.

Well, with very little rancor. She began to roll curlers in Miranda's hair. *Curlers.* Miranda wasn't sure about that, but when Adrienne started talking again, she didn't dare interrupt.

''Maybe you were too busy to hear the rumors. They did their best to keep it quiet, naturally. And I guess they were pretty successful. The school trustees never found out, at least. And Miss Flemming never lost her job.''

''Miss Flemming!'' The high school English teacher had been young and very pretty. Miranda knew a lot of the guys had crushes on her. But she'd never guessed the rather shy, retiring woman had been seeing one of her students.

''They didn't go out on dates!'' Where could they be together without being recognized? Maybe a drive-in movie, but even those could be risky with the way kids were always moving around, checking out the occupants in the various cars.

''Remember the school paper? Warren wrote practically the entire thing. Word was the two of them had many a saucy editorial meeting after school hours in the staff room.''

''No kidding...'' Wow. If something like this happened today, Miss Flemming could find herself being sued for sexual harassment or worse. Depending, of course, on what exactly had transpired at those "editorial meetings."

"Time for the dryer." Adrienne led her to a third chair, where she lowered a plastic bubble over Miranda's head.

Hot air pulsed around the tiny rollers and into her ears. Adrienne chatted away as she set a timer, but Miranda couldn't distinguish the words. God, what they said about small-town hairdressers was true. They really did know everything.

After a comb-out, which seemed to require the use of about half a can of hairspray, Adrienne let Miranda have a peek in the mirror.

"Isn't that lovely? Got to say it's wonderful to have someone with your looks to work with. Women come in the door, expect you to perform miracles. We stylists can only do so much. You, though. You could be on the cover of one of my magazines."

Miranda barely heard a word of the gushing. With a combination of tight curls and copious back-combing, Adrienne had transformed her into...her *mother.*

"What do you think?" Adrienne untied the cape with a flourish. Her cheeks were pink with the flush of her success.

"I can hardly believe this is *me.*" She put a hand to the side of her head and was amazed when it didn't stick there.

Adrienne smiled broadly. "Probably the best fourteen dollars you ever spent, right?"

"Fourteen dollars?"

"Well, it did take more than an hour...."

Miranda fought not to laugh. "I only meant that you deliver such good value."

She passed over a twenty from her purse, then had to practically wrestle Adrienne to the floor to convince her to keep the change.

Outside again, the cold air bit at her newly exposed ears. Miranda tried to run her fingers through the mop of curls to loosen them up, but to no avail. Every single strand of hair was lacquered into place.

Oh, well, she'd wear a toque skiing, then shampoo her hair at home. Dashing for her car, she almost didn't notice the big gray truck until the screech and grind of pumping brakes filled the air.

Miranda skidded to a halt just as the truck slid sideways on the ice and stopped on the sidewalk in front of Adrienne's house.

The driver unrolled his window. "Hey, shouldn't a city girl like you know to look both ways before you cross a street?"

CHAPTER SEVEN

WARREN ADDISON SPOKE FROM the lowered window. With her heart rate still in the cardiac-training zone, Miranda put a hand on his door. That was a close call. Why hadn't she been paying attention?

Because she'd been thinking about all she'd learned from Adrienne. About Warren.

"You okay, Miranda?"

"Oh, I'm fine." She gave him another look—a closer look. In his smoke-colored sweater and fleece-lined denim jacket, he appeared masculine, relaxed. The glint in his eyes, as always, was vaguely unsettling. Yet something about him was different.

After a few seconds of pondering, Miranda realized it wasn't the man who had changed but her perception of him. Hearing about his early romantic relationships, she realized, had smashed her preconceptions.

She'd thought of him as a loner at school, maybe a bit of a misfit. Yet an intelligent, popular high school girl and then a sensitive, beautiful grown woman had been interested in him back then—a skinny, intense young man years their junior. Obviously Warren had qualities that she, Miranda, had underestimated.

"I'm sorry. Had my head in the clouds, I'm afraid."

"Looks to me like you had your head in Adrienne Jenson's hair dryer."

Oh, no, she'd forgotten about the new "do." She put her hands to her helmet of curls and managed a small smile. "So. What do you think?"

Warren laughed. "You're a good sport, Miranda. Want to grab a coffee at the café? I've got a scarf in here I can lend you."

"What? Ashamed to be seen with me like this?" As she joked, she wished that she could say yes, that she hadn't already made plans with Chad to go skiing. She tamped down the impulse to jump into the passenger seat of Warren's truck and shrugged. "Can't this afternoon. Next time you're in town, though, give me a call."

"Hey. No problem."

Despite his casual words, she saw the question in his eyes: what could she have on her agenda that was so pressing she couldn't take a minute for a coffee? She knew he was waiting for her to explain, but she forced herself to keep quiet.

Not that she didn't want Warren to know she was skiing with Chad. Hell, she didn't care if the entire town knew.

So why hadn't she said, "Sorry, but I promised

Chad I'd ski around the golf course with him. Maybe another time?''

"Well, I'd better let you go. It's damn cold today."

"Yes." Reminded of the chill, she put her hands to the collar of her ski jacket and nodded as Warren closed the window of his cab, then backed off the sidewalk and drove down the road toward Main Street.

Miranda got into her car and sat for a moment, not at all sure why her previous good mood had dampened. She watched Warren's truck make a lumbering left at the intersection, as she turned the ignition and waited for the car's engine to warm up a little. It was ten past twelve. She hoped Chad wouldn't be upset that she was late.

After grabbing the toque on the passenger seat next to her, she pulled it on over her ears. For the first time since elementary school, she wasn't at all worried about what wearing a hat might do to her hair.

FIVE MINUTES LATER WHEN Miranda pulled up to the clubhouse, she found Chad waiting, already in skis. He had on a blue windbreaker, black ski pants and a toque. A pair of skis and poles sticking upright from a nearby snowbank were obviously meant for her.

"I haven't done this in years," she reminded him,

tugging on the rim of her hat as he approached. He carried a woman's ski boot in each of his hands.

"I'll give you a refresher course."

His smile reminded her that there were other activities she hadn't tried in a while.

"I guessed at the size." He passed her the boot for her right foot, and she checked the number stamped on the inside.

"You were right." Sitting sideways in the driver's seat, she slipped out of her fine leather footwear and into an extra pair of cotton socks and the boots. Chad bent to tighten the laces, then held out his hand to pull her upright. For a moment they stood inches apart.

Was he looking at her differently than usual? She felt the familiar heart-pounding of her adolescence, then almost laughed at herself as he gave her a casual wink.

What was the matter with her? She had to stop being so sensitive around him.

"Let's get you in some skis and see how much you remember."

A double set of tracks had been groomed into the packed snow. Standing at the beginning of the trail, Miranda glanced back at the clubhouse. "What if you get some customers while we're gone?"

"No sweat. We work on the honor system here. I have a lockbox just inside the door and a guest book beside it. People know to leave five dollars and to sign their name."

"Five whole dollars, huh?" She could live a long while in Chatsworth on the money from her last project if she divided her time between the beauty salon and the ski track.

"My expenses are pretty minimal. Our big money-makers are the golf course and the swimming pool. Maintaining the ski track gives me something to do in the off-season."

"I'm not complaining. I'll put in my five dollars when I get back."

"My treat."

With her skis in the tracks on the right-hand side of the path, Miranda eased into her stride. Chad glided up beside her in the other set of tracks. Leaning over, he put a hand to her back. "Looking good, Randy. Just like riding a bike, isn't it?"

The technique *was* coming back to her. "Not bad for a city girl?"

"Acceptable."

"Oh, really?" She sped up as they approached a gentle curve, then realized her mistake as a long downward slope appeared from behind a grove of poplars. Faster she went and faster. With her skis trapped in the tracks, how was she supposed to slow herself?

Ahead of her, Chad zoomed down the hill. She didn't have the same confidence. She tried digging her edges into the sides of the tracks, then gambled on lifting one foot out of the track to attempt a half snowplow.

Miraculously, she kept her balance. Angling her newly freed ski into the packed snow, she was able to provide some resistance and slow her speed marginally. At the bottom of the hill, she let out a whoop of victory.

"Now, what do you have to say about *that*." She pushed gently against Chad's chest.

"Full points for courage, but we'll have to work on the style. I like your hat, by the way." He tugged on the top and a couple of curls sprang out from around her neck.

"What's this? A new hairdo?" Before she could stop him, he'd yanked the hat entirely off. He stared at her for a moment, then broke into a belly laugh.

"Oh, my God... What *happened* to you!"

"Adrienne Jenson happened to me, that's what. And stop laughing. It's not *that* funny." She tried to grab her hat from him. Chad skied backward a couple of feet, dangled it tauntingly in front of her.

"Our local hairstylist. Well, that explains it. You look like half the ladies in Chatsworth. The ones over fifty."

A suspicion hit her. Had Adrienne *purposefully* tried to make her look older and out-of-date?

"It may not be the greatest hairstyle, but I got my twenty dollars' worth of information out of that woman. I asked her about Warren and she was more than pleased to fill me in on the details of his love life."

"Really?"

Chad tossed her the hat, then took off skiing. She watched him, exasperated. Wasn't he interested in what she'd learned? Really, men were so strange sometimes, Miranda thought as she struggled to catch up. She was breathless by the time she reached him.

"Aren't you—" *gasp* "—the least bit—" *gasp* "—curious about what Adrienne said?"

Chad shook his head. "This is old news already. So Warren preferred older women when he was a kid. Or maybe older women preferred Warren."

Was that still the case? she wondered. If so, how much older did they have to be?

"I won't say that some of the guys weren't jealous," Chad added. "Especially when it came to Miss Peaches-and-Cream Flemming. It was bad enough that he snagged hot little Bronwyn Jenson. She was always walking around with her sketchbook in her hands, totally oblivious to the guys drooling in her wake. Then, when she finally does bother to take a little notice, who does she pick?"

Warren. A man who was becoming a bigger enigma the more Miranda found out about him. "So, Chad. Did you like Bronwyn, too?"

"What hot-blooded male wouldn't? I never managed to go out with her, though. Her sisters, yes, but never Bronwyn."

Miranda knew that he'd dated both Adrienne and Tammy. Hell, she could recite the entire list of Chad's past girlfriends if she had to. Chad had never been particularly discriminating in selecting his girlfriend-of-the-moment. Which only made her wonder all the more why he'd never even glanced in her direction.

He thought she was attractive. She knew he did. And he obviously *liked* her. They'd been friends practically forever, for heaven's sake!

Maybe she should just ask him, get it out in the open. The question formed and reformed itself in her mind: *Say, Chad. Did you ever think about dating me?* Or, *Isn't it funny that not once in all these years have you and I...?*

But she couldn't, because right from the beginning of their friendship they'd been able to talk about anything when they were together except their feelings for each other.

Chad referred to her as his buddy. Even when they flirted, there was always a line they couldn't cross. A few times they'd come awfully close, but afterward, both had pretended the incidents had never occurred.

In a little over an hour and a half, she and Chad completed the circuit. Pretty good time, Chad assured her. When they returned to the clubhouse, they found a couple of cars next to Miranda's in the parking lot and a few new names in the guest book.

Chad provided a brief explanation. "The Thompson boys. They usually work on the oil rigs in the winter, but I heard they wouldn't be starting until January this year."

"'Henry Bateson and Sue Duncan,'" Miranda

read over his shoulder. "I remember Henry. Chris's and Libby's father, right?" The terrible car crash that had taken both Henry's wife and son had sent Henry into a terrible depression. "Is he doing all right?"

"Yeah, finally. Word is he's interested in Sue Duncan—her husband died from a heart attack last spring. He brings her out here about three times a week, and to the café for coffee afterward."

Miranda was amused. "You make fun of me, but I notice you're up on the local gossip...."

"Hell. This isn't gossip. It's current events." Chad brushed off her teasing as he pulled out a handful of loonies from his pocket. "Can I buy you some more of that lovely hot chocolate?"

Miranda glanced at the vending machines and sighed. "You can buy some for me, but I won't promise to drink it."

They settled at the same table where they'd sat before and he downed his hot beverage in about three swallows. She wondered if he was eating all his meals at the café, or whether his mother occasionally softened enough to cook him dinner. Miranda would have loved to invite him to her mother's, but could only imagine what the bridge club would think of *that*.

Come to think of it, didn't the bridge club meet on Wednesday nights? "How about I bring you dinner tomorrow evening?"

"Here? To the clubhouse?"

Miranda felt embarrassed to admit she didn't dare

invite him home. She shrugged. "Why not?" If the
dishes were piping hot when she left, the food would
be plenty warm enough to serve when she arrived.

Only—what would she put in those dishes? Funny,
in some ways she knew Chad so well, but they'd
never eaten a meal together—discounting lunches at
school and burgers out with the gang.

"Anything special you're craving?" she asked.

"I take it we're not talking sex here."

"Chad!"

"Hey, it's been two weeks."

She rolled her eyes. "Two whole weeks, huh?"

Chad raised his eyebrows. "Don't tell me it's been
longer for you?"

"You know I haven't had a boyfriend for a
while."

"Only because you're so damn picky. Hon,
you've always had men lined up, waiting to be the
lucky one."

Lined up? Hardly. Chad didn't have a clue, but
she couldn't blame him. They never discussed *her*
love life. This was a real exception. Normally when
she sat down at the computer or picked up the phone
to talk to him, it was as if other men simply didn't
exist.

"What can I say, Chad? None of the guys I've
met could ever measure up to *you*."

"Can't argue with you there." He laughed and
patted her hand.

He thought she was joking. She wondered what

his reaction would have been if she'd told him she wasn't kidding. She'd meant every word. Chad English *was* her ideal. He had been since she was fourteen years old....

But here she was, dreaming about the past, when she ought to be focusing on the future. She'd lain awake so many hours last night, fretting about Chad's current situation. Tossing restlessly beneath her covers, she'd wondered if Bernie, too, was having difficulty sleeping.

Miranda suspected she was.

"I ran into Bernie last night at Lucky's."

A beat of silence, then, "How was she?"

Awful would have been Miranda's guess. "She's pretty unhappy, Chad."

"Yeah?"

Miranda couldn't tell how he felt from that one gruff word. Especially since he'd turned his face away from her. Obviously he was reluctant to talk further about Bernie and their problems. Was this macho male posturing? Or was it possible he didn't care?

No, that couldn't be. Although, Chad did appear to be coping with this separation better than Bernie. Despite his distress, his insistence that he didn't want a divorce, Chad didn't seem to be doing much to win Bernie back. He certainly didn't look as though he spent his nights crying, the way Bernie did.

Poor Bernie. The girl Miranda remembered from school had been trim, cute and full of spunk. Miranda had caught her at her worst at Lucky's, true, but there was no denying Bernie had gained at least ten pounds since high school. Or that there were definite streaks of gray in her hair. Surely Chad couldn't be so shallow as to care about those superficial changes, though.

"Chad, have you given any further thought to Bernie's three conditions?"

"I should never have told you about those."

She touched his arm, willing him not to withdraw from her. "No. I'm glad you did. I thought about this all last night." Seeing Bernie yesterday had been the catalyst. She'd promised to help Chad get his family together. Now she meant to deliver.

"You've got to take this seriously, Chad. Tell her you'll go back into the mixed curling league with her."

"That would be easy enough to do. But you know that's not her only demand. What about us? We've been friends a long time, Randy."

Here was the hard part. Miranda wished she could see an option. But she knew she had no choice. "Bernie is your *wife*, Chad. You have to put what she wants first."

She waited while he thought that over. Finally, he looked her in the eyes. "Randy, how can you even suggest that we stop being friends?"

Well, it hadn't been easy.

"You do understand what Bernie is insisting on?

We'd have to cut off all communication. No visits, no letters, no *e-mails*. Nothing.''

Right now Miranda couldn't stand to think what that would be like, how empty her life would become. Chad had been her best friend for so long.

It did seem strange, though, that Bernie was so vehemently opposed to their friendship. Yes, Bernie had never liked her much. But zero communication between her and Chad was definitely extreme.

''You're sure Bernie doesn't have the wrong idea about us?''

Chad dropped his gaze to the paper cup he was holding. ''I don't know how that woman's mind works these days. As far as I can tell, she'd just trying to see how high I'll jump.''

''But you *have* explained that our relationship is completely platonic? Maybe she imagines we're having cybersex or something.''

Miranda blinked and stared into her own cup of cocoa. They'd skirted that very activity a couple of times. But had never gone beyond the bounds of friendly flirting.

Well, there'd been that one night. Last New Year's Eve, Miranda had returned home late from a party—she'd gone without a date and that had been a mistake, leaving her an open target for all that kissing at midnight. For some reason, after brushing her teeth at one-thirty in the morning, she'd checked her e-mail messages. Chad's name came up on the screen.

Vicky had taken sick, forcing Chad and Bernie to cancel their plans for the evening. It was eleven-thirty in Saskatchewan, and so Miranda had spent the next hour instant-messaging, bringing in the New Year with Chad.

At midnight he'd given her a cyberkiss. And hinted that if he was with her he'd be tempted to do more.

That night she'd gone to bed imagining what Chad might have meant by "more." It wasn't the first time he'd starred in one of her nighttime fantasies.

But that was all they were, all they'd ever been. *Fantasies.* And Bernie couldn't control those as easily as she could e-mail and phone calls.

"Look, Bernie knows I've always been faithful to her. I can't explain why she has this bee in her bonnet when it comes to you. Maybe she feels threatened because you're so damn gorgeous." He pulled off her hat and tossed it in the air. "Usually, that is."

"Not fair!" She reached over to snatch the wool cap back and ended up in a tug-of-war. "Give that here!"

"Make me." He pulled the hat to his chest, drawing her closer.

She caught her breath. His mouth was so close. Surely he had to be thinking the same thing she was. Just one kiss—then Bernie would really have something to complain about.

Bernie. Vicky. Reminding herself of his family and that she wanted to help bring them *together,* not tear them apart, Miranda cleared her throat.

"My hat?"

He put it on her head himself, adjusting the wool band snuggly around her ears. "I'm not going to give up our friendship, Miranda. No wife of mine is going to tell me who I can and cannot be friends with."

She couldn't deny the rush of relief she felt at his words. "As long as you know. If you need me to disappear from your life—I'll understand. Just say the word."

"I'm never going to say that word," he reassured her. After a moment, he peered into the cup she still cradled in one hand. "You haven't touched your hot chocolate. Mind if I drink it?"

"Be my guest." She supposed that was his way of telling her this conversation was now over. So much for her attempt to help his marriage.

Miranda wished she could find out what Bernie's third condition was. That had to be the key. What this separation was really about. Miranda couldn't believe it was only a night of curling, or even her relationship with Chad.

Something else was behind the problems between these two. And how could she help if she didn't know what it was?

BERNIE ALMOST STARTED a new notebook. That seemed wasteful, though, so she decided to just flip over several clean pages. She selected a different pen, with green ink for a change. After that fiasco at Lucky's yesterday, it was important to her to make a completely fresh start.

For instance, from now on she would no longer write in her journal unless she'd showered and dressed and put on her makeup.

> Okay, this is it. Today I become a new woman. From now on I'm only eating healthy foods, and no more snacking. I'm going to exercise—five times a week.

Bernie jotted down the words on a clean page of her journal. It was hard to believe that she had been going to bed alone, sleeping alone and generally wallowing in despair for almost two-and-a-half weeks now.

Her journal was twice as thick as it had been the day she'd bought it. She'd stuffed the thing with her ranting, raving, whining and finger pointing. The pages were warped from thousands of tears and stained with all sorts of foods, from chocolate to coffee. This book was a testament to all she'd suffered since she'd had that showdown with Chad.

And to how pathetic she'd become in the process.

It had to stop. That disastrous run-in with Miranda James at Lucky's yesterday had been a humiliating wake-up call. She'd gone over ten years without seeing her old classmate. Didn't it figure that the day she decided to run out in her old sweats and greasy hair would be the day she'd cross paths again with her old nemesis.

Not that she *hated* Miranda. After all, they'd hung out in the same gang throughout high school, gone to the same parties, dated some of the same guys. But something about that girl had always rankled.

Too much went her way, and when it did, she took it for granted. Miranda had never had to try hard for anything. And she'd always had a special relationship with Chad that defied Bernie's efforts to understand or contain it.

Whenever Bernie tried to explain how their friendship made her feel like an outsider, Chad made fun of her. As far as he was concerned, if he wasn't sleeping with the woman, his wife had no reason to object to their phone calls and e-mails.

Still, if their relationship was so innocent, why did he go to such lengths to keep it private? Miranda never called him at home, never sent her letters to their house. Bernie remembered a terrible fight she and Chad had had last New Year's Eve.

They'd missed the annual curling club party because Vicky was running a high fever. Bernie hadn't really minded. She'd chilled a bottle of wine, lit a fire and turned on the television so they wouldn't miss the countdown.

At eleven-thirty, though, Chad had disappeared into his office with the laptop he'd brought from work and hadn't come out until almost an hour later.

Bernie had had only herself to toast when the New Year rang in. She'd *known* her husband was instant-messaging with Miranda in Toronto, but what could she do? Break down the office door and demand he disconnect?

She'd stewed about the episode for several days,

until her resentment had finally boiled over and they'd had a huge fight.

And now that woman was here, in Chatsworth, washing Chad's sweaters, no less. This was not a good sign. Next thing she'd be vacuuming the clubhouse and cooking his meals.... And sleeping with him on that lumpy pullout couch. Maybe she already was.

And what could Bernie do about any of this? She'd been the one to kick Chad out. She couldn't welcome him back with open arms, especially when he hadn't met even one of her three conditions!

No, like it or not, she was now in competition for her own husband. And her rival? None other than the one girl who always got what she wanted.

Bernie knew she needed heavy artillery to even stand a chance. And she had it, splayed out on the kitchen table in front of her. Several books from the library and a one-week rental from the video store.

She was going to starve away those ten blasted pounds with *Thirty Days to a Slimmer You.* Reshape what was left over with power yoga. Then, using *Beauty Tips From an Expert,* she would determine the proper hairstyle for her face shape and figure out whether her wardrobe belonged in the spring or the summer palette.

She couldn't turn herself into a supermodel. But she would make Chad English stand up and take notice.

And she would accomplish all this by December 22, the night of the annual Chatsworth Christmas potluck and dance.

CHAPTER EIGHT

WARREN WONDERED WHAT Miranda would want to talk about this morning. She'd carefully set a copy of his book atop her notepad on the kitchen table. Trying to hide the list of questions she had written out? That she'd spoken to Adrienne yesterday worried him. He could well imagine the topics they'd covered.

"Here you go. One double, no-fat cap." He mimicked coffee shop lingo as he set the mug beside her papers.

"Mmm. Smells delicious. But you're sure I'm not interrupting?"

Having Miranda's company for his midmorning cappuccino might be habit-forming, Warren suspected. For him as well as Miranda. Only, his reasons for enjoying her company had nothing to do with caffeine.

"Your timing was perfect." He'd suggested midmorning for her interviews since his favorite writing hours were very early and very late. "Maybe we can go out for a walk later."

"I don't know about that. It felt pretty cold out

there. My car wasn't too happy about starting this morning—even though it was plugged in all night.''

He went to the window to check the outdoor thermometer. ''You're right. Almost thirty below.''

''Feels like forty with the windchill.''

He'd forgotten how frosty winters were on the prairies. With the old woodstove fired up and the modern gas furnace running, too, they might do well to stay in the kitchen all day.

Miranda certainly looked comfortable where she was. She had one foot tucked under her as she leaned over her fragrant coffee mug.

''You're addicted, you know.''

She scooped a spoonful of froth from the top of her mug, the foam so dense it was almost like cream. When she touched it to her tongue it evaporated.

''I suppose I am,'' she admitted. ''But as addictions go, this one is far from the most dangerous.''

He settled onto his chair with his coffee, trying to ignore the camera that Miranda had placed on a tripod for today. The lens was pointed right at him, he knew. Miranda seemed to think if she wasn't holding the damn thing in her hands, he'd be less self-conscious.

''But have you considered that your weakness for cappuccino puts you in my power? To my knowledge, I'm your closest source for at least twenty miles.''

''Then I'm doubly under your power. Because I

need your cooperation to make my video. I guess I'll have to be very nice to you, Warren Addison.''

''Sounds good, but somehow I don't believe it.'' He leaned back in his chair, eyeing her notepad under his book. ''So what torture do you have planned for me?''

''Please. Talking to me isn't that awful, is it?''

''Talking to you? No. Having that glass-eyed beast glaring at me?'' He indicated the camera. ''Yes.''

''Come on, you'll forget all about being filmed once we get going. Tell me about your morning. Did you get much writing done?''

''A few pages.'' Not as much as he'd hoped. Probably because he kept checking the time and counting the hours until Miranda would arrive.

His work was suffering, he knew, because he'd decided to cooperate on this video. But he wasn't sorry. At least, not yet. He had months to finish his first draft. The opportunity to spend time with Miranda, he figured, was a once-in-a-lifetime thing.

He'd been curious, initially, to see if she would hold the same appeal for him now as she had when they were schoolmates. To realize that if anything she'd only become more charming, more beautiful, hadn't taken him long.

''Do you follow an outline when you're writing?''

He'd guess these weren't the questions in her notepad. She was warming him up, priming the pump. ''I try to. For the first draft, at least. The second time through I get adventurous, mix things up a little.

Sometimes the whole bloody plot gets turned upside down at that stage.''

"The fictional town you created in your book felt so real. How do you do that?''

"To me Runnymeade is real. So are the people.''

"I notice you say people, not characters. When I read your book I had the strangest experience. As if I had once known everything that happened, but somehow managed to forget it all, and now someone was reminding me.''

"You amaze me, Miranda. The things you say.'' What amazed him even more was that most of the kids they'd gone to school with had considered her a bit of a lightweight. He knew damn well she'd fostered that illusion. And he thought he knew why. At least in part.

"Well, you, too, amaze me. I still can't believe a boy I went to school with wrote this book.'' She patted her copy of the hardcover on the table. "I've been racking my brain trying to remember how you did at school, which subjects were your favorites. English lit, I suppose?''

"Maybe. I wasn't all that focused on schoolwork. Spent most of my time daydreaming. Never got the marks that you did.''

"Pardon me?''

"What's the matter, Miranda? Don't you remember that you graduated with the highest average in the class? That Garland, our old physics teacher, practically begged you to take the scholarship you'd been offered and go to university?''

He could tell he'd made her uncomfortable bringing this up. Shifting in her chair, she reached for her coffee, then changed her mind and pulled out her notebook, holding it to her chest.

"My marks weren't *that* great."

"They were, too. I always wondered how you did it. You didn't spend much time studying at school, and from all accounts your social life was very...social."

"I may have put on a bit of an act in class," she conceded. "But face it. Getting high grades wasn't exactly cool."

"Miranda, you set the standard for cool in Chatsworth. Weren't you proud of your marks? Weren't your parents proud, too?"

"Maybe my dad..."

She stared out, past his shoulder, recalling how gratified she'd felt whenever her father had smiled at her report card. But her mother had always managed to bring her down to earth.

High marks aren't what counts in this world, young lady.

She'd heard these words so often growing up she'd assumed they represented a truth that everyone subscribed to.

But Warren didn't seem to. Her grades had impressed him. Enough so he remembered, all these years later, what her standing in their class had been.

"A high grade-point average doesn't guarantee you'll be a success in the real world, does it? Look at what you've done. I'll bet your editor didn't care how you'd performed in high school when he was reading your manuscript."

"I guess the same could be said for your videos," he countered.

"Please. My videos aren't exactly in the same league as your books."

"Oh, you think you're that much better, do you?"

She scrunched her nose at him. "Stop making fun of me."

"But I'm not. Hell, just because you're beautiful doesn't mean you can't be smart, too. And talented."

Did he really think she was smart? Talented? So many times she'd heard people rave about her looks. But not too often did anyone make comments on her other qualities.

"I have this theory about you, Miranda."

"What do you mean...theory?" A theory implied thought; it implied study and reflection. When had Warren spent all this time thinking about her? And why was a part of her flattered that he'd bothered?

"You're an interesting case," he said. "You always have been. I'm sure you believe that you're beautiful. But I don't think you're as cognizant of your other assets. Your intelligence, or your talent. Why do you suppose that is?"

"I have no idea. And what's more, I don't care. You've managed to spend the past twenty minutes avoiding my questions. That's what this has been about, hasn't it?''

"Don't be annoyed with me. Can I help it if I find you a much more interesting topic of discussion than I could ever be?"

"Well, let me guarantee you that Catherine Cox at the CBC is much more interested in *you*."

"Fine, then. Let's talk about *me*. Would you like to know my first words? The age when I mastered potty training?"

She grinned. "Roll forward a few years. Adolescence. How about we start there. You're fifteen years old and you're in love. Tell me about Bronwyn, Warren. How did you come to date a girl three years older than you?"

Warren's teasing smile dissolved into open-mouthed disbelief. "How the hell did you—" He snapped his fingers. "Of course. Adrienne. That explains the horrible hairdo."

"Speak for yourself. My mother thought I looked quite lovely. But yes, somewhere between the shampoo and the hair dryer Adrienne did mention a few words about you and her sister."

"I see."

As Warren stuffed more wood into the cast-iron stove, Miranda settled herself again at the scarred Arborite table, resisting the urge to reposition her camera. Even if much of her footage ended up being of an empty chair, at least this conversation was being recorded.

A full minute passed before Warren faced her again, brushing dirt and slivers of bark from his hands to his jeans.

"We don't need to discuss Bronwyn, do we? I mean, really. We were just kids. And I wouldn't want to embarrass her by talking about something that was so private."

"I sympathize with what you're saying, Warren, but only to a point. A man's first love can have a powerful impact on his life."

"In some cases, maybe. But Bronwyn and I..."

Hearing him link his name to the other woman's gave Miranda an odd feeling.

"I admired Bronwyn's talent. She had a true artistic sensibility. And she liked my stories. No, *loved* my stories. I guess I was a little intoxicated by that."

"Didn't the age difference matter?"

"Not to us."

"Do you still prefer older women?"

"Do I— Hell, Miranda, what kind of question is that?"

"Well, Bronwyn was three years older than you, and Miss Flemming was more than that."

Warren's eyebrows shot up. "Her, too? God, you've been thorough."

"And you were a virtual high school Don Juan," she countered. Then wished she hadn't sounded so disapproving. In her job she'd uncovered romantic entanglements far more compromising than Warren's early love affairs. In the past, she'd made it a policy to distance herself, to be nonjudgmental.

"Then what were you, Miranda?" Warren sat opposite her—finally within camera range!—and leaned over the table. "You must've dated five guys for every girl I looked at."

"That was different. That was just *dating*. None of those relationships was ever serious. I didn't *sleep* with those guys."

They both fell quiet as the topic of sex settled heavily in the air around them.

"Do you have proof that my relationships with these women were sexual?" he challenged.

Of course she didn't.

"Miss Flemming…Evelyn…is now married and has two children," Warren said finally. "She sent me a card congratulating me on my book. She said she'd always believed I would accomplish something special. And she also mentioned that she's still teaching."

He stared across the table at Miranda, and she knew what he intended for her to understand. This video wasn't to compromise Evelyn Flemming's reputation. Well, that was fine. But in Miranda's opinion the woman was still important.

"It sounds to me that both Evelyn and Bronwyn offered early encouragement that helped shape your future writing career. Their feelings may be hurt if I film this biography without any mention of their contribution. Do you want them to feel they didn't matter?''

He rubbed the side of his face, his sigh hinting at weariness. ''You're manipulating me. And you're damn good at it. How about this? Talk to Evelyn and Bronwyn and see what they say. If they're willing to discuss our relationships with you—fine. But I'm not saying anything more on the subject.''

''Not even about the age-difference thing?''

''I don't see that it was such a big deal.''

''There are *six* years between you and Miss Flemming.''

''I was in grade twelve, eighteen, an adult. Believe it or not, in many ways Evelyn was more naive than I was.''

Miranda had no difficulty believing that, none at all. She considered the man across from her, realizing that every day he proved himself so very different from her initial preconception of him.

What had happened to Warren the loner? Turned out he'd had a much richer love life, at a much younger age, than she—with all her friends and her so-called popularity—ever had.

''Didn't any girls your age interest you?'' The question was already out there, when Miranda realized what she really wanted to know.

Had Warren been interested in *her?*

From the new sharpness in his gaze, she could tell he, too, had figured out what was behind her question.

"But, Miranda, you barely knew I was alive in those days. So what would have been the point?" He stood, stretched his legs. "I may be a dreamer, but I'm also a realist. Why turn down a fulfilling relationship with a flesh-and-blood woman, just to yearn for someone who's completely out of your reach?"

This had to be hypothetical talk. He wasn't saying that he'd spent his high school years yearning for *her*. Still, Miranda felt her body reacting to the images his words provoked. If she had taken the time to get to know Warren when they were younger, who could tell what might have happened.

"Looks like the temperature is warming a little." Warren was at the window, checking the outdoor thermometer again. "It's only twenty-three below zero now. Practically beach weather. Interested in taking that walk?"

She knew she couldn't. She needed time alone to assimilate what had just happened. This had to be the strangest interview she'd ever conducted. Most of the discussion had been about *her,* not Warren.

Again, she had to wonder if he'd done this intentionally. If so, she'd better pull herself together, and soon, or her project was in big trouble.

"Not today. Sorry." She went to pack up her camera. "I've committed to making a lasagna for dinner tonight. I never cook so it's going to be a challenge."

"But isn't Wednesday your mother's bridge night?"

"How do you know that?"

"I may spend a lot of time on my own, but I do read the local paper. Used to be in the newspaper business myself, after all."

He was referring to the school paper. The one he'd worked on with Evelyn Flemming's guidance. Miranda hated the image that immediately came to mind. Warren and his teacher embracing behind a closed classroom door.

Why did it bother her? She didn't really think Warren's teacher took advantage of him.

Was it jealousy, then? But that was equally absurd. Why should she feel jealous about a guy she'd barely even known was alive, to use Warren's words.

"So who's going to eat the lasagna?"

"Oh, Chad will. He's been taking his meals at the café since Bernie kicked him out. I felt sorry for him."

"Oh, really. You felt sorry for him."

Warren's tone was mild, yet she sensed disapproval. "Is there some reason I shouldn't?"

"Maybe you should ask Bernie that question."

She caught and held Warren's gaze. "I hope you're not suggesting it's wrong for me to offer Chad a meal. He's one of my best friends. And I stand by my friends when they're in trouble."

"Admirable."

She couldn't discern a trace of sarcasm in his voice. After zipping up her camera case, she unhooked her jacket from the rack by the door.

"Tomorrow, same time?"

Warren nodded, and she backed out the door, grateful for the reprieve.

She would have her emotions under control by the next day. And she would not deviate from her list of prepared questions.

Whatever Warren had done to her in that room would not happen again.

CHAPTER NINE

MIRANDA DIDN'T like cooking. She preferred restaurants. When pressed, however, she made lasagna from a recipe she'd begged off the chef of her favorite vegetarian bistro.

She ran into a slight problem, though, when she stopped at Lucky's for groceries. No Portobello mushrooms. No eggplant. No feta cheese, for heaven's sake! Lucky's was too pared-down a store to stock these items, and Yorkton was too far away.

She made do with substitutes. Regular button mushrooms, zucchini and shredded Monterey Jack. She supposed she should be grateful for decent-quality canned olives and fresh spinach leaves.

Back at home, she found her mother's kitchen spotless and empty. Good. Annie had already gone to bridge club.

Miranda put on music and drank a glass of wine as she cooked. She told herself not to think about the dreadful conversation she'd had with Warren. If she didn't focus on her cooking, something was bound to go wrong.

The wine helped her relax. Soon, she found herself looking forward to the evening ahead. When the casserole was finally tucked into the oven, she cleaned the kitchen, then herself. Generally, Miranda wore black. Tonight it was a sweater and jeans, spiced up with a leopard-print belt.

She sprayed on perfume, eager for the timer on the stove to buzz. Chad was expecting her shortly and she didn't want to keep him waiting.

Unbidden, Warren's disapproval came back to her. Did he really have a problem with a man and a woman having dinner together as friends? The idea was ridiculous.

Just because Chad was special to her—and no question he was—didn't mean there was anything wrong with her seeing him tonight. It wasn't as if she wanted anything to happen between them. In fact, just yesterday hadn't she offered to end their friendship if it would help his marriage?

And he'd turned her offer down.

The timer on the stove went off just as she was putting on her lipstick. She popped the tube into her purse, then went to pull out the casserole. The liquid at the edges was bubbling; the cheese on the top was melted and slightly browned. Perfect.

She put on the glass lid, then wrapped the steaming casserole in a towel and zipped it inside an insulated picnic bag. In a separate box she packed salad fixings and bread and ice cream for dessert. Soon she was on the road, her car filled with the enticing scent of roasted vegetables and cheese and Italian spices.

First thing she noticed as she approached the clubhouse were the colorful lights on the three evergreens grouped to the right of the main entrance. Chad had decorated for Christmas.

She parked, then hauled out their dinner, leaving the carton of ice cream in her trunk. At fifteen below zero, her car would be colder than whatever refrigeration Chad's clubhouse kitchen could offer. Since her hands were full, she tapped at the kick plate with the toe of her boot.

Almost immediately the door opened. Expecting Chad, she was speechless when she saw Vicky. His twelve-year-old daughter wasn't surprised to see her, however.

"You're here! I've been waiting and waiting!" She stepped back so Miranda could enter. Chad came striding into the room from his office.

"Let me take that." He scooped the food effortlessly into his arms, then glanced behind her. "You didn't happen to bring my sweaters, too?"

"Sorry. Forgot the sweaters." Darn! She'd left them drying on towels near the heat register in her room. Not in the laundry room, where her mother would see them. The small deception nagged, even though she knew it was necessary. Her mother just wasn't wired to understand modern-day thinking.

"I'll bring them tomorrow."

"That would be great. Say, Vic, could you go to the kitchen and grab us some plates? Knives and forks, too, I guess."

When the young girl had left, Miranda said quietly, "Your night with Vicky?"

"Yeah. I get her every Wednesday after piano. Didn't I tell you?"

Yes, he had, but she'd forgotten. Not that she minded. No, she was pleased to have this chance to get to know Chad's daughter better.

Vicky returned from the kitchen with a loaded tray. "I just love your car," she told Miranda as she set the tray on the table. "Dad, when I turn sixteen you've got to get me a punch-buggy."

"Is that before or after I buy the big-screen TV and DVD player for your bedroom?" Chad went to the vending machines. "What would everyone like to drink?"

She should have brought a bottle of wine, Miranda realized. She'd expected Chad would have something, but maybe he wasn't comfortable drinking with Vicky present. Especially when he had to drive her home later.

"Root beer," Vicky ordered.

"Water's fine for me." Miranda glanced around the room. While the view from the large picture windows would be wonderful in the summer, those thin panes of glass let in a lot of cold air. The room's large dimensions didn't help create any sense of coziness or comfort.

"Could we possibly eat in your office? It's warmer in there."

"You've been in Dad's office?" Vicky asked.

Oops. Had she said the wrong thing? Chad, popping loonies for drinks, didn't seem perturbed.

"Randy's dropped by a couple of times. To say hi when she first arrived, then later for a ski."

"So you guys were, like, friends in high school?"

"Even longer than that," Miranda said. "Do you remember when we started hanging together, Chad?"

"Shortly after I figured out that there really wasn't such a thing as girl germs and you didn't get them sharing the same pencil."

Chad passed Miranda the drinks, then picked up the container of food. "Bring the tray, okay, Vic? We'll humor Randy and eat in the office. I'm warning you, though. No tables or chairs."

"We'll sit on the floor around the coffee table. It'll be fun!" One thing she *had* thought of, and that was candles. She placed them randomly on the table, as Chad unwrapped the still-steaming casserole dish.

"Hmm. Looks like green stuff in here," he said. "Smells good, though—hey, Vic?"

"Just let me toss the salad and then we can eat. Chad, would you slice the bread? I think I packed a knife."

"You sure did. What I want to know is if there's anything left in your mother's kitchen."

"Maybe it would have been easier if we'd come to *your* house for dinner," Vicky said.

Miranda didn't comment.

Chad cleared his throat and glanced at the space heater. "Should I jack up the temperature a little?"

The room was plenty warm, but Miranda didn't object. Sitting cross-legged on the floor, she began to dish out the casserole.

"Just a small piece, please," Vicky said. "I'm not a very big eater."

Or maybe Vicky didn't like the look of the casserole. Miranda wished she'd known she was cooking for a twelve-year-old.

"Two more days till the weekend." Chad held out his plate next. "What do you want to do, Vic?"

"Go shopping in Yorkton." She shot Miranda a shy, pleading look. "Maybe you could come with us."

Miranda smiled at the invitation. She'd love to go. But would her inclusion in a family outing send the wrong message? "I don't know, Vicky. Wouldn't you rather have your dad to yourself?"

What did Chad think? She couldn't tell. But Vicky didn't give him a chance to voice his opinion.

"I see him *all* the time. Plus, I *love* the way you dress. Your belt is just so awesome. Could you help me find something for the Christmas dance?" She shot her dad a glance. "*Not* a cute little-girl dress. I'm *way* too old for that sort of thing."

Vicky had to be referring to the annual Chatsworth Christmas potluck and dance. Miranda wondered if Bernie would be there, and realized the event might be very uncomfortable for the newly separated Englishes.

"Well, of course you are. And I'd love to come along. If it's okay with your dad."

"Hey, fine with me," Chad said. "We'll hit the mall for an hour—"

"Only an *hour?*"

"Well, maybe two," he compromised. "If you guys promise to let me take you to dinner and a movie after. And not a chick flick, either. Something with *action.*"

"I heard that *Lord of the Rings* movie is showing," Vicky said.

Miranda had already seen it. But Vicky and Chad were keen, so she acquiesced. She questioned Vicky about other movies that she'd enjoyed, then asked about books. Vicky didn't care much for reading; she preferred listening to music.

"Hey, Miranda… Want any more casserole? We need to wind up here. Vic has homework and she left her stuff at home."

Vicky was clearing off her plate. She'd made a neat pile of all the unwanted vegetables—which seemed to be most of them. Even Chad had picked out the olives and mushrooms. Between the two of them, though, they'd demolished the loaf of bread. At least something on the table had met with their approval.

"Sorry, guys. Guess you would've liked a standard ground-beef lasagna better, right?"

"Yours was good," Vicky insisted, despite the evidence to the contrary. "Are you a vegetarian?"

"Yes."

"Wow. I've never met a vegetarian before."

Miranda had to laugh. "It's really not that glamorous. Or that rare." At least not in Toronto. But in Chatsworth it probably was.

Chad wrapped the towel around the glass dish. "When did this happen? You had no trouble with hamburgers and hot dogs when we were younger. I bet some guy in Toronto converted you."

He made her dietary choice sound like a religion. "Actually, a female roommate I had a couple of years ago, before I could afford my own place, was a vegetarian. We were both short of cash and you wouldn't believe the money you can save when you cut meat out of your diet. Eventually I just came to prefer eating this way."

Chad snuffed out the candles, then packed them. "Sorry if we're rushing you. I promised her mother I'd have her home before eight."

"No problem. I was finished, anyway." The ice cream would keep for another day. She took her plate to the kitchen, where she helped Vicky wash up. When they were done, Chad met them at the front door.

"I could drive Vicky home," she offered. The English house was just a few streets from her mother's.

"Yeah!"

Chad took his daughter's arm. "Thanks, Randy, but it's probably best that I take her."

What an idiot she was. First she'd struck out with the vegetarian lasagna. Now she'd tactlessly offered to drive Vicky home. Bernie, undoubtedly, was expecting Chad. Perhaps they had matters they needed to discuss.

"But I want a ride in the punch-buggy...."

"Maybe this weekend, Vic. Thanks for dinner, Randy. You'll keep Saturday open for us?" His smile was warm, and suddenly the evening didn't feel like a disaster at all.

"I look forward to it," she assured them. Then, winking at Vicky, she added, "Just make sure your credit card is in good working order, Chad."

THE NEXT DAY MIRANDA TOOK some footage of the schools—not only the high school, but also the brick elementary building where Warren had taken grades one through six.

She interviewed a couple of the teachers who had known him—silently marveling at how they could still be teaching twelve years later at the same school in the same small town. They probably knew more about Chatsworth and the people who lived here than anyone.

Keith Garland, who'd taught her grade twelve sciences, was now the high school principal. Other than stooped shoulders and a little less hair, he was unchanged. They chatted about Warren's success, and he professed himself pleased but not surprised.

"That kid always approached a subject from left field. I knew that whatever he did, it would be different."

She would include that quip, Miranda thought as she pulled back from the close-up. "I'd like to talk to some of the other teachers. Miss Flemming, for instance, since she taught us English."

"Oh, she left Chatsworth long ago. Year after you graduated, I believe." Mr. Garland ducked out of his office, beckoning for her to follow. In the wide hallway, class photos in black, glass-covered frames spread out along either wall.

The principal headed for the one hanging above the water fountain between the doors to two washrooms—girls on the right, boys on the left. God, she'd had her first try at smoking in there!

"You were class of '90, right?"

"Absolutely." There they were, all eleven of them! She was almost smack in the middle, with Bernie right in front of her and Warren and Chad in the back row. Adrienne was there, too, next to Bernie... She needed a minute to retrieve a few of the other names.

Keith Garland put a finger on the picture of the teacher standing off to the side: Miss Flemming, their homeroom teacher. She stood in her knee-length skirt and buttoned-down blouse, bangs curled demurely over her forehead. Who could have guessed she was romantically involved with one of her students!

Warren's photo proved equally misleading. In it he looked like an overgrown, gangly puppy with his long, skinny arms, prominent nose and disheveled dark hair.

"Yup," the principal said. "This was the last year she taught at Chatsworth. I believe she transferred to Yorkton for a term, then Regina."

"I'd love to talk to her. I bet she'd have plenty of insight into Warren's…writing potential." She'd paused deliberately to see if he picked up on any other meaning. But he appeared oblivious.

"Well, I could see if she's still working for the Saskatchewan Board of Education."

"That would be so helpful. If you do track her down, you can reach me at my mother's."

"How is Annie?" her former teacher asked with more than passing interest. "We had a few memorable interviews when you were a student."

"I don't remember getting in that much trouble."

"Of course not. You were my top student. I was determined that you should go on to university, but your mother was very definite in her plans where your future was concerned."

Oh, yes. Annie James had known what was best for her daughter, all right. And thought she still did.

"But obviously you found your niche, anyway." Garland nodded his approval. "Good for you, Miranda."

She was only a videobiographer, with just a handful of completed films to her credit. Still, his approval felt good.

She left the school, then checked her watch. She had time to visit the library, two streets away. Years ago, the white clapboard house had been abandoned by its owners. The town had taken it over for unpaid property taxes.

Her mother's morning shift was long over. In her stead Miranda found Mrs. Jenson, Adrienne's petite, late-fiftyish mother. Miranda couldn't believe her luck.

"Hi, I'm Annie's daughter, Miranda."

"Miranda!" She could not have sounded more delighted if she were greeting her long-lost best friend. "I was hoping I'd get a chance to see you while you were in town. Look at you, still the beauty."

A brief, friendly interrogation followed, before Miranda could finally squeeze in a few questions about Mrs. Jenson's daughters. Eventually, she focused on the one of most interest to her at this moment.

"I hear Bronwyn and her husband have a graphic design firm in Calgary."

"That's right. We're so proud of them, although grandchildren would be nice. But those two are always so busy."

"Could I possibly get her address and phone number? Mom may have told you I'm working on a biography of Warren Addison, and apparently..." She had to tread gently here, not sure if Bronwyn's mother had known of the relationship.

"Oh, yes, Bronwyn was quite impressed with that boy. Told me he would write a book one day, mark her words."

"Well, she certainly was right. Do you think she'd mind talking to me?"

"Not at all." Mrs. Jenson printed the address and phone number neatly on the back of a due-date reminder, already stamped with that day's date.

Before heading back to her mother's, Miranda detoured by the clubhouse to drop off Chad's sweaters. He wasn't around so she left them just inside the unlocked doors, on a table. At home she found Annie peeling vegetables in the kitchen. They hadn't had a chance to chat since the previous morning.

"How was bridge club last night?" Washed salad ingredients were on a nearby cutting board, so she started to chop the cucumber.

Annie shook her head. "Had terrible cards all night. A tasty dinner, though. Diane made that casserole recipe of her mother's…. Seems you were cooking last night, too."

She turned toward her daughter, with an *aha!* look in her eyes. Miranda thought back, trying to figure out what clue she'd inadvertently left for her mother to find.

Annie took great pleasure in telling her. "There was a lingering odor in the oven. Plus a zucchini in the chill drawer that *I* didn't buy."

Miranda could see that she'd have to 'fess up.

"I made a vegetarian lasagna for Chad and his daughter. He's been taking most of his meals at the café."

"And how is that your problem? Miranda, I appreciate that you were friends when you were younger, but I don't think it's wise for you to spend too much time with that man. You can be sure Bernie kicked him out for good reason. There's another woman…has been for years. You don't want to get in the middle of something ugly."

Miranda diced the cucumber. "That's just malicious gossip." She'd *know* if Chad was up to something, even if he hadn't had the nerve to tell her.

"I stopped by the school today to interview some of Warren's old teachers."

"Hmm?"

Her mother didn't sound very interested. But what else were they going to talk about?

"I spoke to Keith Garland at the high school. He remembered you."

"Really?"

It was kind of cute—that coquettish lilt in her mother's voice.

"Was he your mathematics teacher?"

"No. Sciences. Biology, physics, chemistry…"

"I know what sciences are, Miranda. He was the one who wanted you to go on to university." Now that she'd pinpointed him, her tone sharpened.

"I believe so."

"The man was totally outrageous. To think a woman with beauty like yours would choose to squander her most valuable years in classrooms and libraries…" Annie transferred the peeled potatoes to a pot on the stove. "A woman's prime lasts a mere ten, fifteen years. Such a precious, short period."

She adjusted the dial on the stove, then stopped to look at her daughter. At thirty-two, Miranda realized, she must seem already over the hill to her mother.

"I've been a disappointment to you, haven't I, Mom?"

"Well." Annie wiped her hands on a clean towel. "I'm sure you tried your best. Show business is very competitive. Maybe if I'd sent you to Los Angeles instead of Toronto. But it's a big city and I was scared what might happen to you."

This was *her* life Annie was talking about. Yet Miranda couldn't dredge up any anger or resentment. Her mother was the way she was. And a part of Miranda actually felt guilty. She hadn't really tried her hardest to excel at modeling and she'd barely given acting a shot.

She didn't want those careers. She never had.

"I was married at twenty-one." Annie stood by the mirror that hung over the table. Every room in this house, Miranda realized suddenly, had a mirror. She watched as her mother ran a hand down the side of her face, her hand smoothing the wrinkled skin as it went.

"I squandered my best years in this small town."

Miranda tensed, waiting for the rest. How Annie had devoted the prime of her life to her husband, only to have him abandon her in middle age. Now she was trapped in this small town, too poor to move to a bigger city. All men were bums, none more so than Miranda's father.

"You're still beautiful, Mom."

"You think?" Annie tilted her head to the side and back, lengthening her neck. She held the pose a second, then sighed and turned away.

"Oh, who am I kidding? I'm old enough to be a grandmother." She glanced again at her daughter, and Miranda caught the unspoken message.

She hadn't delivered in that department, either. All in all, Miranda James was one disappointing daughter.

CHAPTER TEN

BERNIE'S COFFEE was too hot.

"Hey, Donna! Can I get some skim milk over here?"

Donna Werner and her husband owned the café. In the kitchen Jim fried eggs, bacon and hash browns. All of which smelled sinfully good. Moving languidly between tables and the counter, Donna covered more ground than she appeared to. Within seconds she stood at Bernie's table with a pitcher of cream.

"I said *skim milk,* Donna."

"Don't stock the stuff. Might as well add cold water to your coffee. Would you like a glass of water, Bernie?"

"Whatever. Just please take that cream away." She couldn't stand the temptation. Coming here had been a stupid idea. As if she wasn't having a hard enough time sticking to her diet.

But she hadn't wanted to be home when Chad came to pick up Vicky for his weekend. Apparently Miranda was included in their plans for the day.

And night?

Surely Chad wouldn't sleep with the woman while his daughter was with him.

But then, who knew what Chad would do anymore? She sure didn't.

Nothing was working out as expected, her new beautification plan included. So far she hadn't lost a pound, even though she was starving almost all the time.

She'd pored over those books from the library but hadn't been able to figure out where she fit on the color wheel. Her hair wasn't dark and it wasn't light. Her eyes were blue, but also had flecks of green and gray. As for her skin tone, she couldn't tell if it was golden or pink. Actually, gray seemed the closest match. But there was no gray listed on the chart.

Maybe she didn't fit into any of the classifications because no color existed that could possibly suit her.

So much for that new wardrobe she'd planned on.

And she was in a similar quandary about her hair. According to *that* chapter, she needed a feathered cut, parted at the side and framing her petite, slightly squared face. Highlights would probably help. But who was supposed to work this magical transformation? She wanted to book an appointment with Yolanda's in Yorkton. From what she'd heard, Yolanda was the best.

But what would Adrienne say if she went to another hairdresser? There was no way she wouldn't notice. Her feelings would be so hurt.

A table of men, farmers in work clothes and ball

caps, stood up from their yolk-stained empty plates. She didn't recognize the one with a toothpick in his mouth, but nodded to the father of one of her students from last year. After they'd exited, she realized she was the only one left in the café.

Donna shuffled the men's dirty dishes to the counter, then wiped the table. Eventually, she made her way to Bernie with that glass of water.

"Everything okay?" Donna settled into the opposite side of the booth and slipped her feet out of her rubber-soled white shoes.

"Just peachy." Bernie sipped at the water as she waited for her coffee to cool. How much longer before she could head home? She checked her watch and decided to give Vicky, Chad and Miranda another five minutes to be sure. She'd been in such a rush she'd gone out in her sweats and without a shower—again. No way was Miranda James going to catch her in this condition a second time.

"So where's Vicky?"

"Spending the weekend with her father. They're off to Yorkton for shopping, then dinner and a movie." Bernie traced the flecked pattern on the table with her finger. What she wouldn't give for Chad to spend a day like that with her.

"The James girl going, too?"

For the first time that morning Bernie focused on Donna. She saw the older woman's gray hair, up in her usual bun, and her pale, lined skin and thin, colorless lips. In her neutral eyes was no malice, only commiseration.

"Yeah."

Donna wagged her head disapprovingly. "I suppose you heard she cooked them dinner on Wednesday night. And went skiing, just her and Chad, the day before that."

How did these stories get spread? Someone noticed a parked car where it didn't belong; someone else overheard a conversation or a one-sided phone call...whatever. The one thing Bernie could be grateful for was that she had no need to hire a private investigator. This town was more than capable of itemizing every last one of her husband's wrongdoings.

Bernie picked up her mug of Donna's boiled coffee and took a sip.

Too cold.

"I guess I'd better get going. Should vacuum the place and do laundry." She put change on the table and nodded farewell to Donna. At the door she paused while the two Browning girls wandered in from the street.

"Hello, Nicole, Allie. Your mom in town doing some shopping?"

"Yes, Mrs. English. We get to order ice cream, even though we haven't had lunch yet." Allie, the blond one, spoke. Her stepsister, always quieter, just smiled shyly. Bernie smiled back. Nicole had been one of her favorites when she'd had her in grade two—a few years ago now.

"Well, have fun. I'll see you both on the playground Monday."

Bernie set a brisk pace back to her house, wondering if she could consider this her workout for the day. The yoga tapes weren't panning out. She'd like to see one person over the age of twenty-five in Chatsworth who could contort her body into those poses.

Well, one person might be able to. The person who was sitting in the front passenger seat of her ridiculous yellow car, which was parked out front of Bernie's house right this moment. No sign of Chad. He must be inside, collecting Vicky.

Damn! Why were they so late? Probably Miranda had kept them waiting while she dried that cute blond hair of hers and put on her makeup. Even through the slightly frosty window, Bernie could tell the other woman looked perfect. Ignoring Randy's halfhearted wave, Bernie stomped up the front sidewalk in her heavy, practical winter boots. At the door, she almost collided with Chad's chest.

"See you later, Mom!" Vicky breezed past her parents as she dashed toward the waiting car.

Chad, handsome as ever in his *clean* Nordic sweater and unzipped leather coat, swallowed nervously.

"I see you don't have the Christmas lights up."

A criticism would have to be the first thing out of

his mouth. "They didn't make the priority list this year."

"I'll swing by some night next week and string them up. I'd like to check the furnace at the same time. Filters could probably stand with a cleaning."

Bernie scrutinized the face that was so familiar, yet so unfathomable. By offering to do those jobs was he telling her he still cared? Or was he just worried about making Christmas nice for Vicky and keeping up the maintenance on their home?

She gave a noncommittal nod. "If you want."

"Maybe we could…"

She waited, part of her hopeful, part of her angry. Was he going to suggest they have a meal together? She'd love the chance to cook for him again—whatever Miranda had going for *her,* Bernie, at least, had Chad's favorite pot roast recipe.

Yet, why should she make a meal for her vagabond husband? He'd been skiing with Miranda and having her over to the golf course. In flagrant disregard with one of the conditions she'd set on his moving home.

Anyway, she—Bernie—shouldn't be cooking for him. He should be wining and dining her. If he loved her, that is. If he wanted to get back together.

A honk from the Volkswagen startled them. Vicky unrolled the window. "Come *on,* Dad."

"I'll have her home before dinner on Sunday."

A wave of his hand and then he was down the sidewalk, sliding into the driver's seat next to Miranda. In the back, Vicky leaned forward with something to say, not even bothering to wave goodbye to her mother.

Watching them drive off, Bernie could only think about the color of their hair. Matching. Three blondes!

IF YOU LOVED SHOPPING and if you were very good at it—and Miranda qualified on both counts—then you could view Yorkton as either a fashion wasteland or a bargain-hunter's paradise. Miranda chose the latter. In their allotted two hours, she and Vicky scoured the discount outlets, department stores and retail chains in the city's largest mall.

They put together the perfect holiday outfit for Vicky. Black pants—the kind *all* the girls were wearing—and a sweater in an exuberant red that worked magic on Vicky's pale coloring. Chad even sprang for black platform shoes, and Miranda steered Vicky toward one of the less-clunky styles.

Passing a department store display of Christmas sweaters for men, Miranda noticed a cream-colored, ribbed cotton turtleneck.

She thought of Warren. Like her, he tended to wear mostly dark colors. But the camera would love him in this lighter shade. She picked up a Large and carried it to the till.

The three of them snacked at the food court, then Miranda and Vicky trailed after Chad as he made stops at the hardware store, the bank and the Ford dealership.

"Looking for a new car?" Miranda guessed that his truck was a pretty recent model.

"I wish." Chad left them to speak to a salesman about a part that he had ordered for some equipment at the golf course. Miranda and Vicky took turns behind the wheel of a leather-seated Thunderbird, a high-riding Windstar van and a spacious Crown Victoria.

"I don't know." Miranda pretended to be torn by indecision. "The van is practical, I suppose, and the Crown Victoria has every luxury. Somehow, though, the Thunderbird feels more *us*. What color should we get, Vicky?"

Finally, Chad was done and they went for their pizza—Vicky's choice—then a movie, the sci-fi one. Driving home, Miranda reflected that the day had been very pleasant. She dropped father and daughter off at the entrance to the clubhouse, wondering if she'd get an invitation for vending machine coffee.

But Chad waved goodbye with just a "Thanks" and "See you again soon."

She drove off into the dark, alone, her cheery mood dissipated. The outing was over; it was back to real life for her.

Still, it had been fun while it lasted. More than a few times she'd noticed the three of them attracting a smile of approval from a stranger or shop clerk. *Nice family,* she could read in their eyes. And she'd enjoyed pretending it was true. That Vicky was her daughter and Chad her spouse.

Another one of her fantasies. She was very aware that she had merely "borrowed" another woman's husband and daughter. Bernie should have been with them today.

Not her.

MIRANDA'S DOWN mood lasted all Sunday, and Monday morning, too. After her mother had left for her morning shift at the library, Miranda settled at the kitchen table to make some calls. Periodically, she stared out the window into the backyard of her childhood.

Snow lay over Annie's rectangular garden patch and frosted the branches of the prolific raspberry bush that divided one yard from the next. Miranda remembered the many times she'd been sent out by her mother to pick the berries that popped out by the hundreds every night in the summer. She'd brought them in by the gallon pail full and her mother had canned some, made jam and jelly with others, and still ended up giving the majority to neighbors.

She wondered if Bernie grew raspberries in her backyard. She'd bet that she did. Probably had a garden, as well. Miranda pictured Chad digging it up in the spring, then Bernie and Vicky planting the seeds.

Even though she'd never seen the three of them together, Miranda just knew that they were the kind of family who did things like that.

She made another long-distance phone call and talked to the woman on the other end of the line for a good half hour. After hanging up the phone, Miranda jotted down a list of questions, preparing herself for the day ahead.

It was time to go to Warren's. Time to stop indulging in this funk and concentrate on the work she'd come here to do.

Resolutely, she packed her equipment into her car. The drive went smoothly. No snow had fallen in the past twenty-four hours and the roads were clear, with perfect visibility.

Adrenaline surged as she pulled into the now-familiar lane. With Warren, she never knew what to expect. After a day and a half of lethargy, she needed a little excitement.

She stepped out of her car, then lugged out her camera, her notebook and the bag with the new sweater. Warren met her at the door.

"Good timing. I just backed up my disk."

She paused on the doorstep. Was it possible the man became better-looking every day? She turned her mind from the distracting thought. "Is that fresh-brewed cappuccino I smell?"

"As I said, good timing." He hung her coat up as she struggled out of her boots.

Miranda passed him the bag. "I bought you a present."

"It's only November." He nodded toward the

counter, where an extra mug of cappuccino sat waiting.

"It's a *just because* present." Miranda sipped her beverage. It was so, *so* good. Watching Warren pull the sweater from the bag, she added, "Actually, it's a self-serving present. I wanted to get some footage of you wearing a lighter color. It seems everything you own is black."

Warren held the sweater up for inspection. From his expression, she couldn't tell what he thought.

"You wear a lot of black, too," he pointed out.

His gaze skimmed her tight sweater and hip-hugging pants. Both were indeed black. But she hoped he also noticed the chic silver belt that she felt emphasized her slender waist.

"I'm the one who stands *behind* the camera," she reminded him.

"Despite your mother's very best efforts to the contrary." He settled his cup of coffee in the palm of one hand, then leaned against the far counter in a relaxed posture that belied his ever-alert eyes.

"So, Miranda, what's in your notebook today?"

"Questions. And they're all about *you.*" She pointed a finger at his chest. "And you're not allowed to distract me. When I left here on Friday I felt as drained as if I'd just endured a marathon therapy session."

"Not a bad analogy. When you start winging your questions at me, that's exactly how *I* feel."

"Well, maybe a little therapy is what you need."

"Having you around has helped me identify several needs." He raised his dark eyebrows. "Therapy not being one of them."

Was he flirting? Miranda could hardly tell; he hadn't cracked even the smallest of smiles.

"Well, that sounds interesting. Want to tell me more?"

"Not really. But you'll probably pry the details from me eventually. You're like a black hole, Miranda. Your force of gravity draws me in. I gush and gush and you just keep absorbing. I'm not at all sure it's healthy. I'm going to start thinking I'm the most fascinating man on earth."

"To me you are," she said.

"Please, Miranda. Don't feed the fantasy."

"But it's true." Surprisingly true. She was always superinterested at the beginning of a new project. But with Warren, her creative energy seemed to be hitting an all-time high. That he served the best coffee this side of the Regina airport didn't hurt. Was it the caffeine that made her feel so buzzed whenever she was around him?

"Still, I would have to say 'gush' is quite an exaggeration. I only wish you would." She slipped her camera out of its case, powered it on. "You'll never guess who I spoke to this morning."

He eyed the camera warily. "I'm afraid to ask."

"I'll bet you can guess with just one clue. Both seem to have found you just as fascinating as I do."

Through the viewfinder, he looked unruffled. But

she could sense his tension as he waited for her to elaborate.

"I'm talking about Bronwyn and Evelyn Flemming, of course. You'll be interested to know, they were more than happy to talk about you."

"You didn't use scare tactics? Threaten to have Adrienne give them a perm?"

"I'm surprised you think I would stoop so low. Actually, they were pleased that I'd called. Both want to help with the video." She couldn't resist teasing. "In fact, I'd say they're still a little in love with you."

There'd been something in their voices when they'd spoken of Warren. A tenderness that implied happy, magical, sweet memories.

She didn't want to be jealous. The emotion had always struck her as so negative, so selfish. And yet it was hard not to envy those women the magic of their first love. She herself had managed to miss out on that milestone. Of the guys she'd dated in high school, none lingered in her memory as particularly special.

Even the man she'd lost her virginity to, during one of her brief stints at modeling, had become blurry in her memory. Their relationship had been short and embarrassingly superficial.

"Why do you think they feel that way about you, Warren?" She wasn't sure that this urge to probe had anything to do with her video now. She just wanted to know. Where did the magic come from? Why had she never found any of her own?

"First love, I guess. They say a woman never forgets hers."

She lowered the camera. "Is the same true of men? Do you still carry a torch for your ex-girlfriends?"

"At the time they meant the world to me. And I still care about them, of course."

She noticed he didn't mention love. "You're lucky. So many relationships end bitterly."

"Speaking from experience?"

"Not really." None of her relationship had ever been serious enough to cause much of a splash when they ended.

"We've talked about my love life, inside and out. Not a word about yours…"

"You ought to be grateful I haven't bored you with the details. I'm beginning to believe some people are born unlucky in love."

"And you figure you're one of them?"

She shrugged.

"You don't know yourself very well if you think that."

"Oh, really? And who does?" She could guess the answer. He thought he did. Of all the nerve. She'd sworn she wouldn't let him get under her skin today, and look what was happening already….

"I'll bet you haven't even admitted to yourself the

real reason you came back to Chatsworth,'' Warren continued.

''To do this biography—''

''Like hell. I was just a convenient excuse. Just for once, Miranda, why don't you admit the truth? It might do you a world of good.''

WARREN COULD TELL HIS question had startled Miranda. She glanced away from him, while her thumb worried the silver ring on her pinkie. Reaching out, he grasped her hand, and her fingers immediately stilled.

''Of course I'm here because of the biography. I've never had a project I felt more committed to.''

''But you have another reason for being here.'' Miranda was an expert at avoidance, but he would get the truth out of her this time.

''Well, my mother hasn't been well.''

''Right.'' He dismissed that excuse impatiently. ''And what else? Or should I say *who* else did you want to see when you decided to come home for a few months?''

''What are you driving at, Warren? Let go of my hand—you're squeezing too hard.''

Reluctantly, he released his hold on her, but he kept up the eye contact. Finally, she let out a sigh.

''I guess I was interested in seeing Chad again. It's been a lot of years.''

''You knew he and Bernie had separated?''

"Not until I arrived. My mother told me the news during dinner my first night home."

That was hard to believe. "Good timing on your part."

"I don't know what you mean. Chad and I kept in touch, but he never confided his marriage problems to me."

Well, there was something to be thankful for. She hadn't shown up like a vulture, in for the kill.

"I don't see why you're looking at me like that. As if I've done something wrong. Chad and I have been friends for a long time. I feel badly about the problems he's been going through lately. I've been trying to help…."

He had to laugh at that. "Do you really think you're helping Chad and Bernie's marriage by cooking Chad meals and taking his daughter shopping in Yorkton?"

"I can't believe this town! I might as well post my every movement on the Internet. Only, gossip circulates around here much more efficiently than it ever could on the Web."

"Look, Miranda. I agree with you on one point. This is your business—you don't have to answer to anyone else. But just be honest with yourself about what you want."

"You think I want Chad, is that it? That I'm *glad* his marriage is in trouble, that I'm hanging around hoping to catch him on the rebound? Well, I think that's totally *disgusting*."

"Are you telling me that you don't care about Chad? That you aren't in love with him?"

She twirled away, but not before he caught the surprise that rounded her eyes. "Don't be ridiculous."

"And don't you insult my intelligence. You've always loved Chad. I figured that out in grade ten and it's still true now."

"Well, maybe I did."

He'd known it, but hearing her admission still hurt. God, he wasn't a kid anymore. Why couldn't he have more control over his feelings?

"But even if I did love Chad, even if I still do…that doesn't mean I'd want to cause problems between him and Bernie. If I was that sort of person, don't you think I would have tried before they were married?"

"I did sometimes wonder why you didn't. If you'd made a play for Chad, I doubt he would have resisted." He honestly didn't understand how the other man could have even tried.

"At times I was tempted. But it would have been a mistake. So what if I managed to seduce Chad with my body? I was interested in his heart. Bernie always had that."

She blinked and glanced away from him. Warren felt frustrated. Furious. It wasn't right. None of this. Yet, what could he say to make her see what she was doing to herself?

There was only one reason for a woman like Miranda to have spent all these years pining after a man like Chad. It wasn't his boy-next-door good looks, or his surface charm, either.

Miranda had set her sights on Chad because he was unattainable.

She hadn't planned this consciously, but it didn't matter. The result was the same. By her own admission Miranda had reached the age of thirty-two without having ever experienced a truly fulfilling and loving relationship with a member of the opposite sex.

She claimed to be unlucky in love.

No. He didn't think so.

"It's because I care about Chad that I want him to be happy. If he loves Bernie, I want to help him save his marriage. You can believe that or not, but it's the truth."

Seeing her earnest expression, Warren couldn't remain angry. Gently, he cupped her face between his hands. "I believe you, Miranda. But just tell me this. Supposing Chad didn't love Bernie. What would you want in that circumstance?"

She lowered her eyes from his. "You're just playing games with me, Warren. It isn't a fair question."

He took both her hands this time and pulled her inches from his chest. "Why not? All I'm asking is if you can imagine being married to Chad. Living in this town full-time, giving up your career. Do you think you'd be happy?"

He wanted her to confront her fantasy and see just how ridiculous it was. She didn't belong with Chad.

She belonged with *him*.

CHAPTER ELEVEN

MIRANDA FELT DIZZY, disoriented, confused. It wasn't just the twisting conversation, but a physical reaction...to Warren.

Had she ever been this close to him? A minute ago he'd touched her face so gently. Now he was holding her hands, pulling her forward to him. And she liked his touches—all of them.

"Warren, I can't answer that question. I can't even understand why we're talking about this." She'd promised herself that today she'd stick to her questions about Warren. How had they ended up discussing her feelings for Chad?

She crossed the room, needing more distance. Holding out her hands to the stove's warmth gave her an excuse to turn her back on Warren for a moment while she regained her composure.

"If we could just get on track with the biography," she finally said, "I would really appreciate it."

"Miranda..."

"I don't want to waste time that you could be spending on your writing." The muscles in her neck and shoulders were so tense that her head had begun to ache.

What was Warren trying to prove? She hated knowing that he'd guessed about her feelings for Chad. Had she been that obvious? Or maybe Warren was more observant than most people.

"Look, it's getting late already. Why don't I leave my list of questions with you. Mull them over and we can talk some more tomorrow...."

Despite her best efforts, this session was even more of a disaster than the last one. She was in deep, deep trouble and she knew it. She put her camera back in the case, wondering if her career was on the verge of ending. If she couldn't get a better grip on her emotions...

Warren watched, unsmiling. After a few moments, when she was ready to walk out the door, he nodded at the window.

"You want to drive in that?"

"What?" She shifted her gaze, then couldn't stop from moaning. "Oh, no." Snow was falling by the bucketful and a northeasterly wind had it buffeting the pane of glass. Already the ground was covered. She couldn't even see the car she'd parked just twenty feet away.

The morning forecast *had* called for snow, beginning in the afternoon and continuing throughout the night. She hadn't expected a dump like this, though. "I'd better leave now, while I'm able."

"Not in that little yellow tin can of yours." Warren sounded incredulous.

She pulled her coat off the hook. "The storm just started. The roads will be fine."

"With that wind? I doubt it. And what about visibility? You won't see five feet in front of you—even with headlights you'll be risking a head-on collision."

She didn't want to listen. As she opened the door, the wind almost forced the knob out of her hands. Using her shoulder, she closed the door behind her—practically in Warren's face.

Ice crystals bit at her eyelids, her cheeks, her lips, as she lowered her head and waded through snow already above her ankles. Her car looked like a giant snowball. She brushed the powder from the handle, then leaned inside to start the ignition. With a mittened hand, she set to work clearing off the windows, while the tailpipe shot pungent gray fumes into the air.

She was covered with thick white powder by the time she sat behind the steering wheel. She shifted to Drive and felt the tires spin for a few moments before gaining enough traction to move her VW forward. The car's back wheels slid sideways, then straightened. She peered out the front window with narrowed eyes, but she couldn't even tell where the lane was anymore. With her luck she'd drive into Mrs. Addison's old garden or hit the drainage ditch that ran alongside the main road. She shifted back into Park.

The air blowing out of the heating system was still

cold. Still, the snow on her hair and eyelashes had begun to melt. She brushed a wet mitten over her face and smeared the moisture across her cheek. In Toronto, when these freak storms hit, she relied on the subway. Out here, she couldn't even call a cab.

She was stuck. Stuck in an eighty-year-old farmhouse with poorly insulated windows and an old wood stove in the kitchen for heating. Stuck with Warren Addison and his million annoying questions.

With a twist of her fingers, she switched off the engine. Towing her camera and bag along, she left the car and headed back to the house.

Warren—annoying man that he was—had a fresh cappuccino waiting, just for her. How could she remain angry with him now?

"You were right. I couldn't see a thing." She set her wet mittens on a chair next to the fired-up wood stove, then sat at the table. It seemed she and Warren had no choice but to spend the next few hours together. She took the fresh coffee as his peace offering, and tried to summon a smile.

"It's cold out there." She shook her head and droplets of melted snow scattered around her.

"Warm yourself by the stove," Warren advised. "I'll just be a few minutes."

He slipped out of the room, and Miranda relaxed deeper into her chair. This time she was going to enjoy her cappuccino. She took a sip, then sighed. This beat digging a small yellow Volkswagen out of a snowdrift. Indeed it did.

Seconds ticked by on the old clock above the stove. Seconds turned to minutes and soon her mug was empty. Energized by caffeine and her brief outing in the cold, Miranda tidied the kitchen, then pulled out her notes to update them.

Reviewing each of her carefully worded queries reassured her. She was good at her job, knew what she was doing. This project differed from her others because she'd grown up with Warren. They had a common history that prevented them from remaining in the roles of interviewer and subject. If she was smart, she could use this extra level of complexity in their relationship to her advantage.

All she had to do was keep her cool and her confidence.

"I'm sorry I was hard on you earlier." Warren entered the room, wearing the new turtleneck she'd bought him and carrying a towel. He tossed it at her. "Your hair is wet."

She rubbed the plush fabric over her short tresses, focused still on him. She'd been right. The light color of the sweater emphasized his dark complexion and gray eyes. The camera would gobble him up. And her female viewers would fantasize about doing the same.

"I was too sensitive." She was happy to smooth over the highly charged emotions from earlier. "And it's not like you're the only one who doesn't approve of my friendship with Chad. My mother keeps warning me to keep my distance. She'd far rather I spend my time convincing you to cast me as your leading lady. Laughable, isn't it?''

But as their gazes connected, neither one of them so much as smiled. In that moment, Miranda realized Warren's questions alone weren't responsible for the tension she felt around him.

An awareness was growing between them. More and more she was thinking of Warren not as her biography subject but as a man.

Suppose the two of them had run into each other in Toronto. Say she'd shown up at one of his book signings. She imagined he might have asked her out for coffee. And after…would she have invited him to her apartment…?

"Maybe we could…" She cleared her throat. "Do you think we could take a second stab at my questions now?"

Warren blinked, and his expression relaxed. "Why not? Let's move to the living room, where we'll be more comfortable."

They'd never spent time in that part of the house before. Just off from the dining room, the sitting area was shabby, but cozy. Curtains were pulled back on a big bay window that provided a view of the swirling snow. Hearing the wind whistle through small cracks in the old house's wood frame made Miranda shiver. Although in truth, the central heating was quite successful in keeping out the cold.

She sat on one end of an old floral-patterned sofa,

right leg tucked under so she could face Warren, who'd settled at the other end.

"I don't know anything about your life in New York."

"How would you like to go there with me?"

She started at the unexpected offer. Was he kidding? No, he appeared totally serious.

"But I—" She stopped herself as she realized what a wonderful opportunity this was for the video.

"How about the first week of December?" Warren continued. "It would be nice to get back into town for some Christmas shopping. You could meet my editor and my agent, maybe get some interviews for your film. What do you think?"

This was a business proposal, nothing more. Warren's smile, the lazy interest in his eyes, held no hint of an ulterior motive. Still, she wondered. Where would she sleep? Would they eat meals together? What would it be like to be with Warren for days at a time?

The prospect was not unappealing.

"Where do you live?"

"I have a small apartment on the Upper West Side. Two bedrooms," he added, with raised eyebrows.

"Ah."

"You'll be moderately safe," he promised.

"Moderately?"

"I'm not making promises I can't keep."

He was flirting. Or maybe not. There was no teasing glint in his eyes; the man was dead serious. Miranda knew her heart was racing; knew, too, that the heat she felt right now came from her own internal furnace.

Two adults alone in New York City. Anything could happen, really. Wasn't that what Warren was saying? After all, they were single, available…

And she couldn't be thinking this way. Had she lost all common sense? This was Warren Addison, the loner she'd known from high school, the subject of her next biography, definitely not a man for her to take a romantic interest in.

Bronwyn had, though. And so had Evelyn Flemming. Obviously they'd been drawn to something about this man so strongly that the pull hadn't faded in the more than ten years since they'd last seen him.

What was that pull? And could it explain why she was suddenly wondering what it would be like to kiss Warren Addison? To make love with Warren Addison…?

Her thoughts were as out of control as the storm outside, as the howling wind. *Think video. Think business. Think keeping your advance.*

"It sounds like the perfect opportunity to meet your agent. She was quite keen to participate on this project when I called her. I'd love to get some footage of your apartment, too."

"Sure, why not."

Something she'd said had amused him. Or maybe it was the something she hadn't said. Could he possibly have guessed the thoughts that had raced through her head a minute ago?

So what if he had? Men weren't the only ones allowed to think about sex every now and then. And if the statistics were accurate, he'd already thought about it a dozen times since she'd stepped in the door.

"IT'S A TERRIBLE STORM."

Chad stood at the front door of his own house. The wind at his back drove fingers of snow onto the tiles at the entry, but still Bernie didn't invite him in.

"Vicky told me you were taking her to her friend Chelsea's birthday party tonight," he added.

Chelsea, Vicky's friend from swimming lessons, lived in Yorkton. Bernie had contemplated canceling the trip, given the lousy weather. But all she said was "So?"

She was still angry about the weekend. No. *Angry* didn't begin to describe the fury she felt when she thought about Chad taking Miranda along on his weekend outing with Vicky. It hadn't helped that, since that weekend, all Vicky had been able to talk about was that very woman.

Miranda's so pretty, so funny, so nice! Bernie had longed to tell her daughter, *That woman is trying to steal your father from me, break up our home for good.* Oh, maybe not consciously, but Bernie had no doubt where this renewed friendship between her husband and *friend* was headed.

Of course she hadn't said anything to Vicky. Anyway, her daughter would probably be thrilled to find out Miranda was going to be her new stepmother. Since yesterday, Bernie had been subjected to a replay of every second of the shopping trip that had meant so much to Vicky. Worst of all, she'd had to admit, to herself as well as Vicky, that the clothes Miranda had chosen for her daughter were pretty special. Or they made Vicky look special, which was what clothes were supposed to do, right?

Bernie knew the cords, turtleneck and vest that she was wearing right now, that she'd worn to school that day, were nice. But they were also a little on the bland side. And at least five years old. How many times had Chad seen her in them? No wonder he gazed past her in that blank way that told her he wasn't really seeing her at all. Next to Miranda, she was boring and dull.

"So, I don't think you should go." Chad's voice had a familiar, authoritarian ring. "The roads are awful. I wouldn't be surprised if they closed the highway."

Oh, she wanted to argue! But she happened to agree. No party could be worth the risk of traveling in these conditions.

"Vicky will be disappointed," she said.

"Let me talk to her." Pulling the door closed behind him, he stepped onto the inside mat, hesitating when she didn't take a step back to make room. His eyes narrowed and his lips thinned. ''What's the problem, Bernie? Want me to wait outside in the bloody blizzard?''

Much as she tried not to, Bernie saw the situation from his perspective. The house he'd planned, helped to build and still paid the mortgage on was now off-limits. That had to sting.

Good! She wanted him to suffer, and so far, by all that she'd seen, he'd done precious little of it. She was the one who cried her eyes out every day. And look at him. Clear eyes, good skin, no new lines to bracket that oh-so-perfect smile of his.

The smile that she'd once woken up to every morning. Chad was a cheerful early riser. She missed the pot of coffee he usually had waiting for her, the sound of him and Vicky chattering at the breakfast table as she put together sandwiches for their lunches.

Did Chad miss anything about their life together?

''Aren't you going to call Vicky?''

''Of course.'' She turned as she blushed, and hoped he didn't notice her embarrassment. His un-expected visit had befuddled her. Usually she had Vicky waiting at the door when her father was ex-pected, to avoid awkward moments just like this.

She went to the foot of the stairs and called out with enough volume to be heard over Vicky's stereo, but not so loud as to alarm neighbors. ''Vicky, your dad wants to talk to you.''

"Daddy?" Vicky appeared in jeans and a too-tight T-shirt that Bernie had thought she'd tossed into the giveaway pile in the basement.

"Hey, Vic." Chad held out his arms, and Bernie pretended to shake dust from one of her plants so she wouldn't have to see them embrace. God, she felt like crying, but she couldn't. Vicky would be mortified. So, probably, would Chad.

"I'm sorry, Vic, but you're going to have to skip this party in Yorkton," Chad said. "The roads are too dangerous."

"But—"

The doorbell rang and Vicky carried on as if she hadn't heard it.

"That's so unfair! I've been looking forward to this party forever. And I've already done my hair!"

The style was new, with a zigzag part and a half-dozen cute little clips. Miranda's influence again, no doubt.

Bernie went to the door, puzzled at this second interruption to her evening. Outside, she found an attractive woman in a camel-colored coat and a black scarf.

"Danielle!" They'd gone to school together, been best friends at the time, but Danielle, like so many others, had ended up in a city—in her case, Edmonton. She usually came home to visit her parents for the holidays. But Christmas was still more than a month away.

Bernie hustled her guest inside and closed the door

quickly to block out the snow and wind. Danielle's cheeks were ruddy. Her thick brown hair was covered with white.

"Sorry to just drop in. I tried calling a few times, but…" She smiled at Vicky, guessing, correctly, the cause for the busy line. Danielle herself had a couple of daughters at home.

Chad stepped forward to give her a hug. "Is Gary with you? And the girls?"

Danielle's smile faded. "No. I'm here to help Mom get my dad to the doctor. Apparently he hasn't been that well, and she's worried. We all are."

Two years ago Danielle's father had retired from his job at the potash mine in Esterhazy. Since then, he'd been suffering from a depression that was controlled as long as he stayed on his medication.

"Come in and have coffee." Bernie took Danielle's coat, then paused when she noticed Chad still standing in his ski jacket and boots. Vicky, apparently accepting that she wouldn't be going to the party in Yorkton, had disappeared back upstairs.

Had Danielle heard about the problems between her and Chad? It didn't seem so, as she turned to him and said, "On your way out or in, Chad?"

He hesitated, glanced at Bernie, then away. "In."

She should have been angry that he was taking advantage of their visitor in this way. But Bernie couldn't help feeling the very opposite. She led the way to the kitchen, thankful that she'd already cleaned up from dinner and actually had a plate of cookies to offer with the coffee.

From habit, Chad took care of making coffee, while she laid out cups and plates for the ginger snaps. Bernie felt the poignancy of each little act of her husband's, right down to his selecting his usual chair at the kitchen table.

"The reason I was so eager to talk to you guys," Danielle said, "was that Mom told me both Warren Addison and Miranda James are in Chatsworth right now!"

And this was good news? Bernie went to the cupboard to get sugar for Chad's coffee.

"A regular class of '90 reunion, huh?" Chad said.

Even before Danielle replied, Bernie guessed what she had on her mind, and could hardly stop from groaning.

"Counting Adrienne, that makes six from a class of eleven. We *should* have a reunion of some sort, don't you agree? Oh, nothing fancy, but I was thinking, why not organize a cross-country ski, followed by a potluck up at the golf course? What do you say, Chad? Could we use the clubhouse?"

Bernie stared at her husband, willing him to come up with an excuse. Any excuse. She'd back him, no matter what he said.

But he didn't even glance in her direction as he gave Danielle one of his high-voltage smiles. "That's a *terrific* idea. Of course we can use the clubhouse."

"WILL YOUR PARENTS ever sell their farm?"

Miranda and Warren were back in the kitchen, eating by the warm stove. Warren had made pasta and stir-fried vegetables. Compared with her, he was a master in the kitchen. For one thing, he was able to cook and carry on a conversation at the same time. Another point in his favor—he hadn't glanced at a single recipe, and everything tasted delicious.

"No. Even though they know I'll never be a farmer, I doubt they'll part with the farm. To them, owning land really means something."

"After they're gone, will you sell?"

"Not as long as I can afford to pay the property taxes and keep the house in reasonable condition. I can't imagine living here full-time, but it's not a bad place to escape to for a binge of writing."

No, it wasn't a bad place at all. In fact, the lonely little farmhouse was beginning to grow on her. Miranda shifted her chair another inch closer to the heat-generating stove. They'd abandoned the coffees they'd savored over the long afternoon for a bottle of very decent Shiraz. Warren now held the bottle above her almost-empty glass.

"Why not? I don't have to worry about driving." Neither the snow nor the wind had abated in the past five hours. Miranda had phoned her mother earlier to tell her not to expect her until morning.

"Besides," Warren continued, "coming back to Saskatchewan keeps you grounded. People in cities are very consumption-oriented. Folks here wouldn't dream of spending three dollars on a single cup of coffee, or a hundred dollars in a restaurant when it isn't even a special occasion.''

''Or fifty dollars for a haircut.''

''Precisely.''

Warren glanced at her hair, probably remembering the fiasco Adrienne had made of it last week. Now Miranda tried to spike up the short strands behind her head, which had been flattened by the melting snow and subsequent toweling off.

A particularly strong gust of wind rattled the kitchen window. Miranda half expected the lights to flicker. ''Sounds like the storm is getting worse. Is there any chance the electricity and phone lines will go down?''

''The wires have been underground for years.'' As if to prove his point, the telephone rang. It was an old-fashioned rotary model, attached to the wall by the back door.

While Warren took the call, Miranda cleared and washed the dishes. There weren't many. Warren was a clean-as-you-go kind of cook.

''You'll never guess who that was.''

''Not my mother.'' Please, not her mother.

''Danielle Morris. She's in town and wants to organize a mini class reunion. Remember her?''

''Of course I do. She was Bernie's best friend.'' Miranda reflected on that fact for a moment. Both Bernie and Danielle had been part of the gang of kids she hung out with, but neither had been very friendly to her. But they hadn't been unfriendly, either.

"Did you have a best friend in high school?" she asked Warren.

"My dog," he said without hesitation. "Gone now." He sighed, his gaze dropping to the floor by the stove as if he could almost see his old companion curled up there for a winter nap.

"I didn't have a big circle of friends the way you did," he added. "But of course you knew that."

"Maybe you didn't have a huge group of friends. But the relationships you had were deep." And she was still a little envious of that.

Warren reached for a plate in the sink just as she folded the dishcloth over the faucet. Their hips bumped, then their hands. She felt the rush of heat she'd experienced earlier when they were sitting on the sofa.

She glanced sideways at the same time as he did. Her quick, automatic smile faded when she noticed the way he was looking at her. His gaze moved from her mouth, to her eyes, then back to her mouth.

How many men had she kissed in her life? Enough, so the act was no longer all that meaningful to her. But kissing Warren—it was on his mind, just as it was on hers—seemed way more significant than all those other times.

He put an arm around her waist and gently pulled her closer, until mere inches separated them. Her heart began to thud bass notes in her ears.

Yes, she wanted this kiss. On some level she'd hungered for it since the first time she'd stepped foot in this kitchen.

And yet, her cautious side warned her to be careful. Did she really want this relationship to become intimate? Was she ready for the consequences of that?

No. Feeling like a coward, she ducked her head and gently eased back from his embrace. If Warren was upset with her decision, he hid his disappointment well.

"What's the matter Miranda?"

"I've never become…involved with one of my biography subjects. I'm worried I'll lose my objectivity." Although, in truth, she suspected, she already had.

"I've never met anyone like you, Warren," she continued. "You've always had this ability to make me feel…unsettled." It wasn't just his questions, upsetting as they could be. It was his very presence. The way he looked at her, the way he touched her.

"Maybe a good unsettling is just what you need."

She felt the warmth from his eyes pour over her skin, her arms, her breasts, her legs. What if she'd spent some time getting to know him when they were younger? Could she have been his Bronwyn? His Miss Flemming?

What would that have been like?

CHAPTER TWELVE

WARREN HAD KNOWN THE DAY would come when he would regret agreeing to let Miranda do this damn video biography. If anyone else had suggested such a project, he'd have rejected them outright. But he hadn't been able to resist the opportunity to spend a little time with the girl who'd been the focus of so many of his teenaged fantasies. A girl he'd never quite forgotten. And probably never would.

He thought about her all the time now. Sometimes those thoughts helped to inspire his writing. Other times all they did was distract him.

Like this morning.

Rising early from his sleepless night, he noticed the snow had stopped. Although the mid-November sky was still dark, he dressed for the outdoors and took his shovel to dig out Miranda's car.

She would want to leave as soon as she woke up, he guessed. And frankly, until she was gone he didn't think he could focus on his writing. He should have realized his fascination with her wasn't something he could control.

Bronwyn had guessed at his feelings for Miranda

back when they'd dated. She'd felt secure enough in his affections for his interest to amuse her.

"You like that girl, don't you?" she'd asked him once, when she'd noticed him staring.

He'd been too mortified to answer.

"She's cute—admit it," Bronwyn had goaded him.

He'd been confused at first. Wasn't Bronwyn jealous? Then her next comment had explained everything.

"Thank God you're not the kind of guy who only cares what a girl looks like. Miranda James may be pretty, but she's about as deep as a first-grade reader. You could never be happy with a woman like that—

"Which is why I'm so crazy about you. Unlike most of the guys in this school you've got real thoughts, real feelings. Warren, I couldn't put down that story you gave me to read last night. Where did you ever get the idea?"

But Bronwyn had been wrong. Not about his story—it turned out to be the first he ever published—but about Miranda. She wasn't shallow—just self-deluded. In his opinion, Miranda would benefit from doing a video biography on herself. She needed to confront the false self-image fostered by everyone who'd ever assumed, like Bronwyn, that a pretty girl couldn't be very smart.

The damage, he was sure, had been mostly inflicted by Miranda's mother. Warren had never particularly liked Annie James. As he was growing up, she'd been the librarian, and every time he'd wanted to borrow a new batch of books, he'd had to do so under her disapproving glare.

He couldn't recall the woman ever making a positive comment. She nattered constantly. How did he go through so many books? Did he really read them all? If so, he ought to be taking in more exercise and fresh air.

Later, his tastes had graduated, and she'd frowned on the adult subject matter. A couple of times she had refused to let him have a specific book until his mother gave her approval. This had continued right up to grade twelve.

He didn't know how Miranda's cheerful disposition and good humor had survived that woman. Her father had cut out from the scene when Miranda was in high school. Rumors had abounded, but Miranda and her mother had substantiated none of them. And as far as anyone knew, neither Annie nor her daughter had ever heard from the recalcitrant Mr. James again.

Warren stopped shoveling. He'd uncovered the car; now he needed to start up the tractor and clear a path to the main road. A hint of dawn showed on the eastern horizon, but the house remained dark.

Miranda still slept. Well, they'd stayed up late last night. They'd finally moved away from their personal lives to discuss movies and books. A topic both of them had more than enough opinions about to sustain a vigorous conversation that only faltered when Miranda could no longer keep her eyes open.

He'd shown her to the spare room. She'd paused in the doorway for a moment, her hand on the arm that still wore the sweater she'd bought for him in Yorkton.

He'd thought, *Maybe.* Wondered briefly if making the first move himself might be construed as taking advantage of the situation. Decided he didn't give a damn; she was an adult, and she could say no if she wanted.

Then she'd kissed him. On the cheek.

"Good night, Warren."

"Um, need anything? I could lend you a clean T-shirt to sleep in."

"I'll be fine. I keep a toothbrush in my purse."

A toothbrush. But no pajamas, he was sure. Which meant she'd be sleeping in the—

She'd closed the door, and the heavy thud had punctuated his thoughts and longings perfectly. He'd stood there a few minutes before heading to his own room, rubbing the spot where her lips had pressed against his skin.

And that had been that.

MIRANDA WOKE UP IN THE spare bedroom of Warren Addison's farmhouse. Her first thought was that this would have been *his* room when he was growing up. What stories had he dreamed when lying in this plain, metal-framed bed?

She raised herself onto one elbow and noticed on the bureau a framed, slightly blurry photo of a black-and-white border collie. Warren's dog, obviously. On the wall hung a 1990 calendar—the kind the grain elevator operators handed out, with landscape photographs arranged by season marking the individual months. This one remained on July. The month Warren had left home.

The same month that she'd packed all her belongings into two suitcases, then taken the Greyhound bus to Toronto.

Glancing at her watch, still strapped to her wrist, Miranda saw it was ten minutes past eight. She tossed aside the covers, and swung her feet to the cold floor. First she groped for her socks, then her jeans and sweater. Treading across the linoleum flooring, she made her way to the window and pulled back thick, lined curtains.

The sunlight hurt her eyes initially, but the good news was the storm had ended. She would be able to leave. Knowing she was no longer stranded ought to have brought relief. But her feelings were more complicated than that.

The final few hours of last night had made up for the tense back and forth of Warren's questions earlier in the day. While discussing movies and books— pretty much neutral territory for them both, even though they'd defended their favorites in both categories pretty ferociously—something had sparked between them. Miranda wasn't sure what exactly had happened. Only, that after this video was finished, she hoped she and Warren would remain friends. They had so many common interests and shared passions.

Still, this morning she craved distance from Warren's strong personality. A little quiet, reflective time would help her put the past twenty-four hours into perspective.

As soon as she opened the bedroom door, she could hear the familiar melody of Pachelbel's *Canon,* which she assumed came from the radio in the dining room downstairs. She trod the stairs carefully, avoiding the worn, squeaky spots, clinging to the handrail, her camera bag bumping against her hip with each step.

In the kitchen, the stove put out warmth and a faint golden glow. One empty coffee cup sat next to the gleaming stainless steel espresso maker. Next to that was a plate with a scattering of crumbs.

He'd had his breakfast. And judging from the pooled moisture by the back door, he'd been outside, shoveling. Sure enough, from the kitchen window she spotted her bright-yellow car, swept clear of snow.

She stepped farther into the room, and suddenly heard the clatter from a keyboard, as well as the classical music. He was working, then. Probably, he'd been at his writing for at least an hour. She shouldn't interrupt, no matter how badly she craved one of his delicious espressos. Just leave a note of thanks on the table and slip out the back door.

Alternatively…

She dug in the case for her camera, powered it on, then brought it up to her eye. Moving as silently as possible, she headed for the arched opening to the dining room.

He'd said she could film him writing as long as he wasn't aware of her presence. Well, unless he was purposefully ignoring her, he had no idea she was standing in the next room. He tapped away at the keyboard frantically, slowed his pace, then sped up again. She zoomed in to catch his expression, and when she did, her fingers trembled.

She'd seen him like this before. In the middle of a discussion, as he stopped to gather his thoughts. But this time no other person was in the room with him. The characters in his mind had him so preoccupied.

She stood captivated for minutes, amazed by his concentration, fascinated by the bursts of typing followed by long moments of thought. He came to something that made him smile, and oddly, she felt jealous. What had happened to give him that look, to soften the line of his mouth and cause the corners of his eyes to crinkle with indulged amusement?

Feeling the emotion, recognizing the emotion, she immediately chided herself. If she was going to envy a fictional character, then she was even more confused than she'd been afraid of.

She powered off the camera, and the slight click turned his head. She smiled guiltily, as if she'd spied on something she shouldn't have. But he'd said if she caught him unaware, she could tape him. And he didn't look annoyed at the interruption.

"You're awake."

"I would have to call that a slight exaggeration given my present caffeine-free state."

"Is that a subtle hint that you'd like an espresso?" He rose as he spoke.

"No. Don't stop. I think I've seen you work the machine enough that I can manage on my own. Would you like me to make you one, too?"

He paused. Assessing her offer? Or just assessing her? She hadn't yet washed her face or brushed her hair. Given that it had been a mess when she went to bed last night, she didn't suppose its being squashed against a pillow for hours had improved it much.

"Sure, a coffee would be great. Sleep okay?"

"Surprisingly, under the circumstances. I mean the unfamiliar bed and setting and everything…" She let her words fade away, aware that she was rambling. God, they hadn't made love last night; this wasn't one of those awkward morning-afters. So what was going on here?

She couldn't look at him anymore, so she glanced through the window, instead.

"You shoveled out my car."

"Don't take it the wrong way."

"As in, you're in a hurry to get rid of me? Warren, I'm crushed." She laughed as she turned back to the kitchen, lightly, as if she'd been joking. But actually she felt a small pricking of hurt.

But of course she had no right to feel that way. This was his time. By the terms of their agreement, she had no business being here. Besides, she wanted to leave.

Didn't she?

At the kitchen counter, she scooped whole beans into the grinder and checked the water level in the espresso machine. This one was slicker than her machine at home, but it operated similarly. Soon she had two cups ready.

She brought his to the table, so he could enjoy it hot, then tried to slink back into the kitchen. He caught her hand before she made her escape.

"Sorry for not being a more hospitable host."

"I'm sorry that I'm interrupting your writing time."

His amused smile reminded her of the one she'd captured earlier on film. "You couldn't help the blizzard. I was glad to offer you shelter for the night. Don't think I resent your presence this morning."

She was surprised at how relieved she felt to hear him say these things. And to sound as though he meant them. "It's been a bizarre twenty-four hours. And you've been the very best of hosts. But I really should be going. We'll talk soon," she promised, backing out of the room.

In the kitchen she gulped her espresso, then pulled on her coat and boots. Warren remained in the dining room, but there were no clacking sounds from his keyboard. Probably she'd derailed his train of thought.

Silently, she ducked out the door and ran to her car. It wasn't until she was halfway home that she realized why she felt so strange.

She'd never spent a night alone with a man without him coming on to her. Aside from that one moment in his kitchen when he'd almost kissed her, Warren hadn't made a single advance. Even her mother would have said he'd acted like nothing but a gentleman.

And some part of her—her womanly vanity?—was very annoyed that he'd played the part so perfectly.

AFTER SHE LEFT, WARREN didn't try to get back into his writing. He went to the room where she'd slept and stood at the doorway.

She hadn't made the bed. The sheet and quilt were tangled, the pillow still indented from her head.

She must have forgotten. She'd left the kitchen spotless, and generally was quite organized and tidy.

Or maybe she'd left her bed like this so that he could remember she'd been here. To tempt him into imagining her lying in this spot, naked, or perhaps in her underwear, all last night while he'd pretended to sleep in the master bedroom across the hall.

Warren laughed softly to himself. As if Miranda

had any interest in seducing him. Still, he found that he was. Seduced. Slowly he crossed the floor of his boyhood bedroom. He sat on the edge of the mattress, then eased his body down, until his head rested on the pillow in the same spot where hers had been.

He could smell her here. Closing his eyes, he could picture her here.

Miranda. Miranda James.

Come back.

BUT MIRANDA DIDN'T come back. She phoned the next day to tell him she was flying to Regina to interview Evelyn Flemming; then Calgary, to speak with Bronwyn Jenson. Both women, apparently, were eager to be included in the video. Go figure.

From Calgary, Miranda would head to Vancouver Island and his parents. She'd call him when she returned.

Warren hung up the phone, mired in negative emotions. Couldn't she have discussed these plans with him last night? In person, he might have talked her out of them. Over the phone, he hadn't a hope. Now the idea that in a few hours she'd be speaking to his *old girlfriends* about him was almost unbearable.

God, what would they say? And what would his parents discuss the next day when she got to them? He could just imagine the drivel his mother would come up with. Probably some sappy stories about how precocious he'd been as a baby and what promise he'd shown in kindergarten....

Why had he ever agreed to this crazy project? He was used to mining other people for his material, not vice versa. Miranda was way more thorough—worse, way more insightful—than he'd anticipated, although he should have known better, since those were the very qualities he'd admired in her previous work.

Now he had to accept that she'd be delving into his past secrets. Worse, that he wouldn't see her for days.

In fact, the next time they'd be together, he calculated with dismay, would be at that blasted reunion party Danielle was organizing for the weekend. And that wouldn't be the same, because Chad would be there.

Warren had become quite used to Miranda's undivided attention. He wasn't at all interested in sharing. Especially not with Chad English.

Oh, the guy was decent enough. And he had a surface charm that people warmed to on sight. But Warren couldn't see enough depth in the man to sustain Miranda's continued fascination with him. Because she still was hooked, no matter how much she tried to deny it.

Not that he seriously believed Miranda intended to break up Chad's marriage. But her unexpected appearance in Chatsworth, Warren was afraid, might have just that result.

Chad was the kind of guy who thrived on the devotion of women. Despite his looks and charm he needed constant reassurance about his importance.

Besides his mother, it was Bernie, not Miranda, who filled this need in him.

Still, Miranda was quite a temptation. And if Chad did end up leaving Bernie for her, then Warren feared the consequences would be dire.

At stake were a marriage, a child's future and Miranda's happiness. As for Warren's own prospects for love and contentment, he was afraid he would lose regardless.

As long as Miranda held on to her childhood passion for Chad, she would be out of reach for any other man.

BERNIE DECIDED she wouldn't attend the reunion. As an adult, after all, no one could force her. Chad deserved to be shot for having agreed to this crazy scheme. And since she knew where he kept the key to the cabinet in which he stored his hunting shotgun...

Too bad she was a law-abiding citizen at heart. There had to be some other way out of this mess. She could claim she'd contracted a flu bug. But everyone would *know* it was an excuse. And what would they say when she didn't have the nerve to show up at the gathering? Worse, what would they think?

Bernie pulled off the Nordic sweater that matched Chad's and substituted a fleece zip-up in powder blue. If this wasn't one of her colors, she didn't care.

It was almost twenty below outside and the jacket was warm.

She'd hoped the temperature would dip even lower. Minus forty would be nice. Then the excursion would definitely be canceled.

Shrugging into her matching windbreaker shell, she passed through the kitchen to collect her casserole for the potluck. Vicky sat leafing through her latest *Twist* magazine.

"These outfits are totally awesome, but I can't get any of this stuff in Yorkton. When are we going to Regina to do our Christmas shopping?"

Usually the whole family went in late November or early December, depending on the weather. This year, though... Bernie sighed. "I don't know if we'll be going. With your father and I...separated...finances are a little tighter." From the oven she pulled her prettiest ceramic dish containing the beef-and-bean chili she'd made that morning.

"What do you mean—tighter?"

"Just what I said." If this separation turned out to be permanent, they'd be living on her teacher's salary alone. Oh, sure, Chad would pay support for Vicky, but would it be enough for them to keep the house?

Bernie slid open one of the deep drawers on extension hardware, which she'd insisted on when planning the kitchen. This was her home—her dream home—and Bernie thought she would almost rather give up groceries than have to move out. After selecting a wicker basket large enough to hold the casserole dish, she faced her daughter.

"Isn't Karen expecting you?"

"Yeah." Vicky tossed the magazine aside. "I just figured I'd hang around until Daddy got here."

Bernie frowned. "Your father isn't coming over."

"But I thought you were going to the same party?"

"Yes…but we're not going as a couple."

"Oh." Vicky pushed away from the table, turning her back to Bernie. "I'll grab my coat."

"I can give you a ride. I'm just on my way now."

"Never mind. It's only two blocks."

Vicky disappeared with a curt "Bye" as Bernie was putting her skis on the roof rack of the Buick. After making sure she had her neck warmer, toque, mitts and ski boots, Bernie backed out of the garage and headed for the clubhouse.

Outside, piercing sunlight reflected off the mounds of new-fallen snow. Bernie slipped on her sunglasses and lowered the car's visor, and still had to squint as she followed the familiar route around the lake. Five vehicles were in front of the clubhouse when she finally arrived fifteen minutes late. Miranda's yellow punch-buggy stood out cheerfully from the crowd, and Bernie felt a familiar, ugly resentment as she pulled her own stately navy-blue sedan up next to it.

She'd no sooner turned off the ignition than her former classmates—including her soon-to-be-former husband—spilled out of the building. Adrienne took Bernie's casserole, volunteering to put it in the oven to stay warm. While Danielle engulfed her in a big hug, Chad removed her skis from the rack.

"I'm so sorry," Danielle whispered. "I didn't *know*."

Oh, please. Bernie didn't believe her former best friend for an instant. Danielle's parents had probably passed on the information over the phone weeks ago. After all, Chad moving out was front-page stuff for a town of this size.

"Hi, Bernie." Warren's handshake, even through warm thermal mittens, was firm. "Nice to see you again." His smile seemed genuine, and so was the trace of concern that put a faint line between his brows.

She blinked away the ever-threatening tears and smiled back. "Congratulations on your book. I really enjoyed it." She'd been amazed that the quiet boy she remembered from school had written something so exciting and complex. Looking at the mature man now, however, she thought *exciting* and *complex* could describe him as well as his novel.

"You look very pretty today, Bernie. I like that color on you." Miranda's compliment, though genuine-sounding, grated on Bernie's nerves.

"Thanks." She couldn't summon a generous reply from her suddenly stiff lips. Probably because *pretty* would be a totally inadequate adjective to convey the picture Miranda made in her classic white-and-black ensemble.

"It's cold," Adrienne said, crossing her arms over her down-filled jacket, "but at least the snow should be in good condition. Have you groomed the trail since that big dump last week, Chad?"

"You bet. Say, Bernie, did you wax your skis yet?"

Bernie nodded, unable to look her husband in the eyes. In the past, he'd always been the one to take care of their equipment. He'd seemed to enjoy the process of measuring the temperature of the snow, selecting the correct wax, then scrubbing it onto the bottom of the skis.

Chad dropped the skis on the snow in front of Bernie. They fell with a *thwack*. "Time to hit the trails."

It didn't take long for everyone to fit boots into skis and start the circuitous route that began with the slightly hilly terrain of the golf course and would end in a final, flat two miles along the lake.

Bernie took off first, deciding she'd rather lead than watch the others. Thankfully, she had the skill and the strength to be out front. Most winters, she skied this trail every day, back before she'd had to worry about avoiding her own husband.

A glance over her shoulder confirmed her guess. Chad had taken the rear, skiing behind Miranda. She could hear him shout words of encouragement. Closest to Bernie was Danielle. The brunette struggled to catch up to her.

"What's the hurry? It isn't a race!"

Bernie slowed her stride, allowing Danielle to come up on the tracks to her left.

"It's cold. I need to work up a little sweat."

"Or maybe you just want to put as much distance as possible between you and Chad? Look, Bernie, I really am sorry about this. My parents told me you were having troubles, but they didn't mention that you'd actually kicked him out. What happened? Was he having an affair?"

No sooner was the question out of her mouth than Danielle shot a glance behind them. Bernie knew she was looking at Chad and Miranda and wondering...

Damn it! This was all wrong! Danielle had once been her best friend, but Bernie could tell she didn't really care anymore. Danielle didn't want to know how Bernie was feeling, whether there was anything she could do to help.

What interested Danielle were the titillating details of what had gone wrong. Nothing would make her happier, Bernie was certain, than to hear that Chad *had* been unfaithful. She'd love to know how many times, and with which women, and exactly how Bernie had figured it all out.

Bernie understood that was what Danielle wanted because she'd been guilty of the same base curiosity about other marriages that she'd heard of going sour. Usually some excuse or another was put out as the official reason for the divorce. *We'd grown apart* or *we fought all the time*—something bland like that.

But always she'd wondered what the *real* story was. Had there been an affair? Some other form of betrayal? Was one of the parties in love with someone else?

With a friend, though, Bernie hoped she would be capable of a different reaction. With a friend, surely she would *dread* hearing those kinds of details.

"It isn't Miranda, is it?" Danielle whispered loudly. "Surely Chad isn't sleeping with *her!*"

"I don't know, Danielle. Perhaps you'd like to ask him for me?"

CHAPTER THIRTEEN

WARREN'S FEAR THAT CHAD would monopolize Miranda's attention proved well founded. He could hear them chatting behind him as they skied. About five minutes ago Bernie had broken ahead of Danielle and she was securely in the lead now. Occasionally, she fired scorching glances back at her husband, but Chad didn't notice. His tone as he conversed with Miranda continued to be light and good-humored.

Either Chad didn't care about his wife's mood or he was somehow oblivious to it.

Miranda was not. Warren heard her say, more than once, "Don't worry about me, Chad. I know I'm slow. Go catch up to Bernie."

But he wouldn't.

Damn it, he wouldn't.

Warren spent the entire hour and a half hoping for the chance to fall back and ski with Miranda, but Chad never once relinquished his spot.

By the home stretch, along the lake, Bernie was at least ten minutes ahead. She was loading her skies back on the roof rack of her car when Warren skied up to the clubhouse with Chad and Miranda at his heels.

"Wasn't that fun?" Danielle kicked snow from the bottom of her boots.

"Great snow!" Adrienne exclaimed.

They tromped inside, Adrienne and Danielle picking up the conversation they'd begun on the trail, which Warren had been unable to follow, other than to discern that it had something to do with crafts. Warren was right behind Miranda when she pulled off the white band she'd been wearing over her ears. Something tiny caught the light, then fell on the carpet near his boot. As Warren scooped it up, Chad took Miranda's coat, then Adrienne and Danielle's.

"Anyone hungry?" Chad asked.

"Starved," Adrienne said.

"Can't have that. I'll put out the grub." Chad headed for the kitchen, leaving behind his estranged wife, who balanced on one foot by the door, struggling with her boots.

"Let me help." Warren gripped a heel and pulled hard. Bernie almost went flying.

"Thanks, Warren." She accepted the boot from his hand without so much as a smile. Her attention was on Miranda's back as the other woman followed after Chad into the kitchen.

Warren could almost see the jealousy flare in Bernie's teal eyes. Then he glimpsed a welling tear, and felt compelled to squeeze her shoulder.

"You looked great out there, Bernie. Do you do a lot of cross-country?"

"Usually."

Warren guessed he hadn't asked a tactful question. Bernie was probably avoiding the golf course ski trail this winter given the problems between her and Chad.

"Something smells good," he said, at a loss to fill the conversational void.

Between them, Chad and Miranda had set out all the food. Adrienne and Danielle were already filling their plates. Warren waited for Bernie to precede him before joining the informal buffet line.

Appetite revved by all that exercise, Warren heaped food onto his plate. Bernie had made chili; Chad had purchased whole grain bakery buns. Miranda and Danielle had brought salads; and Adrienne, a cake for dessert. For his contribution, Warren had supplied beer and wine as well as baked fiery-hot chicken wings.

"More salad, Randy?" he heard Chad ask from behind him in the line.

Bernie snorted. "What's the matter? Is Randy too delicate to lift the serving spoon?"

The biting comment severed Danielle and Adrienne's conversation. Into the silence, Warren replied, "Didn't you see how hard she was poling up those hills, Bernie? Of course she's tired. Here, Miranda, let me give you a roll." His fakely solicitous tone turned the episode into a joke—almost.

And still Chad remained glued to Miranda's side. Didn't he realize he was humiliating his wife? Miranda did. Warren saw the strain behind her smile as she squeezed between Danielle and Adrienne with her full plate of food. This move forced Chad to take the one remaining seat at the table, next to his wife.

Good for you, Miranda!

But the damage was done. Bernie sat rigidly in her chair, making no attempt to eat the food on her plate.

"Great chili, Bernie," Warren said after his first mouthful.

"Thanks."

"Yeah, it's very good." Danielle turned to Warren. "So tell us what it's like—being a famous author and all...."

He fielded the usual questions, such as where he got his ideas and how much money he'd made so far on that first book. Soon conversation returned to Chatsworth matters—changes in the past decade or so.

"Pass me another beer, would you, Warren?" Danielle asked.

Warren stood up from the table to meet her request. Most of them were still on their first drink. This was Danielle's third. He snapped the tab back and passed her a can, then set several more in the center of the table in case anyone else wanted one later.

"To old friends," Danielle said.

"Old friends." Only a few of the voices around the table sounded enthusiastic. One of them belonged to Adrienne. Of the six of them, she seemed the least affected by the tension in the room.

"Remember grad night?" she asked.

For a second all were silent. Each recalling, Warren supposed, his or her unique experience of the night.

After the awards ceremony at the school, they'd enjoyed dinner at the town hall, followed by a dance. Later, the entire class and their dates had gathered at the beach on Chatsworth Lake and partied until morning.

Warren—who certainly hadn't been about to bring Evelyn Flemming as his escort—had gone dateless. As a result, he'd seen more than most people.

"Didn't you push your date off the dock into the lake that night, Miranda?" Adrienne seemed oblivious to the terse silence. She sopped up chili juice with a portion of her roll, then popped it all into her mouth.

Miranda glanced at him then. To Warren, it felt like the first time she'd really noticed him that day. He hated to admit to his own childish pique about this. Once again he acknowledged that he'd grown used to having her rapt interest all to himself. But maybe he'd needed this reminder that her apparent fascination with him did not extend to a personal level.

"That was Warren," Miranda said.

"What? You mean Warren pushed him in the lake?" Adrienne sounded confused.

"I'd say he intimidated him into it."

Warren didn't confirm the story, although he recalled the event in every detail. He'd noticed Miranda's date coming on to her, and noticed even more the way she'd tried to put him off. First with words, then with a shove.

That was when Warren had shown up on the dock, advancing on the shorter but huskier boy without fear. All he'd done was raise his fist—with every intention of planting it in the other fellow's gut—when Miranda's date had taken his only escape route. Into the lake.

Later, the coward told everyone Miranda had pushed him in. And no one, not Miranda, not Warren, had disputed this explanation for his dripping wet clothing.

Now Miranda reached across the table to touch his hand. "I never thanked you for coming to my rescue."

He could tell that, until Adrienne had brought it up, she'd forgotten the entire incident. "It was my pleasure."

"And much appreciated. My date thought grad night entitled him to a guaranteed roll in the back seat of his car."

"*My date,*" Danielle echoed, her tone cutting. "Do you even remember who your date was that night, Miranda?"

Miranda seemed not to notice the derogatory edge to Danielle's voice. "I have his picture in my scrapbook—brown hair, a crooked nose. He played defense on your hockey team, Chad. What was his name?''

Did she have any idea, Warren wondered, how her blasé forgetfulness irritated the other women? None of them had had so many dates that they couldn't still name each of them. Especially the boy who'd escorted them to the grad celebration.

But of course Miranda's attention hadn't been on her escort that night.

''Oh, for God's sake, it was Derek Sorrelson!'' Bernie pushed aside her empty plate. ''Though I didn't see his swan dive into the lake. After Chad asked me to marry him, the rest of the party sort of passed in a blur.''

She lowered her head, hiding the sad smile that Warren had glimpsed.

Danielle's hand trembled as she reached for, then opened, her fourth can of beer. ''Was that before or after you told him you were pregnant?''

After seconds of silence, Chad finally spoke up. ''It was before. I asked her to marry me before I knew about the baby.''

''Before *I* told you,'' Bernie agreed. ''But Randy had already spilled my secret. Hadn't you?'' Her eyes glittered as she glared at Miranda. ''She saw me in the school bathroom with the pregnancy kit on the last day of classes.''

Bernie's bottom lip trembled. ''I was scared to take the test at home in case my parents found out.''

Miranda's cheeks reddened. ''I knew you were

pregnant, but I had no idea Chad was the father. You two had broken up months earlier.''

That was true, Warren remembered. Bernie and Chad's high school romance had been one of those "on-again, off-again" affairs. It had just so happened that when grad rolled around they were both dating other people.

"How I found out about the baby doesn't matter," Chad said. "Either way, we would've gotten married."

Bernie stood up from the table. "Is that so, Chad? Frankly, I've always wondered." Shoulders tightly squared, she headed for the door, grabbed her coat and left. Seconds later, they heard her drive away.

Danielle bit her lip. "Me and my big mouth. I'm going after her."

"You shouldn't drive." Adrienne glanced at the almost-empty beer can still in Danielle's hand. "Let's take my car. You grab Bernie's casserole. I'll get her ski boots."

On the way out the door, Adrienne turned back to her remaining three classmates. She sighed. "Well, *I* had a good time at grad."

THE ROOM WENT QUIET after Adrienne and Danielle left, but as far as Miranda could tell, the tension didn't ease a bit. Chad, his expression grim, went to stand by the window. Was he hoping Bernie would come back? Regretting that he hadn't been more attentive to her when he'd had the chance?

Warren started to clear away the paper plates. She sensed anger behind his quick, economical movements.

''I forgot how mean Danielle can get after she's had a few drinks.'' Miranda piled the empties back into the cardboard case.

''She sure outdid herself today,'' Chad said.

''I'm afraid none of us has grown up much since high school.'' In her opinion, Danielle wasn't the only one who'd succumbed to immaturity.

''That might explain why high school reunions are rarely as much fun as people think they're going to be.'' Warren slipped on his navy ski jacket. ''I think I'll head out now, too. Walk you to your car, Miranda?''

If he'd avoided eye contact earlier, now his gaze was downright probing. Was he warning her not to stay alone with Chad? But she couldn't leave her friend now, not like this, not after what had happened.

''I'll be right behind you,'' she said.

He raised both eyebrows and she wondered what he was thinking. He'd avoided her today, almost as if the very sight of her was painful to him.

Strange that she'd forgotten how he'd come to her rescue on grad night. The whole thing had happened so quickly. One second Warren was standing on the dock beside her. The next Derek was splashing in the water and Warren was gone. She hadn't seen him again that night.

But the memory had reminded her of something else. That hadn't been the first time Warren had come to her aid. There had been another occasion, when they were in grade ten. He'd found her in a corner, at the far end of a hallway. It was lunch hour. She'd just seen Chad end his most recent fight with Bernie by giving her a tiny sapphire promise ring.

How many times had she witnessed those two kiss and make up—dashing, over and over, her secret dreams? Yet this time, for some reason, she'd been unable to hold back the tears.

And Warren had seen her...

"Are you sure you won't come?" Warren stood at the door.

"Not yet," she repeated.

"Fine." Just before striding outside, he slipped something tiny into her hand. He was gone by the time she realized it was one of her pearl stud earrings.

She put her fingers to her earlobes and confirmed one was bare. She hadn't even noticed the earring fall. Thank goodness he'd found it! Kicking aside the carton of beer bottles, she went to join Chad by the window. With his finger he traced patterns in the frost, his expression morose.

"Part of me is glad Adrienne brought up that stuff about grad night," she confessed. "I've always wanted to apologize for telling you about the baby. I wouldn't have said a word if I'd known you were the father." She'd been so sure he wasn't!

She'd had her own plans for that night. After making certain that Chad had nothing to do with Bernie's baby, she'd intended to finally tell him how she felt. How she'd *always* felt.

But Chad's stunned reaction to the news had made that impossible. He'd gaped at her, then finally sputtered, "Bernie's p-p-pregnant?"

Miranda had nodded.

"You're sure?"

When she'd nodded the second time, he'd taken off, running. And that was the end of all her hopes and dreams. The next time she saw him, about an hour later, he and Bernie had their arms looped around each other.

The meaning had been obvious.

"I'm glad you told me," Chad admitted. "I'm not sure Bernie would have. She didn't want to trap me into marriage. Her words—not mine."

Poor Bernie. What a predicament she'd been in. "But you loved her. You would've married her even if she wasn't pregnant."

Chad's answer surprised her.

"How can I know for sure?"

"But you just said to Bernie—"

"What choice did I have but to tell her I would have married her with or without the baby? That damn Danielle!" He took a deep breath. "Things are what they are. All I can say for sure is that I've never been sorry we had Vicky."

Miranda wondered if that explanation would be

enough for Bernie. It wouldn't be for her. She'd want her husband to have married her for love, not out of a sense of responsibility.

But then, she'd never been eighteen and pregnant, so who was she to judge the choices they'd made back then?

"I'm glad you stayed." Chad took her hands, squeezed them, then let them go. "I'm glad you were here. Do you know you're my only friend now? Not just from our old high school group, either. My mom's still angry with me. Even my curling buddies have been standoffish lately. I guess everyone in Chatsworth is siding with Bernie."

He looked so vulnerable, so sad. In that instant Miranda forgot about her own wants and desires. All she cared about was seeing him happy again. Chad was a gregarious, fun-loving guy. He *needed* his friends. And he needed a family.

Why was everyone in town shutting him out? It didn't make sense. Not when Bernie had been the one to kick *him* out.

"No matter what happens, Chad, you know you can count on me."

It was a promise she meant with all her heart.

CHAPTER FOURTEEN

WARREN HAD ALWAYS wondered about Miranda's pearl earrings. He noticed them peeking out from her short blond hair when he picked her up at seven in the morning, two days after the reunion.

"My, but this is an early start, isn't it?" Miranda covered a yawn with one hand. Five minutes later she was dozing.

He drove them to Regina, where they caught a flight to Toronto and just made the connection to New York. Safely on the last leg of their journey, Miranda sighed into the luxurious seat and sipped from her complimentary glass of wine. "I could get used to traveling like this."

In that second Warren knew the extra money for business-class seats had been well spent. "You have on your earrings."

"Thanks to you, I do. The only thing that could have made that awful reunion party worse would have been losing one of my favorite earrings. I'm so glad you found it."

He'd always been curious about who had given her the pearls. Someone important, he thought.

"You've had them a long time. You wore them to grad."

"Please, don't mention the *G* word."

"No kidding. A hell of a lot happened that night...."

"Too much."

"Probably poor Derek Sorrelson would agree."

She laughed, then patted Warren's hand on the armrest between them. "How did you happen to be at the right place at the right time that night?"

If he told her the truth—because he'd been watching her all evening—it would freak her out. So he had to shrug it off as coincidence. "Just good luck, I guess. I was on the beach when I heard you tell him to back off. Only took me a few seconds to run up the dock."

A flight attendant stopped in the aisle beside them. "Finished with that wine, ma'am?"

It was time to prepare for landing. A different flight attendant came by offering a basket of hard candies. A voice over the speaker system required them to tuck away trays and straighten their seats. On the ground, Warren shouldered both their carry-on bags and hurried her into a cab.

"What's the rush?" She scooted over on the torn vinyl seat to make room for him next to her.

"Nothing really. For some reason I always feel like I'm in a hurry in this town." He gave the driver directions to his apartment on the Upper West Side. Turning back to her, he outlined their agenda.

"We're meeting my agent for dinner at eight. Then tomorrow, my editor is taking us for lunch at one. Other than that, the slate is clear until our ten o'clock flight the following morning."

"Would I seem terribly unsophisticated if I admitted how exciting that sounds?"

"Not missing Chatsworth yet?"

She laughed. "Warren, Chatsworth is a nice town, but *please*. This is *New York*."

"No place like it," he agreed. "But after a few days, or let's say for the sake of argument, a couple of months...wouldn't you get tired of the fast pace? Wouldn't a small prairie town start to appeal?"

"As a weekend getaway, maybe. Although a drive to Vermont would accomplish the same purpose with far less travel time involved. But I'm a city girl, Warren. Living in Toronto is great. New York City would be even better."

Miranda adjusted the zipper on her leather coat as she gazed out the front window at the approaching skyline. She felt an ache for the missing World Trade Center—she hadn't been in the city since the September 11 tragedy. Then she glanced at Warren.

No trace of their native small town clung to the man. From his clothes—all black—to his assured posture, to his obvious ease at getting around in the city, he seemed like a native New Yorker.

"You like it here, too," she said.

"Admittedly. Although I do need frequent trips to the country to clear my head."

She tried to imagine Chad in the seat beside her. No way. It wouldn't work. For all his complaints about small-town attitudes, Chad thrived in the community where he'd been born. Before his problems with Bernie, she knew he'd been happy.

What would have happened to him, though, if Bernie hadn't gotten pregnant when she did? If Miranda had been given a chance to tell him how she felt on grad night, how would he have reacted?

She'd never know the answer to that question. But sometimes, she liked to speculate on the effect that moment could have had on their lives. Maybe Chad would've come with her to Toronto. Maybe they'd both be living there now.

Or maybe he would've convinced her to move back to Chatsworth after his father died. They might have decided to have children. Maybe with a family to raise, she'd feel differently about small-town life…

Yet, if she'd told Chad the truth about her feelings on grad night, he might have turned her down. Maybe the reason he'd never asked her out was simply that he didn't want to. She wasn't his type— romantically speaking, at least. For some reason that possibility didn't hurt as much today as usual. Miranda made herself a promise. Tonight and the next couple of days as well, she was going to forget about Chad and his broken-down marriage. She was in New York! With a man who while at times was very annoying was also extremely fascinating. What new

snippets would she learn about Warren Addison tonight? she wondered. She was almost afraid to find
out.

MIRANDA WAS looking forward to dinner in a New
York restaurant until she saw Warren's apartment.
Here was her first surprise.

"Oh, my Lord..." She did a three-sixty in the
foyer. "Who decorated this for you?"

Warren took her jacket and tossed it on the zebra-
striped chaise longue that stood on the opposite wall.
Hanging above the chair was an antique mirror—the
frame had to be ten inches thick easily. A potted
orchid—moss dripping from the terra-cotta container—sat on a glass-covered table to the left.

"No decorator. I just collect stuff."

"Collect stuff, my eye! Come on, Warren. *Some-
body* had to have helped you with this." What about
the linen-colored wallpaper and wooden window
shutters and thick wool carpets? Even though the
building seemed very high end, this wasn't standard
apartment issue, she was certain.

"I promise you not."

As he guided her to the next room, his hand
skimmed so lightly down her silk-clad back that she
shivered. "Cold?"

"No. Perfect." The next room was small, denlike.
Here were two love seats, built on a grand scale, and
stuffed with enough down to fill the chicken coop
from the Addisons' farmyard. When Warren waved

a hand, she sank into one, then found her gaze caught by the framed oil above the wide-grated fireplace.

"Hmm. I don't know if I like that."

"It may grow on you. Or may not. It *is* different, I'll admit. Want a drink?"

She jumped up and followed him to the next room—the kitchen. Here was lots of granite and maple and copper. "Well, no wonder you like to cook. You have such an inviting place to do it in."

One interesting feature of the room was bookshelves built around the window on the far wall. A small table and two fully upholstered armchairs were positioned by the window.

Warren noticed her interest. "I like to read when I'm eating. An indulgence of living alone...."

She needed to film him here, too, she realized. Maybe tomorrow morning, if she was lucky... Oh, coming to New York had been such a great idea!

"What shall I pour you?"

"A martini?"

"Done."

She strolled around the island, running her hand along the speckled rock surface. Through an arched opening she saw the dining room. The walls were burgundy, the chairs covered in rich velvet. *What a dramatic setting! I wonder...*

"Do we have reservations for tonight?"

"I'm not sure. Why?"

"I'm thinking it might be fun to eat in. I could get some footage of you in the kitchen. What do you say?'' She could shoot the agent in the dining room, against the rich, wine-colored backdrop. She was willing to bet that conversation between them would flow more freely in this intimate, almost sensual setting, than in a restaurant.

''I thought you were eager to experience New York.''

But the video came first. And instinct told her dinner in Warren's apartment would produce some exceptional footage.

She strolled back to the window, ran a hand over some of the book spines. At random she selected a pristine hardcover. Leonard Cohen. *Dance Me to the End of Love*.

''You've read this?''

Warren, still dealing with bottles and delicate cocktail glasses, gave her a distracted glance. ''Hmm? Oh, yes, of course. Beautiful illustrations by Matisse.''

''You *are* full of surprises.''

He passed her a glass—clear liquid containing a speared green olive.

She put two fingers around the slender stem of the glass, but he didn't let go from his end. Up close, he exuded such intensity. She was used to seeing him from a distance, she realized. Through the camera lens.

''Now that you're back in town, is there anyone you need to call?''

"As in a woman, you mean. No, there isn't. I've already told you that."

She'd thought she'd been so subtle, but of course he saw through her.

"Yes, well…"

"Ever probing, that's my Miranda." His voice, as smooth as vermouth, felt like a physical caress as he finally released his hold on her glass and lifted his in an understated salute.

"Welcome to my home."

WARREN'S AGENT ARRIVED at seven-thirty, not put out in the least by the change of plans. Phyllis Bolder was not what Miranda had expected. Although by now she ought to have known better than to set up any expectations whatsoever when it came to Warren and his life.

At six feet tall, and with a girth to match, Phyllis almost appeared to be tackling Warren when she gave him a welcoming hug at the door. Warren put tentative hands to her shoulders—whether returning the embrace or pushing her away, it was difficult to say.

"Warren is not the huggy-kissy type," Phyllis informed Miranda. An abundance of makeup and gold jewelry could not hide a face of experience and savvy intelligence. As they shook hands, she beamed at Miranda.

"I can't tell you how thrilled I was to hear that our dear Warren had agreed to this video. He wants so badly for his books not to sell that he's forever running from cameras and journalists.''

Warren ignored her hyperbole and handed her a drink. Phyllis settled herself, and her voluminous black caftan, into one of the love seats, leaving the other for Warren and Miranda.

"I arrange dates with up-and-coming young actresses—these are not homely women, you understand—and he won't call them. I organize dinner parties with publishers and book reviewers—and he won't accept. What am I to do? Why does he bother to pay me if he won't let me do my job?"

Miranda's fingers itched for the power button of her Canon. At the first pause in Phyllis's diatribe, she asked, "Would you mind if I filmed some of this?"

Of course Phyllis didn't object. Phyllis was delighted to accommodate Miranda's project in any way she could.

"Let's move to the kitchen," Warren suggested. "I'm making pasta. Miranda wants to film me working the dough with my hands."

"Oh, good idea! Very sensual!" Phyllis grabbed each of them by the elbow and virtually plowed them into the kitchen. She settled in one of the upholstered chairs to watch, while Miranda circled the island with her camera.

Soon, fantastic smells began to entice her appetite. Warren pulled a round of Brie baked with garlic and pears from the oven for them to snack on while he hand-rolled the pasta and cut it into thin, fettuccini-style strips.

She zeroed in for a close-up as he tenderly worked the soft dough. He could have been a pianist with hands like that, she thought.

Or a marvelous lover…which he probably was.

"So, Warren," she murmured, while Phyllis concentrated on her wine and the cheese. "Why do you give your agent such a hard time? Perhaps you don't care for starlets."

"I don't need my dates arranged for me. At least not yet." He glanced straight into the camera lens, as if he could see right through to her eyes. "Anyway, I prefer intelligence over beauty. Always have."

For a moment Miranda froze, remembering the day he'd put her on the spot with his questions. Aside from her old science teacher—and her father—Warren was the first person who'd ever made a big deal about her intellectual capabilities.

"So you say, Warren. But as I recall, Miss Flemming was very pretty. And Bronwyn was…"

"Well endowed. Yes, and she hated the way the boys stared and all the lewd comments they made. But there have been women since those two."

Oh, she could well imagine.

"And not all of them had outstanding physical characteristics. In fact, you'd probably consider my last girlfriend quite plain—"

"Indeed she was," Phyllis interjected. "I was so

thankful when that ended.'' She spoke at Miranda's camera, now trained on her. ''They dated for almost six months. I was worried they might end up married.'' She shook her head disapprovingly. ''Not that I had anything against the woman, but she simply wasn't photogenic. Who would have been interested in the wedding? Certainly not *People* or *Entertainment Tonight*....''

Miranda swung the camera back to Warren. He made a face at her.

''The pasta is al dente. Sit down now,'' he commanded.

She and Phyllis scurried to obey.

''THIS PLAIN WOMAN,'' Miranda asked, after Phyllis had left, at about one in the morning. ''What was her name?''

''Forget it. I think you already have more than enough details of my love life for your video.'' Warren shifted on the love seat, making room for her to settle next to him.

He'd dimmed the lights after Phyllis left, and the CD player had shifted to a selection of romantic jazz classics. Miranda slipped her feet out of her three-inch heels and leaned back against the cushions, humming a few bars of ''They Can't Take That Away From Me.''

They'd had a very busy day. She ought to be longing for bed. Yet she felt she could stay up all night.

"Perhaps you're avoiding discussing her because you haven't gotten over her."

He rubbed his forehead. "You're doing it again."

"What?"

"Making me feel like I'm in a therapist's chair." He groaned. "It's been a long night, Miranda. Can't we finally take a break from the question-and-answer routine?"

"Okay. For the rest of the night anything you say is off the record. Satisfied?" She rarely made an offer like this when she was in the middle of a project. But this didn't feel like work. Not at all.

She felt other things. Pleasantly tired, yet keyed-up, too. Despite her casual posture, she was aware of Warren's thigh next to hers, of their bare feet just inches apart on the low table in front of them.

"So. About this woman…"

"Miranda!"

"I said we were off the record. I never promised to stop asking questions."

"Oh Lord… Her name was Sally and I was fond of her. Still am, actually."

"Fond." Miranda took a last sip of wine and set down her glass. She thought she was a little drunk. That they both were. "Please don't ever tell me that you're fond of *me*. Fondness is such an insipid emotion."

"To me it implies great warmth and affection."

"As I said, insipid. Women want you to think of them with much stronger emotions than that. I suspect this woman of yours would like you to look back on her with longing and painful stabs of regret for what might have been.''

Warren finished off his wine, then set the glass down right next to hers, crystal clinking against crystal. ''Watch out, Miranda. Your romantic side is showing.''

''Well, it's true. Any woman would feel that way.''

''Including you?'' He leaned back into the love seat, but strangely, she felt as if he'd drawn nearer. ''What would you say, Miranda, if I told you I feel that way about you? That I look back at the years we went to school together and I wonder...

What? She ached for him to finish his sentence. In his dark cashmere sweater and well-tailored pants he appeared sophisticated, elegant, totally assured. Any woman he desired he could have in an instant. No longing required.

He was toying with her. Flirting, skirting the bounds of their friendship *and* their professional relationship.

And she didn't mind a bit.

''I've wondered, too,'' she admitted.

''Well, now's our chance. We could find out exactly what we missed out on.''

His words thrilled her. Scared her. She ran her fingers over the fine weave of a cushion. ''Don't tease me, Warren.''

''Why do you think I'm teasing?''

She could feel the drug of sexual attraction pulling her under. To stare into his eyes was easy—as always they drew her in. But to read the emotions they contained *wasn't* so simple.

"When we were sixteen, you found me crying in the hall. Do you remember?" She hardly ever cried anymore, but back then she'd been more emotional.

Warren picked out a gold thread in the upholstery fabric and followed it until his fingertips met hers. "You were hiding in the alcove by the storage room. Tears poured from your eyes, but you were so quiet, your face so composed. I'd never seen anyone cry like that."

"I was mortified to be found out," she said. "But you were very kind. Do you recall what you said to me?"

He shook his head. "No, I don't think so. Not exactly, anyway."

"You said it was okay, that I was going to be all right, that my father loved me." All the kids—hell, the entire town—had known that her father had left her and her mother just a few weeks earlier. And she'd been happy to let Warren believe that was the reason she was upset. When really it was Chad.

Chad and Bernie and that silly little ring that Miranda would have given the world to put on her own fourth finger.

Only now, she wondered. Would she have been crying about Chad if her father hadn't just run out on her mother and her? Was it possible Warren had been right all along about why she'd been so upset?

"You were so nice to me. Tell me, was I nice enough in return? I hate to think that I might have hurt you in any way."

"Miranda, those days were long ago. I don't want you to remember the boy I used to be. I want you to look at me and see the man I am. A man who desires you very, very much...."

Here it was, then. The moment they'd been working up to from that very first day when she'd driven to his parents' old farmhouse.

Warren's mouth was a breath from hers. She longed for him to kiss her, yet fear paralyzed her from making the next move.

Instead she closed her eyes and waited, expecting to feel his lips on hers in the next instant.

But his lips only brushed her cheek. The lightest touch. He smelled heavenly, felt heavenly.

Warren, Warren. A bittersweet ache choked her throat. She wished she could understand the emotion and what it meant. All she knew in that instant was that despite all the feelings she had for this man— attraction, respect, admiration—she couldn't kiss him. Couldn't make love with him.

Her reaction didn't make sense. She admired this man and she wanted him. Why was something in her resisting? Was it just the project—her need to be objective? She didn't think so.

It was more than that.

WARREN'S HEART lurched as Miranda pulled away from him.

"I'm sorry, Warren. I'm attracted to you, too. Very. However…"

She trailed her fingers down his arm, letting the tips sink through the silky cashmere of his sweater to the muscles beneath.

His chest rose on a deep, quavering breath. As he exhaled, he took her hand. Somehow he'd known that the evening would end this way. That hadn't stopped him from hoping.

"I care about you, Miranda."

He'd always cared, but she didn't know that. From what he could tell she had no clue that it wasn't just good fortune that he'd happened upon her in high school on the two occasions when she'd needed help.

These past few weeks, that old passion of his had been totally rejuvenated. He'd dared to dream that she might return some of his feelings. She seemed to enjoy his company. And he didn't think he'd imagined the sexual energy between them all evening. Not judging by the conspiratorial wink Phyllis had given him on her way out the door.

Perhaps Miranda's feelings for him just weren't strong enough yet….

That really wasn't the problem, though. She was still holding on. To Chad. To the losses of her past. And he had no idea how to make her let go.

"Warren, you're not upset with me, are you?"

"Absolutely not." He wasn't going to push her.

That would be the dumbest mistake he could make. "I don't want you to think I planned for anything to happen between us. Though I won't deny I might have hoped it could."

She hugged him. "You're a very wonderful guy, Warren. I'm going to be very jealous when some lucky woman captures your heart and I've lost you forever."

CHAPTER FIFTEEN

MIRANDA SPENT THE NIGHT in the spare bedroom. The sheets were beautiful to touch; the down duvet was covered with silk. In the morning she slipped into the kitchen without Warren noticing. Pleased with her luck, she turned on her camera and managed to shoot almost a whole minute of him sipping espresso and eating leftover pasta at his breakfast table. He had the Cohen book open in front of him.

The camera made a small clicking sound when she turned it off.

"You slept well?" He didn't look up.

This made the second night they'd spent under the same roof. In separate beds.

"I did." She set the camera on the counter. The gleaming espresso machine nearby was the same model he had at the farm. All the coffee supplies were close to hand, so she brewed herself a cup and settled in the chair opposite him.

"Will we have time for shopping today?" He'd mentioned wanting to pick up some gifts, so she hoped there would be. All the beautiful things in his apartment had inspired her. And she'd hardly touched a penny of her advance.

"Sure. Our only commitment is lunch with my editor."

For two people on the brink of making love last night they were speaking very rationally, Miranda thought.

"Well then, let's get started. I was hoping you could take me to the gallery where you bought your painting."

He closed his book. "You have to remember I'd just received a very big advance for my book when I purchased that."

"I'm happy just to look." She finished her coffee as he cleared off the counter.

At the front door, he slipped his keys off a hook and into his pocket while she shouldered the stylish suede jacket she'd worn on the plane.

"Bringing your camera?" He eyed the black case at her feet.

"I think I'd better. We're meeting your editor, right?"

"Right." His smile seemed forced, and for once it was she who knew what he was thinking. Last night had been off the record. But today would be business as usual. Obviously Warren wasn't too happy about that right now. But in the long term, he'd be glad that she'd kept their relationship on a friendly but professional footing.

Snow began to fall while they were strolling down Madison Avenue. Flat, sloppy flakes that hit her cheeks like wet kisses. Christmas was everywhere on the streets of New York City. All the windows were dressed for the season and carols played endlessly from one sound system to the next. The hustle of the crowds, the noise from the traffic, even the gritty air, seemed wonderful to Miranda.

Warren took her into the art gallery and introduced her to the owner, a friendly woman in her sixties, who assumed that the two of them were a couple.

After half an hour looking at paintings, they wandered into a shop that specialized in expensive electronic gadgets. Warren tested various models of scooters, then arranged to have several shipped to Chatsworth for the Browning children at Christmas. Miranda checked out digital scales, a pet bath, the latest model of electric toothbrush.

Out on the street again, Miranda felt the snowflakes melting in her hair and against her skin. Worried about her suede jacket, she took Warren's hand and pulled him into the next shop, then the next.

She tried on ankle boots with four-inch heels.

"Oh, yeah." Warren nodded with approval. "You've got to have a pair of those. Consider them my Christmas present."

"Warren, they're more than eight hundred dollars. And I can hardly walk in them. No, thanks," she insisted to the crestfallen clerk.

The next boutique specialized in black T-shirts. "You don't need any more black," Warren pronounced, pulling her back into the wet and cold.

At one o'clock they walked a block east to meet

Warren's editor at Park Avenue Café. Folk art and sheaves of dried wheat decorated the spacious restaurant. "My editor picked this place," Warren told her. "Dale loves dessert and he worships the pastry chef who works here."

Dale Paget had a table waiting for them. He was a small, neat man, with funky, turquoise-rimmed glasses and beautiful teeth. Miranda supposed her mother would have pressed him to be a toothpaste model if he'd been her son.

"Well, now I know why Warren agreed to this video project." Dale was open with his admiration after Warren's introduction.

"Miranda and I went to school together," Warren explained, his voice a little stiff. "She grew up in Chatsworth, too."

"Must be some town. To have produced such a beauty, as well as a first-class author."

Over appetizers and glasses of wine, they discussed the progress on Warren's book. Dale made it clear that while he'd be happy to see whatever Warren wrote, he and his senior editor were still hoping Warren would eventually turn in a sequel to *Where It Began*.

"You've left your readers in the lurch. Don't you agree?" Dale asked Miranda.

"Absolutely. But Warren seems determined to leave Olena's fate hanging in the balance for perpetuity."

"I could change my mind when I finish my current book," Warren allowed. "You never know."

Throughout lunch, Dale made subtle inquiries, obviously trying to categorize more specifically the relationship between Warren and Miranda. When she would have made it clear that they were only friends, Warren covered her hand with his and gave her an intimate smile that was sure to convey the wrong impression.

Immediately she realized he was trying to protect her. And he was right. She didn't really want to encourage the interest of this editor from New York.

So she put her hand on his and sighed appropriately, as the server brought out a towering cream, fruit and pastry creation.

ALL TOO FAST THE VISIT to New York ended. Miranda made notes on the flight back to Regina. Then, on the two-and-a-half hour drive to Chatsworth she and Warren listened to programs on the radio.

When Warren stopped his truck in front of her mother's house, Miranda felt reluctant to get out.

"I've had a marvelous time." Not for one second had she been bored or unhappy. In fact, she had barely thought of anyone or anything else while she'd been away. Now Chatsworth felt like a place she hadn't been to for a very long while.

"Me, too, Miranda."

She smiled, hoping to convey how grateful she was. Not only for his hospitality, but more important for his sensitivity. After the intensity of their first night in New York, he'd struck the perfect note for the remainder of their trip—not too intimate, but still warm and friendly.

"I'm not sure if I'm ready for real life yet." Thankfully, it was Wednesday, so her mother would be at bridge club. She'd have a few hours to settle herself before her mother's inquisition.

Not that she blamed Annie for her curiosity, or begrudged sharing her wonderful experiences in New York City with her mother. She just wanted a few hours to herself first.

"Thank you so much." To lean forward and kiss him seemed natural. A friendly peck, only…she ended up lingering, and not just because of his hand on her shoulder, pulling her closer.

Still, before anything truly significant—or regret-table—could happen, a passing car honked at them. Miranda quickly recognized the wild, fuzzy hair. Adrienne Jenson drove by slowly, obviously drinking in every detail.

Tomorrow the entire town would hear that Miranda and Warren had shared a kiss in front of Annie James's house.

MIRANDA WAS UNSUCCESSFUL in her attempts to get hold of Chad. She phoned the clubhouse several times, then remembered this was his night with Vicky. Probably they were at the café, lingering over dinner before Vicky's eight-o'clock curfew.

Now Miranda felt guilty that she hadn't thought about Chad or his problems while she'd been away. She wondered how he was doing, if he'd talked to Bernie since that awful reunion party.

With time on her hands, Miranda unpacked, then washed a load of delicates. For a late dinner she scrambled eggs and made toast. Emerging from the bathroom a half hour later, dressed in her robe, she heard her mother unlocking the front door.

"Well, you're home. How was New York? Did you meet Warren's agent?" Her mother drew off her gloves and placed them neatly on a shelf in the closet. In the kitchen, she sat down at the table, obviously expecting a detailed description of the weekend. In particular she wondered if Miranda had discussed the screenplay for Warren's movie with his editor.

"Mom, they aren't even thinking about casting the parts yet. And when they do…I'm sure they'll want to hire professionals."

Annie James frowned. "You need to believe in yourself. That's always been your problem."

"Maybe it has. Would you like some tea?" She went to the sink to fill the kettle. "How was bridge club?"

"Not bad. I didn't have great cards, but I believe I played them well." She pulled a score card from her purse and set it on the table. "Chad's mother wasn't there."

"No?"

"Poor Dorothy must be so upset. I know you scoffed when I told you Chad's involved with another woman. But I'm afraid there's just no doubt now."

"Really?" Miranda knew better than to take this bridge club gossip seriously.

"Yes. Apparently she's been doing his laundry."

"She's been what?"

"Donna Werner at the café had it from a very good source. And when a woman's doing a man's laundry you can be pretty sure—"

"That his sweaters were dirty," Miranda said, just as the kettle began to whistle.

"What did you say?"

"Nothing, Mom." She knew better than to disclose the identity of the mysterious woman to her mother. Annie would have a fit. This living with her mom was proving more difficult by the day.

Thank goodness there were only three more weeks until Christmas. Her interviews with Warren were over now, thanks to those precious days in New York. She had some appointments set up for January in Toronto to round out her research. But first she wanted to edit what she had and made sure she had no more questions for Warren.

At least there was no doubt that she'd have this phase of the project wrapped by December 24. She'd spend Christmas with her mother—and try to act as though she was enjoying herself. Boxing Day, December 26, she'd pack up and leave.

The idea of returning to Toronto filled her with mixed emotions. Obviously she and her mother needed a break from each other. But even though she already had plenty of material, she found it difficult to contemplate wrapping up her video on Warren.

And what about Chad? She'd as good as promised him that he'd be back with Bernie by Christmas. So far she'd done little to help him achieve that goal. Other than offering a sympathetic ear, a little companionship and some sweater-washing skills, what had she done to better his situation?

Time was running out. With only three weeks until Christmas the situation was becoming urgent.

She'd speak to Chad tomorrow, Miranda promised herself. She'd suggest he try flowers, a romantic gift—maybe a weekend getaway for two to Las Vegas.

If he turned on the charm, Bernie might forget all about those troublesome three conditions she'd set for Chad's return.

It might not work, but it was at least worth a try.

THE NEXT MORNING, after her mother had left for the library, Miranda drove to the clubhouse dressed for skiing. She found Chad in his office, only too pleased to put off his paperwork and join her for a ski around the circuit.

"How was New York?" he asked.

"Fabulous!" She forgot to worry about her balance on the skis as she told him about the shopping, about lunch with Warren's editor, about his surprisingly beautiful apartment.

"Didn't catch an Islanders game, then? That's

what *I* would've wanted to do if I'd been stuck in that city for three days.''

She tossed a snowball at him, then attempted to pass him on the left track. He relinquished the lead until they reached the flat homestretch along the lake, at which point he pulled up level to her.

''Chad, how are things going between you and Bernie?'' Skiing was easier now that there were no hills to contend with, and she could concentrate on conversation again.

''About the same.''

She couldn't judge from his voice how he felt about that. ''Only three more weeks until Christmas.''

''I know. I put up the exterior lights on the house last week.''

''Did you talk to Bernie?''

Chad kept his gaze fixed on the path ahead. ''She's been avoiding me even more than usual. Since the reunion.''

She groaned. ''Damn, Danielle. None of that was your fault.''

''It's not fair to blame it all on Danielle. She's been stressed out about her father.''

''Oh?''

''He's been struggling with depression.''

''Well, I'm sorry to hear that. Still, I thought it was gallant of you to insist that even if Bernie hadn't been pregnant, you still would have married her.''

''Well, Bernie didn't.'' Chad swung his ski pole with annoyance. ''I told you she's been acting too sensitive lately. And the way she stormed out of there—like a high school drama queen. I tell you, I've had enough of her theatrics.''

"She was just upset. I'm sure she wants to get back with you as badly as you want to get back with her.''

Chad skied on silently.

"You *do* want to be with Bernie. Right, Chad?''

When he hesitated with his answer, she was so distracted, she crossed the tips of her skis and began to pitch forward.

"Watch it!'' Chad whipped around on his skis, catching her before she tumbled to the ground.

"Thanks. Don't know what happened there....'' She was breathless, and not from exertion. Chad had both arms around her; his face was inches from her own.

"Stopped paying attention to what you were doing.'' He tugged the end of her toque, then let her go.

Not until they were back in the clubhouse, holding cups of that revolting hot chocolate, did Miranda ease into the subject of his marriage again.

"So when do you head back to Toronto?'' he asked her.

"Boxing Day. I'm finished my research here. Now I've got a few weeks to work on editing.'' She was excited, but nervous, too. The video had to be good. She wanted to impress Catherine Cox, of course. But even more, she wanted to impress Warren.

She missed talking to him. Just this morning she'd had to fight the urge to drive out to the Addison farm for one more interview. The truth was, she had no reason to go. Thanks to New York, she had so much material she'd probably end up doing a significant amount of cutting.

"You really think you can stand to leave the excitement of Chatsworth? After this, Toronto is bound to seem quiet."

She grinned. "I'll try to fill the empty moments with lots of shopping, theater and gourmet dining."

"Don't know what it'll be like here with you gone."

Her throat closed over the lighthearted response she'd planned to make. Leaving Chatsworth when she was eighteen had been different. Chad and Bernie had been about to get married, and she'd known putting a lot of distance between her and them was the right thing. But this time...

"I'll miss you." Chad put his hand over hers.

"You'll have Vicky. And Bernie," she added optimistically.

"I don't think so, Miranda."

"Yes, you will. Chad, I had this great idea last night. Why don't you book a holiday for two in Las Vegas. Take Bernie as soon as school lets out for the Christmas break. I'm sure a couple of days of intense romancing will do the trick."

Chad wasn't as excited by the idea as she'd hoped.

"What's wrong?" she asked.

"I don't know." He shrugged. "When Bernie first kicked me out, I thought all I wanted was for our family to be back the way it used to be. But I'm not so sure that's what will make me happy anymore. I guess I'm confused. About a lot of things."

He dropped his head into his hands. Miranda didn't know what to say. Chad looked so miserable. Wrapping an arm across his shoulders, she decided all she could do was listen. Eventually, he started to talk again.

"I love Bernie, and I guess I always will. But she started this and I can't put up with her stubbornness. Being on my own—it hasn't been that bad. Sure, I need to figure out a few things—like hand-washing sweaters and cooking real hot chocolate...." He made a stalwart effort to grin. "But for the most part I've been okay. And Vic is okay, too. I still see quite a bit of her..."

"She's a great kid." And Chad was right. She was surviving this trial seperation amazingly well.

Chad staightened. His eyes were red, but she couldn't see tears.

"I've spoken to a lawyer in Yorkton," he said. "I'm going to ask Bernie for a legal separation."

Miranda felt her jaw drop. "Oh, Chad. Are you sure you want to do that?"

"She started this, Randy. Her and that damn list of conditions. I don't want to live my life with a woman telling me what I can and can't do, who I can and can't be friends with."

To Miranda, wounded pride was talking. But she knew better than to question Chad's priorities at this moment. At least he hadn't mentioned divorce; still, a legal separation sounded so final.

Poor Bernie. She *had* been stubborn, and a little unreasonable, too, in Miranda's opinion. Nevertheless, Miranda felt sorry for her. The one thing she was sure of was that Bernie loved Chad in the forever kind of way that some women were capable of.

"That's a big step, Chad."

"Yeah. But you know what? It feels right to me. It really does." He took her hand again, squeezing it this time.

"When are you going to tell her?"

"I can't decide whether it would be better to get it over with now or wait until after the holidays. What do you think?"

"It isn't up to *me,* Chad." Either way, Bernie would be devastated. Maybe she'd enjoy the holidays more if he waited…. Yet, remembering the misery on Bernie's face the last time she'd seen her, Miranda knew Bernie wouldn't be enjoying anything this festive season. Maybe it would be best to just get the worst over with. At least Bernie wouldn't have to deal with the uncertainty anymore.

WHEN SHE WASN'T AT THE clubhouse offering Chad moral support, Miranda spent most of the next two weeks editing. Her mother gave up the dining room table to this purpose. First, Miranda hooked up her camera to her portable Mac and transferred the material from tape onto hard drive. Then she spread out her notes and her outlines and tried to visualize the completed project.

She'd already decided against a traditional linear approach to her subject. Instead she wanted to contrast Warren the man with Warren the artist. How he lived compared with how he wrote. Or what he wrote.

Over and over, she found herself referring to his novel. She felt differently about it, now that she knew Warren better, and suspected he had a secret passion for his female protagonist, Olena.

Did many authors fall in love with their characters? She made a note to do some research. It could make a nice tie-in to the biography.

In general, her work pleased her. She wouldn't pretend to know Warren inside and out, but she felt she could present some honest insights, in an interesting and creative format.

Immersed as she was in this last stage of her project, she didn't forget about Chad. How could she? Given his most recent decision to seek a legal separation from his wife, he needed her support more than ever. Still, she had to keep reminding herself that when she said goodbye to Chatsworth on December 26, she'd be saying goodbye to him, too.

And that wouldn't be easy.

CHAPTER SIXTEEN

"THERE'S A MISTAKE with the paperwork." The Reverend Leighton led Bernie to her sofa and sat her down solicitously.

Bernie held both hands to her heart, afraid to hear the rest.

The minister's silver-framed glasses slipped a fraction down his nose. "I'm afraid, Bernie, that you and Chad were never legally married."

No!

Bernie awoke from her dream in a sweat. She pushed off her covers and sat up straight. At seven-thirty in the morning it was still dark outside. Overnight, frost had fanned out over her windows. That new cold front must have arrived.

She knew why she'd had the dream. Lately her marriage no longer felt real to her. The years she'd spent with Chad had been a fantasy, a desperate daydream. They never really happened.

Well, of course they'd happened. But they didn't mean what she thought they did at the time. Chad was just going through the motions because it was expected. He'd done his duty. But he'd never loved her.

Now he was gone, and she knew it was forever. She'd seen it in his face this Wednesday when he'd dropped Vicky home after their supper at the café. He couldn't look Bernie in the eyes for more than a second. And when he said he wanted to talk, she'd known exactly what he was going to say.

Coward that she was, she put him off. She told him it was a bad time—she was in the middle of marking exams.

He seemed relieved. Of course, he couldn't be looking forward to that final, irrevocable conversation any more than Bernie was.

When he handed over Vicky's knapsack, which she'd forgotten on the front seat, he was so careful not to touch Bernie's fingers. *Am I that revolting to him now? Does he look at me and wonder how he ever managed to make love to me?*

Oh, God. That last thought hurt, maybe more than all the others. Up until this past six months or so, Bernie would have sworn Chad was more than satisfied with their love life. To think that maybe the act he'd been playing all their married years extended to the bedroom was killing her.

Wearily, Bernie dragged herself from the bed. Tomorrow was the town Christmas party. She'd lost five pounds, not the ten she'd hoped for. A new outfit hung in her closet, even though she wasn't sure she'd have the nerve to wear it. And she had an appointment booked with Adrienne tomorrow for her hair.

Yet none of it mattered. The best that Bernie could

be wouldn't draw Chad's attention for a second. The dance would be just like the reunion—with all her husband's attention focused on Miranda. If Bernie was smart, she'd stay home.

From the kitchen, she heard her daughter yell, "Mom! There's no bread to make toast!"

"Check the freezer." Bernie slipped out of her pajamas, then wrapped her body in a terry robe. Downstairs she found her daughter staring hopelessly at the frozen loaf on the counter.

"I can't get the slices apart."

Vicky had on the Calgary Flames hockey jersey that she wore for pajamas and a pair of yellow duck slippers. Never mind the crazy outfit. She was young enough to look cute no matter what she wore.

Bernie used a knife to pry apart two slices so Vicky could slip them into the toaster. Then she made herself coffee, unable to erase the image of her husband performing the very same job.

"I'm so glad it's the last day of school." Vicky pulled the container of peanut butter from the cupboard. "Can you believe we have a math quiz today? And Christmas is less than a week away!"

"Mmm." Bernie made no comment, her sympathy with the teacher. Getting students to focus on the last day of school before a major holiday was never an easy task.

"Oh, Karen asked if I could sleep over tomorrow after the dance. That's okay, right?" Vicky coated her toast thickly with peanut butter, then raised the knife to her mouth.

"Don't lick that thing," Bernie warned. "You could cut your tongue. And why doesn't Karen come here tomorrow night." Vicky had been spending a lot of time at the Olsens' lately. Well, since Chad had moved out. In the beginning, Bernie had been glad for the solitude. She'd needed those precious hours when she could fall apart and not worry that she was adversely affecting her daughter.

But lately she'd been finding the quiet house oppressive. She missed her daughter, and the friends she usually invited over all the time.

"Tell Karen to spend the night here and I'll make you waffles for breakfast." She also hadn't cooked the family morning favorite since Chad had left.

"I'd rather go to the Olsens'. It's too quiet at home. Boring."

This was the first Vicky had given any sign that her father's departure had upset her.

"I guess we'll get used to the silence eventually."

Vicky put down her toast. Her eyes looked huge in her suddenly pale face. "But you guys said the separation was a temporary thing."

Bernie remembered all too well sitting down with Vicky and explaining that her mother and father had a few things to work out, but that Vicky shouldn't worry. Vicky had obviously accepted that conversation at face value.

Until now. Oh, why did this subject have to come

up when they both had to be at school in less than
an hour? This was not a conversation she wanted to
rush. Besides, Chad should be here. Let *him* explain
to his daughter why he wasn't ever moving back
home with his family.

"Initially that's what we thought. What we
hoped."

"Dad left at the beginning of November. It's almost *Christmas* now. And I miss him. It's not the
same, seeing him at the clubhouse or going to the
café. In the beginning it was kind of fun, especially
getting to eat out all the time. But it's turning into a
real drag."

"I know, honey."

"No, you don't know! You get to stay here, in the
house, all the time. I'm the one who has to pack my
clothes and sleep in different beds, and I'm always
forgetting to bring something with me or leaving
something important behind."

Bernie felt so guilty. Her daughter had seemed to
take her parents' separation so much in stride that
Bernie had almost felt she *approved* of the whole
idea.

"I'm sorry about all that, Vicky. In the beginning
I really did hope your father and I would be able to
sort out our problems very quickly."

"Well, why can't you?" Vicky pushed her chair
away from the table. "We still haven't put up our
Christmas tree!"

Bernie had thought about picking one out several

times when she passed the selection lined up outside the local garage on her way home from work. But choosing and decorating a Christmas tree had always been a family project.

"We'll get one on Sunday," she promised.

"Without Dad?"

She hesitated. "Probably."

"I don't want a tree if Daddy isn't going to be with us on Christmas! In fact, we might as well cancel the entire holiday!"

"Vicky, I'm sorry—"

"It's all your fault! You're always nagging him. That's why he doesn't want to move back in with us. Why can't you be nicer? Why can't you be more like—"

"That's enough!" She could guess who her daughter wanted her to be more like. The double betrayal—by husband and offspring—was more than she could stand.

"Vicky, I know this is hard for you, but the problems between your father and me aren't open to discussion. You know that we love you and that we'll always—"

But Vicky wasn't interested in her mother's false reassurances. She ran from the room, and seconds later, Bernie heard a door slam. Great. Vicky had retreated to her room. She hadn't dressed, hadn't eaten her breakfast, and the junior-high bell would be ringing in forty minutes.

Dropping her head to the table, Bernie wondered

if she'd finally hit bottom. Surely her life couldn't get any worse than it was at this moment.

MIRANDA STOPPED HER CAR at the top of the Addison lane. The sky was clear and so were the roads, but she didn't drive any farther. Suddenly it was obvious that coming here had been a mistake.

She shifted into Reverse and checked over her shoulder before backing up. That was when she spotted Warren walking in the field by the road. He'd seen her and raised an arm in welcome.

Warren! She'd felt so instantly thrilled that it scared her. At the end of every project she experienced a reluctance to move on. This was a similar reaction, only stronger than usual.

Which was why she shouldn't have come. Then she wouldn't have had time to wonder at this strange euphoria that made it impossible for her to stop grinning.

As he came up to the driver's side of the car, she opened her door.

"It's been a while," he said. He wore his heavy coat and thick leather gloves. His dark hair was wind tousled; his ears and the tip of his nose, a little red.

"You look cold. Want to sit in here and warm up?"

He nodded toward the lane. "We could go to the house."

She was reluctant to do that, but given that she'd

driven twelve miles to get here, she knew it didn't make sense to turn down the invitation.

"Okay. I'll walk up with you." She slid out of the car and slammed the door shut. Three feet separated them as they strode along, boots squeaking on the cold, packed snow.

"Been busy?" Warren asked.

They hadn't seen each other since New York. More than two weeks ago.

"Mostly editing. The fun part." Usually that was true. She loved creating a cohesive whole out of the bits and pieces of video. Searching for connections she'd missed when she was in the heat of researching.

"Ah, so that's why you haven't been popping by for your regular visits. I thought maybe I'd lost my touch with the espresso machine."

She'd missed their coffees. But she'd missed more than that.

She'd missed this kitchen. She placed an affectionate hand on the table she'd once considered ugly and listened to the crackling of the fire as Warren added a couple of sticks of wood to the cast-iron stove.

"How is the book going?"

Warren turned from the stove to the espresso maker. "Oh, fine."

She glanced through the arched opening into the dining area. His laptop was closed. The piles of paper on the table were suspiciously tidy.

"That's good," she said.

She'd missed Warren.

Silently, he made their coffees. She watched his quiet efficiency, admiring once again his strong, elegant hands. She felt that there were at least a dozen things she needed to say to him, yet she couldn't string together a single sentence. Once they were both sitting, she still could say nothing.

"Have you made plans for Christmas?" she finally asked.

"My parents want me to fly out to Victoria. But I'm so close to finishing my first draft. I think I'll stay put and visit them when I'm done."

"What about Christmas dinner?"

"Libby and Gibson have invited me. It'll be fun to be around their kids."

"Well, that sounds nice." Why hadn't she invited him sooner? Unlike Chad, whom, she knew, her mother would never consider allowing inside the house, Warren at the Christmas table would have pleased Annie.

And Miranda, too.

"Looking forward to the drive back to Toronto?" Warren asked.

"It's a tedious trip, but it will be good to get home. I'm leaving Boxing Day."

He tapped his spoon lightly on the table, then glanced up at her. "Video's all finished?"

"Mostly. I'll do some polishing at home. Add footage from some esteemed Canadian authors.

Would you like to view it when it's done? I could arrange a private screening before I hand the final version over to the CBC." He could stopover in Toronto, before heading south to New York City. That way, they would see each other again.

"Depends on how my writing goes... Maybe..."

Miranda tried to hide her hurt behind a smile. "Well, whatever."

He didn't smile back.

"I should head back to town." She'd finished her cappuccino. It had been excellent.

"I'll walk you to your car."

"That's okay." They sounded like polite strangers. She wasn't sure why she felt upset, disappointed. Hadn't she spurned both of Warren's advances? So what, exactly, did she expect from him now?

"I insist." In the kitchen he held out her coat and his hand lingered on her shoulder as they stepped outdoors.

"The Christmas dance is tomorrow," he said.

She nodded.

"Going?"

"I'm not sure if it's a good idea." Hands tucked into her pockets, she kept her gaze on the road in front of her, fitting her feet into the tracks she'd made earlier.

"Because of Chad and Bernie." Warren stated this as a fact.

"Chad says he wants a legal separation." She hadn't intended to tell anyone this, and felt immediately disloyal. "Of course he told me in confidence. He still hasn't discussed the idea with Bernie. But he's pretty set in his own mind. He doesn't want to be married to her anymore."

"Well." Warren's hand dropped from her shoulder.

"It's a shock, isn't it? I was so sure the two of them would patch things up. When I first arrived here, that's what Chad told me he wanted. But now he swears he wouldn't go back to her under any circumstances."

"I wonder what happened to change his mind."

Miranda knew he didn't wonder at all. "Don't you dare blame me. Chad needed someone to talk to. I was there for him. It's not my fault Bernie alienated him so badly he's given up on the marriage."

"Come on, Miranda. Do you really believe the situation is as simple as that? Can't you concede that your presence here in Chatsworth has influenced Chad's decision to leave his wife?"

"No, I can't. Have you forgotten that I'm going back to Toronto on Boxing Day? Chad knows that. He isn't leaving Bernie because of me."

She'd thought Warren knew her, understood her, better perhaps than anyone else she'd ever met. So how could he think she was the sort of woman who would purposefully come between a husband and his wife? That he even harbored the thought was an insult.

"If you really want to convince me, tell me this,

Miranda. Tell me you don't love Chad.'' The words came out from Warren's mouth in a cloud of frost.

She wanted to. But how could she? She'd *always* loved Chad. And Warren was cruel to bring it up now. A breath of wind scattered the layer of ice crystals that lay over the packed snow. They'd reached her car.

Warren opened the driver's door for her. As she moved forward, he stopped her with a single word.

"Miranda."

His face was inches from hers. He looked terrible suddenly, as if he was in unbearable pain. She thought of the pristine condition of his dining room, and knew that her suspicion about his writing had been correct. Something was wrong.

"Are you okay, Warren?"

He compressed his lips, turned away. "I shouldn't have taken you to New York."

"What are you talking about? New York was *wonderful.* I couldn't have finished the video without New York."

"Never mind. Get in the car, Miranda. I'll see you at the dance tomorrow night."

She needed to see Warren before she left for Toronto. She was confused about many things right now, but she knew that for sure. "What if I don't go?"

"You'll be there," he predicted. "Save me a dance.''

THE TOWN HALL DINNER and dance was potluck. Annie prepared baked beans—a vegetarian version without any salted pork—so that Miranda wouldn't ''starve.''

''I wish you hadn't bothered, Mom. I'm still not sure if I'm going.'' She dabbed raspberry-colored polish on her baby toenail. She'd let herself go when she'd come home and was catching up today. Earlier she'd plucked her eyebrows and deep-conditioned her hair.

''Of course you'll go to the Christmas dance. *Everyone* does.''

''Come on, Mother. The hall can't accommodate the entire town.''

''Well, almost everyone. Wear that red dress I saw hanging in your closet. It's a little dressy for a small-town affair, but I bet you look fabulous in it.''

The red dress that was the same color as the polish she was putting on her toes... Yes, she was going to the dance. Silly of her to pretend she wasn't.

Not much happened in Chatsworth; how could she miss the big annual Christmas bash? Besides, she wanted to admire Vicky in her new outfit, and she'd have a chance to say goodbye, maybe even dance with Warren and...

Chad, too, of course.

She'd make her mother happy at the same time. Annie had her heart set on walking into the hall with her beautiful daughter from Toronto by her side. Miranda supposed she should be glad that her mother was so proud of her.

But it isn't really you she's proud of, just the way you look. It was Warren's voice, inside her head. She wished she could shake it. Lately she'd been seeing lots of things from his point of view.

Except the reasons for the failure of Chad and Bernie's marriage. Warren could blame her if he wanted. But Chad was an adult and he'd come to his own conclusion. Frankly, Miranda thought Bernie had simply pushed the man too hard. Chad was stubborn and he had his pride. Getting kicked out of his own house by his wife had been a blow he'd simply been unable to recover from.

Annie insisted on arriving at the party promptly at six o'clock. Already a dozen cars were in the hall's parking lot. In an hour, the street would be lined on both sides. Miranda walked up the stairs, carrying Annie's casserole dish.

The other members of the bridge club—except for Chad's mother—were already milling around the entrance, most with their husbands. Miranda allowed herself to be introduced around. She smiled and asked questions and agreed that the traffic in Toronto was terrible and that Chatsworth was a much more pleasant place to live. But no, she had no immediate plans to relocate.

After half an hour, a couple walked in the main doors. A blond giant of a man and an attractive woman with long, brown, windswept hair. They had three children in tow. The two girls took their little brother's hand and led him over to meet their friends.

"Libby Bateson!" Miranda smiled warmly as the name suddenly came to her.

"I was wondering if I'd get to see you while you were in town. But I'm Libby Browning now. Do you remember Gibson?" Proudly she put a hand on her husband's arm.

"I sure do. I was so glad to hear you two were married." Libby had had a hard life after her mother's and brother's tragic deaths. She'd left Chatsworth for a while and hadn't been heard of until years later, when she'd appeared with a daughter but no husband. God knows what that must have been like for her. In a town of this size there would have been talk.

"Life has been very good lately," Gibson said. "Now, if only grain prices would improve…"

The noise level in the hall dropped markedly. People turned toward the entrance and stared.

"I didn't think he would come," someone said. She was young and pretty and Miranda had no idea who she was. Her companion, another woman in her early twenties said, "Let's move closer."

Curious, Miranda craned to see over heads. Who in Chatsworth would garner this kind of interest? At first all she saw was Warren Addison, standing at the entrance, extremely attractive in a dark jacket and jeans.

She tamped the impulse to go and say hi as she

realized, with some amazement, that his was the entrance that had created the big stir.

"Good old Warren," Gibson said. "Look! I think all the single women in Chatsworth have set their sights for him. And plenty who aren't single, too."

"He hasn't been in town much, aside from the occasional trip for groceries and mail. I guess people want a chance to admire the local hero," Libby said.

The women who had been standing by Miranda were now in front of Warren. Miranda watched them introduce themselves. They giggled and patted their hair and couldn't take their eyes off him.

Surely they were driving him mad.

"Catch you later," she said to the Brownings. She slipped by several groups of people, smiling and waving rather than stopping to talk. When she finally reached Warren, she stepped between the two girls to give him a kiss on the cheek.

She had to step on her toes to reach. As her lips brushed his skin, she caught a whiff of his shampoo.

"Miranda." His hand touched her waist lightly, then stayed. "That's quite the dress."

For the first time in a very long while, she was glad of her beauty. Glad of her gleaming blond hair, long, shapely legs and winning smile. She sensed the other women backing away, before she turned to verify their absence.

"I thought you needed rescue. Obviously more than a few of Chatsworth's eligible women have their eye on you."

He waved a hand, as if it didn't matter. "Before I published my book, none of them would have given me a second glance."

Miranda wasn't so sure about that. This man had magnetism. She knew she wasn't the only woman in the room who felt it. As they headed to the bar for a drink, she noticed more than a few gazes follow them.

Warren ordered a beer; she opted for a soft drink. At Warren's raised eyebrows, she shrugged. "I don't want to do anything crazy tonight."

"Maybe you should." Warren tapped his glass against hers. "Depending on the sort of crazy things you had in mind, of course."

"I have a list. Maybe we should review it on the dance floor." Being with Warren was so effortless. She didn't worry about his ego, about saying the wrong things, about meeting expectations. They finished their drinks and before she knew it they were facing each other, arms entwined, flying to the rhythm of an old-fashioned polka.

Talking was impossible as they focused on keeping in sync with the fast-moving crowd. As soon as the dance began to wind down, Warren whispered, "That was quite the welcome you gave me."

"Anything in particular meet with your approval?"

"That dress." His gaze dropped the length of her body, then back to her mouth. "Your lips on my skin."

A slow, romantic tune started, and Miranda was certain he planned to kiss her right there on the dance floor. Instead, he held her at a respectable distance and began to dance again, swaying to the beat of Eric Clapton's "Wonderful Tonight."

Something strange was coming over her. She knew her heart was racing, could feel the heat radiating from her cheeks. Holding out a hand, she saw her fingers tremble.

It was happening again, just as in New York... Warren tightened his arms a fraction, and she felt his leg against her hip.

They circled back to where they had started. The lights were dim, but she saw someone familiar standing at the edge of the dance floor. He raised a glass in silent salute and smiled.

Chad was here.

CHAPTER SEVENTEEN

BERNIE WALKED IN THE MAIN door to the hall, then ducked into the cloakroom before anyone could see her. She hung up her long wool coat and pulled a comb from her purse. Peering at the small mirror hanging on the wall, she almost cried.

Why had she let Adrienne talk her into this? She'd just wanted a simple body perm. Not a head full of wild curls.

And the skirt of her new outfit was much too short. Nothing wrong with her legs; they'd always been her best asset. But she didn't think she could carry off the new look. She felt too self-conscious.

She tucked the comb away and settled for fresh lipstick and another spray of perfume. The scent was a new one, a little stronger than she remembered from the sample she'd tried at the department store last week.

With nothing else available to "improve" her appearance, she had no choice but to enter the main hall. Cautiously, she made her way out of the cloakroom. The ladies gathering tickets at a side table didn't see her at first.

"Linda? Stacey?"

"What? Oh, it's *Bernie!*"

She felt the judgment in their appraisals and shivered, waiting for the inevitable reaction. You couldn't buy a new sweater in this town without inviting a comment of some sort.

"Don't you look wonderful," Stacey finally said.

The pause and the way Stacey's gaze couldn't seem to get past the rhinestone choker Bernie had at her neck told her that her new look was a dud. Should she duck out now? But the door behind her opened and her mother-in-law burst in from the cold.

"Bernie, honey!"

Dorothy's effusive approval had started when Bernie and Chad began having problems. Bernie would have expected the older woman to side with her son, but she'd done the opposite.

"Perry," she said to the neighbor who'd driven her to the dance, "please take my coat so I can walk in with my daughter-in-law." She tucked Bernie's hand under her arm and entered the main hall without hesitation.

Fortunately the room was crowded, and no one seemed to notice them at first. People were dancing, and those on the sidelines stood in clutches obscuring the view or nibbling from the buffet set up along the wall next to the bar. Bernie dropped off her jellied salad, then followed her mother-in-law to the bar and accepted wine that was handed to her.

A couple of her mother-in-law's friends snagged them, and for a few moments Bernie could catch her breath while the older women discussed plans for the upcoming holidays.

A fellow teacher noticed her and stopped to comment on the new hairdo. Her tactful comments almost had Bernie convinced her appearance was passable, when Vicky came racing by with her friend Karen. She had on the outfit Miranda had helped her buy. Black pants, red sweater, classy and funky at the same time. The girls were after cola refills, but Vicky stopped dead when she saw her mother.

"Oh, my God, Mom, what happened to your hair?"

"Vicky, shh! I think it looks very nice."

Vicky ignored her grandmother. "And that skirt. It's way too short! Mother, what are you trying to prove?"

Mortified, Bernie froze. If she'd had a magic wand she would have transported her daughter to her bedroom. Better yet, she herself would have vanished. Chad's mother, her friends and the two girls were all staring at her with various mixtures of horror and pity.

Vicky's question was all too appropriate. What was she trying to prove? Beyond making it obvious to the entire town just how desperate she was.

"I've—I've…" Bernie set her wineglass on a nearby table and pushed through the crowd of people standing between her and the exit. She heard Dorothy call her back, but didn't pause. Only once did she turn for a final glance.

And that was when she saw them. Her husband and Miranda, dancing as if they were the only ones in the room. Eyes on each other, bodies moving as one.

The sick, shamed ache in her stomach gave way to an agonizing new pain.

If ever two people loved each other, those two obviously did.

She *had* to get out, and now. Tears blurring her vision, she pushed past yet another clutch of people, past Linda and Stacey at the table, into the cloakroom. Wrapping her coat around her as she walked, she slipped out the main door and down the concrete steps. Her tears were coming so fast she could hardly see, and she had to hold on to the handrail so she wouldn't fall.

"Wait, Bernie!"

A wild, desperate hope had her glancing back at the hall.

But it was only Warren Addison, standing at the hall doors behind her. He wasn't wearing a coat, just a turtleneck and blazer.

She ignored him, headed for her car.

But he ran and overtook her.

"Bernie." He put his arm around her shoulder and squeezed.

She couldn't talk, but he didn't seem to expect her to say anything. He walked her to her car, then took the keys from her hand and opened the passenger door.

"Get in."

"But—"

"You can't drive home. You can't even see."

Well, that was true. But she could sit in her car and cry, couldn't she? Only, then even more people might notice how pathetic she was.

So she sat in the passenger seat like an obedient pupil and didn't say a word as Warren started her car and drove the short blocks to the two-story house in which she'd once been so happy.

Warren picked through the keys on the ring until he found the one to the front door. Inside, he tried to remove her coat.

"No!" She reached to hide the skirt that was too short.

"Bernie." He grasped her shoulders. "You looked great tonight. People were taken aback by the change, that's all. I'm not lying to make you feel better. I don't do things like that."

She'd never known Warren very well. He sounded sincere, but how could he be?

"I made a fool of myself tonight."

"The only mistake you made was running away. I was at the bar, right behind you. I heard what your daughter said, but she was wrong. You were stunning tonight—sexy, pretty and just a little bit wild. Not the way, I imagine, a twelve-year-old girl envisions her own mother."

"But Linda and Stacey at the entrance gave me such strange reactions, too."

"I'll bet they were surprised. And maybe a little shocked. People have perceptions about other people. And they often aren't happy to alter those ideas."

Was it possible he was being honest? That she hadn't looked *that* bad? Allowing him to slip off her coat, she glanced in the hall mirror. Red eyes aside, she thought it possible that some might find her new wild curls sexy.

"Warren, would you like a glass of wine?"

"I'd love one." He slipped off his shoes and followed her to the kitchen.

"Nice house. I see you have an eye for decorating."

Warren was so kind. She felt guilty for not having paid more attention to him when they were kids. She passed him a bottle and the corkscrew, then let him take care of opening the wine while she collected crystal glasses.

They settled on the sofa in the adjoining family room. Warren's gaze roamed over the photographs on the built-in shelves.

Bernie focused on a studio shot of the three of them many years ago. To her eyes, Chad, sitting in the middle, looked like a proud father and husband. "I thought he loved me. That we were happy."

Warren dropped a hand to her shoulder. "He does and you were."

Oddly, his comforting words only made her want to cry. "Yes, *I* was happy," she conceded. "But I don't know if Chad ever loved me. I think for him it was always Randy. Right from the beginning, even on the day he made his wedding vows to me.''

Oh, God, what was she saying? Warren would find her pathetic. But she needed to talk and she was sick of her notebook. And Warren didn't appear to mind listening. In fact, he was damn good at it. ''Did you see them dancing tonight? Randy and Chad?''

''Yes. I saw.''

''It was like being hit in the stomach. The way she looks at him. The way *he* looks at *her*.''

''I know.''

''It's not that I have anything against Randy. But she's always had so much. Beauty, brains *and* talent! She could have done anything with her life. She could have any man she wants. Why did she have to come back here and take my husband? That's what I want to know.''

Tears started again. Warren handed her first one tissue, then another.

''I—I'm sorry. I shouldn't fall apart like this.'' She blew her nose, then took a deep breath and held it. No more crying. She'd done enough of that.

''You have every right to fall apart, Bernie. I know it hurts. It's got to hurt, when the one you love doesn't even seem to *see* you, let alone…''

Something in Warren's voice clued her in. She turned to her guest, to the man so unexpectedly compassionate. Focusing on him instead of herself for a few minutes made everything obvious.

''You're hurting, too.'' Her first thought was that

he'd lost someone, as well. In the next instant, she realized who it had to be. "You're in love with Randy."

Warren took her hand in both of his. He blinked, then regarded her frankly. "That's right, Bernie. I love Miranda and you love Chad. So you see, I know exactly how you feel."

CHAPTER EIGHTEEN

THE SECOND Miranda saw Chad, she tensed in Warren's arms. Something about the way Chad had brandished his glass made her wonder if he'd had a few before arriving—or if perhaps he'd been here longer than she'd known and had already made several trips to the bar.

She couldn't stop worrying. If he ran into Bernie in that state he might say something he'd regret later.

When the song ended, she wasn't sure who dropped their hands first—she or Warren.

''Thanks for the dance.'' Gallant to the end—that was Warren. He'd spotted Chad, too, of course. Definitely he'd noticed the change that had washed over her.

''I just need to talk to him for a few minutes.'' She felt apologetic, although there was no reason she shouldn't excuse herself to speak to another friend.

Miranda was glad she'd stuck to nonalcoholic beverages—she had a feeling she was going to need all her faculties to get through this evening.

Mildly panicked, she searched through the crowd. Then felt a hand on her arm and turned, to see Chad. He held another glass in his hand, empty again. Setting it on a nearby table, he gave her a high-voltage smile.

"Want to dance?"

Suddenly she was eighteen again, and it was prom night, and the boy she'd always wanted was whisking her onto the dance floor.

Now, dancing, his arms around her, she didn't care that all the biddies in the room—her mother included—were glaring at her in disapproval. She was living her fantasy. Dancing with the boy she'd always wanted. Feeling his arms wrapped possessively around her body, his breath warm against her skin.

Chad was different tonight, and the way he looked at her was different, too. He had barely spoken a word so far. She sensed a recklessness that was both frightening and exciting. Perhaps it was the drinking. Perhaps it was something more.

Warren had disappeared. She scanned the crowd, knowing he'd stand out with his height. But she saw no sign of him.

It was strange. For a while when she and Warren had been dancing she'd wondered if she'd made a mistake. If she should have grabbed the opportunity to be with him when they were in New York City. She'd wondered if, possibly, fate was giving her a second chance.

But then she'd seen Chad. And known he was waiting for her. After years and years of pushing her feelings for him to the background, she had no strength to resist anymore.

Chad slowed his step as the current song ended. The romantic Beatles tune, "Something" started next. Chad sang the words softly into her ear as he led her into one of the darker corners of the dance floor.

This song had played at their high school grad. She remembered watching him and Bernie leave their respective dates to dance to it. She'd felt such terrible jealousy she'd had to leave the room, go to the washroom. She'd locked herself in a stall until the song had ended.

Now Chad pulled her tighter to his body. They swayed to the music, but other than that, all pretense at dancing halted.

"Randy." He brushed a hand through her short curls, his expression adoring. "Something I've always wanted to know..."

"Yes?"

"If I'd asked you out in high school, what would you have said?"

"Are you kidding?" He had to be. But he didn't smile as he waited for her answer. "Chad, I was crazy about you. I would have died and gone to heaven if you'd asked me out."

"Really?"

"Come on, Chad. You *had* to know."

"Not a clue," he insisted. "You were so damn cool and confident. Nobody got you too excited."

"That's because there was only one boy I

wanted...." She leaned in to him, letting his chest take some of her weight.

"I can't believe I was such an idiot. Oh, Randy..." His hands tightened at her waist; his gaze lingered at her mouth. "I need to kiss you. You wouldn't believe how badly."

Could bones melt? Hers felt as if they were softening like icicles on a sunny spring day. She'd never known longing like this before. No price seemed too high to pay. And yet...Vicky was in this room. Bernie, too, probably, although Miranda hadn't seen her.

But perhaps Bernie had seen *her*—dancing with Chad. The possibility gave sudden strength to Miranda's legs.

"This isn't right, Chad. We can't. Certainly not here." Pulling away took all Miranda's willpower. But once she was out of Chad's arms, the certainty that she was doing the right thing strengthened.

"I've got to leave. I can't stand this a minute longer."

"Randy..."

She ignored him calling her name; ignored, too, the furious "come here right this minute, young lady" look her mother shot her from across the room. Dashing into the cloakroom, she gathered her coat, not bothering to put it on.

Cold winter air shocked even more sense into her befuddled head. What had they been doing in there? Practically making out is what. God, could they have picked a more public place?

She heard the double doors open behind her, Chad's hurried footsteps. He caught up to her before she could duck inside her car.

"Don't run away, Randy. I can't stand it!" He took her coat, wrapped it over her shoulders, then pulled her in tight.

That weakness she'd felt on the dance floor threatened to engulf her again. She pressed her cheek to his chest, hard enough to hear the wild pounding of his heart.

"Randy, honey, come back to the clubhouse with me. We've got to talk."

But they wouldn't talk. She knew they were past that point. They'd barely been able to contain themselves in a crowd full of their friends and neighbors. Alone at his clubhouse, they'd make love. No doubt about it.

No doubt that that was what she wanted, too.

And why not? If Chad and Bernie's marriage was over—then didn't she and Chad deserve to have their chance?

"You still haven't told Bernie..." She wasn't sure, at first, if he'd heard her. But then he lifted her chin with his finger.

"No. But she knows. I can tell by the way she looks at me. And I will tell her. Tomorrow, if you want." He nudged her gently with his hand, urging her face higher. She could tell he wanted to kiss her, and despite the winter air around them she felt engulfed by warmth and a powerful, insidious need....

She wouldn't go to the clubhouse. But surely one kiss…

His lips were almost on hers, his breath had already claimed her, when she heard herself cry.

"I can't, Chad. It isn't right." She twisted from his arms and threw herself into her car. Chad didn't try to stop her, but he did motion for her to lower her window.

She was almost afraid to do that. Afraid he'd talk her into changing her mind. But she couldn't just drive away.

"You can try to hide from this if you want," he said. "But it isn't going to change anything. I'm crazy about you. And I'm not going back to Bernie."

"Oh, Chad." She had to touch his cheek, then allowed him to catch her hand and press her fingers to his mouth. For a second she closed her eyes and dreamed—

Then pulled back her hand and started her car.

"I'll talk to you tomorrow," he called out as she drove away, her foot barely strong enough to press against the accelerator.

MIRANDA DROVE aimlessly along one of the country roads that fanned out from the small town. The stars were burning up the sky tonight—she'd never seen so many. But the road itself was black and deserted. The only evidence of other humans was a farm light every couple of miles or so.

At first she felt numb. To hold her car on the road

and keep forging ahead took all her concentration. She turned on the radio, found the announcer's voice intrusive, and switched it off again.

Maybe she'd drive all the way to Toronto. Her gas tank was full. She could make it to Winnipeg and refuel there. Day after tomorrow she'd be home and she'd never have to go back to Chatsworth in her life. She'd even move her mother to Toronto.

And never see Chad again? And what about Warren?

Tonight she'd been swept away in the arms of two different men. Two very different men. With Warren she'd felt a cascading joy, like nothing she'd ever experienced before. She'd wondered if this was it— the mysterious connection that had been missing for so long in her life.

The connection, she realized now, she'd been aching to make for more years than she could remember.

Then Chad had appeared, throwing her emotions into a whirl. Because however powerful her attraction to Warren, she'd wanted Chad forever. And tonight he'd offered her the chance to make him hers. After all these years of being alone, wasn't she entitled to an opportunity for love? If she turned him down now, he'd just find someone else. He wouldn't go back to Bernie. That was what he'd said.

But how could she be sure?

She'd been on the road an hour, taking corners at random, when she realized she'd ended up at Warren's. In the glow from the yard light, she could see his truck, so he was home. But the house lights were out, so he was in bed.

She drove in anyway, stopping her car next to his truck. Pocketing her keys, she stepped outside. She pulled off her glove to touch the hood of his vehicle. Still warm. Then she walked round the side of the house, and here, where the dining room was, she found the faintest of lights—a green glow. Warren's laptop?

Was he writing in the dark? She wished he'd left the curtains open so she could peek in and see for sure. But if he was awake and working, he'd have heard her drive up. If he wanted company, he'd come to the door...

She waited a full five minutes. Nothing. And she was getting cold.

Coming here had been no accident, she realized. She needed to talk to Warren. Needed his perspective, his insight, his understanding. Warren had a way of exposing truth with words, the way she tried to do on film. But did she really believe he could be objective enough to help her now?

She already knew he disapproved of her feelings for Chad. And how could she blame him? No one in his right mind would side with a woman who might possibly be jeopardizing another woman's family.

Even *she* didn't approve.

And yet, she simply couldn't turn her back on Chad.

The silent house mocked her despair. And suddenly she decided, to hell with advice. Right now just seeing Warren would be enough.

She marched to the back door. Raised her hand and almost knocked. But couldn't. She waited, interminably, before retreating to her car. Once inside the Volkswagen, she simply sat. Maybe a half an hour passed.

From inside the house, she heard not a peep. Eventually she began to wonder if the green glow she thought she could see was all in her imagination. Perhaps Warren was asleep. Perhaps he'd been sleeping all the while.

She didn't think so, though. She was pretty sure he knew she was out here. He just didn't want to see her.

Maybe this was his way of telling her he couldn't help this time. She had to work this problem out on her own. She had to make a choice.

And maybe he was right.

WARREN HEARD tires crunching in the packed snow of his driveway. Without checking out the window, he knew it was Miranda. He'd just gotten home from Bernie's. Emotions fired up, he'd felt like writing. First time in weeks. Since New York, actually.

He'd only just settled himself at the computer, only just completed the first paragraph, when he'd heard her drive up.

Why had she come *here?*

At least she wasn't with Chad. That was a relief,

but not much. The way those two had swooned over each other it was just a matter of time before they landed in bed. The only obstacle that he could imagine would be Miranda's guilt. Which was probably why she'd come to him, hoping he'd help her to assuage it. But if she expected him to tell her that what she wanted to do was right—hell! She ought to know better!

Damn it, he'd expected more of Miranda James. But maybe he was indulging in a case of sour grapes. He'd had her in his arms tonight—God, he'd been so happy! The Backstreet Boys could have marched up on stage and started to sing and he wouldn't have noticed. But Miranda had picked Chad's face out from the crowd.

And like that, the magic had disappeared.

Or maybe, in Miranda's case, that was when the magic had started.

Was it possible he'd made the wrong assessment where she was concerned? Maybe she hadn't been using Chad as an emotional shield all these years. Maybe she really did love the guy.

Warren left his chair and moved to the window. Through the thick cotton of the curtains, he'd seen headlights when she'd first driven up, but she'd turned them off shortly thereafter. Now he heard a car door slam, her footsteps in the snow.

She walked round his truck, along the house, to the back door. Like a dog on the scent, he followed her there, standing on the other side of the wooden divider, his hand on the knob, waiting for her to knock.

But she didn't. He stood listening for a long time and even began to wonder if he'd imagined the sound of her footsteps. And then he heard them again. Walking away, back to her car.

He let out a long, frustrated breath. What was she playing at? Tempted to open the door and call out her name, he stopped himself. If she came in here, how could he look her in the eye without giving his true feelings away? How could he advise her what to do about Chad, when he wanted her so desperately for himself?

And how could he say, for certain, that what she felt for Chad was wrong? Divorces happened. In all likelihood, Bernie would get over it, marry someone else, eventually. Even Vicky would adjust.

If Miranda and Chad loved each other...

The pain hit him with such intensity he could barely contain it. He paced through the house, fighting back primitive urges. To drag Miranda in here, and make her his, finally. To hunt down Chad and knock sense into the man.

Even as he imagined himself acting in these totally foreign, barbaric ways, a part of himself remained impassively observant. And from that strange corner of his brain came a new discovery.

So this is how a man is driven crazy.

MIRANDA HEADED back to Chatsworth, to her mother's. She entered the dark house on tiptoe and went to bed without even brushing her teeth.

Amazingly, she slept. Deeply, soundly, without any dreams. Four hours later, she awoke with a start.

And remembered the previous night.

Oh, God, what was she going to do?

It was five in the morning. She put on her house-coat and crept to the kitchen, where she made a cup of coffee. It would be dark for hours yet, but still she sat by the window and stared out at a view she couldn't see, mug cupped between her cold hands.

She lost track of time and couldn't say how much longer it was until her mother joined her. Annie sat in a chair across the table, barely a shadow in the dark house.

Almost indifferently, Miranda waited for a lecture. What could her mother accuse her of that she hadn't already blamed herself for?

Annie sighed. Then cleared her throat. "So you were the other woman. I guess I was blind not to see it earlier."

Okay, Mom. Let me have it. Miranda prepared herself for a maternal assault. But Annie remained calm.

"I guess there's no use me telling you what to do. You never listen anyway. You pretend to, but then you just do what you want in the end."

"I already know what I have to do, Mom."

And she did. She had all along, she realized. Right from the very beginning.

CHAD CALLED the house at ten in the morning. Annie had already left for church.

"We need to talk," he said, and she agreed.

She'd already showered and changed into jeans and a sweater. Now she grabbed her coat and car keys and headed out into the cold.

At the clubhouse, Chad opened the door wearing jeans and an untucked shirt. He hadn't shaved; his eyes were a little bloodshot. And still he managed to look gorgeous. He had a cup of vending machine coffee waiting.

She shook her head when he tried to hand it to her. "Honestly, I can't drink that stuff."

He set the drink on the table, and suddenly she felt very awkward. They were standing maybe four feet apart. Totally aware of each other, yet too self-conscious to hug or even smile.

"About last night..."

Miranda waited.

"I didn't sleep all night—I've been thinking..." He took her arm, led her to the office, where they both sat on the sofa. "Randy, when Bernie kicked me out, I thought it was the worst thing that ever happened to me. But lately I've been wondering if it might not be the best."

Even though they were now sitting, Miranda had the feeling of moving too fast. "Chad, tell me you haven't spoken to Bernie about the legal separation."

"I wanted to see you first. I've decided to talk to her tomorrow when I pick up Vic."

"But that's Christmas Eve!"

"I can't wait. I need to have that part of my life settled. So I can... So we can..."

He smiled weakly. "I'm having a hard time knowing how to put this. I behaved badly last night. I should never have put you in such an uncomfortable situation. But lately my feelings for you have been moving in a totally new direction. And I'm hoping that you—"

Again, words failed him. He took her hands and rubbed her palms with his thumbs. Closing her eyes, she could almost hear the music from last night. God help her. Why couldn't Chad have said these things when they were eighteen? Instead of now, when it was too late.

"Am I right about the two of us, Randy? It feels to me that I might be."

Once his words would have filled her with pleasure. She might have been able to fool herself into believing that she and Chad were being swept toward the fate that had been meant for them from the beginning: that they belonged together.

But nothing about this moment felt right now. She was far from deliriously happy. And she wasn't imagining the note of desperation in Chad's voice.

"The past couple of months have been crazy, Chad. Last night especially so... This isn't the time to talk about a future for you and me."

Panic flashed in Chad's green eyes. "When we

were dancing you said you'd always wanted to go out with me. I thought maybe...you love me.''

"Love is supposed to make you feel wonderful. But I don't feel wonderful. When I remember how we behaved last night, I feel guilty and ashamed.'' She examined his face. "And so do you, Chad! I can see it in your eyes.''

"Please don't overanalyze this.''

Chad didn't want to think too deeply about what he was doing. He was *afraid* to think too deeply. But that only made her more determined.

"Talk to me about Bernie, Chad. Tell me why you want to leave her.''

"You *know* why. We've discussed this to death. She's trying to control me. She wants to end our friendship...''

"Well, maybe she has a point about our friendship. Maybe she sensed that our feelings went deeper than we admitted.''

Chad frowned; color stained the high points on his cheeks. "The separation was *her* idea.''

"And maybe you're trying to get back at her for that—using me.'' She thought she'd been groping in the dark, but as soon as the words were out of her mouth, she realized they might be true.

Not that the feelings that had flared between her and Chad last night had been imagined or faked. But infatuation could disguise itself as love—especially in the beginning of a romantic relationship.

And if Chad had really loved her when they were younger, he'd have asked her out.

"Remember what the two of you were like in high school, Chad. You dated other women. But you always went back to Bernie. You loved her. I think you still do."

Dazed, Chad let go of her hands. He went to the window and stood quietly for a long time. Miranda's resolve was sorely tested. Why was she throwing this opportunity for love back in his face? Couldn't she give him a chance? Give them a chance?

Go over there and kiss him. Touch him. Make him want you now and you can have him forever.

Or maybe not. If he really loved her, would he be hesitating right now?

"I guess you could be right. I *do* love Bernie. But I also feel so *angry.*"

"At who, Chad? Who are you angry at?"

"Bernie, of course." He shook his head. "No. Not Bernie." He thought another minute, then his mouth twisted self-deprecatingly. "Me."

"If you stopped being so defensive, you might be able to concede she had reason to be upset with you, Chad. Instead of focusing on being in the right, why don't you try to remember what it was like to live with Bernie. Were you happy?"

"Yeah. Bernie's been a good wife. A good mother, too."

Miranda recalled something Warren had said. About Chad being the kind of guy who needed admiration. Chad would be happiest with a woman who made him the center of her universe, as Bernie had done.

"You can be happy with her again, Chad."

He stared at her for a long moment. Then finally shrugged. "Maybe you're right."

"I know I am. Go talk to her, Chad. You'll see."

"What about you? Will I still see you again?"

She ignored the long-term implications of that question. "I'm leaving town on Boxing Day."

He opened his arms. "Hug?"

As she let him draw her to his big, solid chest, Miranda knew that this was really the end. Whether Chad and Bernie worked things out or not, the friendship between her and Chad would never be the same.

CHAPTER NINETEEN

ON CHRISTMAS EVE, BERNIE finally bought a tree. Stanley at the garage tied the spruce onto the roof rack for her, but at home she had to drag the awkward thing off and into the house by herself.

Putting the tree into the stand, then stringing the lights, were normally Chad's jobs. This year, of course, she did them. And found them difficult, but maybe not so hard as she'd imagined they would be.

She stepped back to gain some perspective. The tree didn't look half bad. "Okay, Vicky. It's time to put on the ornaments."

"I'm in the middle of a show."

Earlier that morning Bernie had dug up the big cardboard box from storage and Vicky had already sorted through to find her favorites. She'd watched Bernie deal with the lights for a while, then had become bored and withdrew to watch TV.

Bernie decided she wasn't going to argue with her daughter about the Christmas tree. After closing the door to the entertainment room, she turned on a rack full of Christmas CDs, then went to the kitchen to make apple cider. By the time she came back with a bowl of homemade caramel popcorn Vicky sat cross-legged in front of the tree.

"Smaller than usual" was her only comment as Bernie set the goodies on a nearby table.

"I didn't think I could manage to get anything bigger into the house."

Bernie was amazed when her daughter rose from the floor and came to give her a hug.

"Poor Mommy," she said, squeezing tight.

Bernie knew this wasn't a good time to cry, even if she felt like it. Vicky had been different since the Chatsworth dance; she could only guess why. Maybe her grandmother had given Vicky a lecture. Or maybe she'd seen her father dancing with Miranda. Or maybe she plain felt guilty for having dissed her mother in front of a roomful of people.

They knelt together over the box of ornaments. "Here's the one you made in kindergarten." Bernie held up the small clay train. A cut-out where the driver would sit held a tiny picture of Vicky with her preschool pageboy.

"I can't believe I was ever that little."

"I can't believe you're already so tall." Almost at eye level. Vicky was going to take after her father's side where height was concerned.

Someone knocked at the front door, then came in before either of them had time to react. Chad stepped into the room. Bernie's stomach knotted with nerves. All day long she'd dreaded this moment. She needed her daughter's company, now more than ever. But she'd promised Chad he could have her—although he wasn't supposed to pick her up until four. "You're early."

Vicky didn't rush to her father as usual. Hands pressed behind her back, she scowled. "We're not finished with the tree. I don't want to go."

Chad glanced from his daughter, to Bernie, to the tree. After a few moments he shook his head. "It's crooked."

Before Bernie could defend herself, he crawled under the sweeping evergreen branches and began unscrewing the holder.

"Stand back and tell me when it's straight."

Now, here was a job she'd had many times before. She moved to the door by the dining room and slanted her head. "A little to the right. Too far… Now back a little. That's it."

Chad tightened the screws, then stood tall. "Better?"

"It looked okay the way it was."

Boy, Vicky was in a belligerent mood. Bernie wondered how Chad planned to celebrate Christmas Eve with his daughter. Dinner at the café? Or would they join Miranda and her mother?

A hot jealousy burned through her veins. She forced herself to think of Vicky. At least she had her daughter. That was the one bright spot in her life right now. As long as she focused on Vicky and what was best for her, Bernie would get through this. She had to.

"Can I speak with your mom a minute?"

Oh, God, here it was. Chad was going to ask for a divorce. Should she tell him she was willing to forget about the three conditions? Should she beg him to give her and their family a second chance?

As soon as their daughter left the room, Chad began to pace—a sure sign he was gearing up for a speech. Bernie sat on the edge of the sofa, hands resting on her knees. She wondered how Chad was planning to break this to her. Would he admit he loved Randy?

Or would he blame the break-up on her, on those three lousy conditions? Why had she ever handed down that stupid ultimatum?

Chad stopped in front of her, squatting so he could see her downcast face. Surprisingly, he took her hands, but even when he tugged at them, she wouldn't turn her eyes toward him.

She didn't think she was strong enough to actually see his expression when he told her he didn't love her anymore.

"Bernie?"

"Yeah?"

"I know I've been a bit of a shit—especially the night of the Christmas dance. But would you consider giving me another chance?"

Her head whipped up. He sounded sincere. He looked sincere. How could this be happening?

"I'll join the mixed league with you. Happily."

He was holding her hands so tightly that her fingers were numbing. She didn't care; she hardly noticed.

"And I'll give up my friendship with Randy."

He would? The memory of the two of them on the dance floor made his words very hard to believe. "Chad, I saw you dancing at the hall."

"A moment of infatuation."

She shook her head, disbelievingly.

"Okay, *strong* infatuation. Bernie, a man's head can be turned by a beautiful woman. You've got to admit, Randy's more beautiful than most. But the point is *nothing happened.* I didn't even kiss her— though I admit I tried."

This ought to be good news. What he was saying was so much better than what she'd imagined had been going on. Still, it hurt. Knowing that he'd wanted Randy was almost as bad as knowing that he'd been with her.

Almost.

"Randy was the one who reminded me what's important in my life. She reminded me of all the fights you and I had when we were dating. She told me that even though I dated other girls, I always went back to you."

Randy had said all this? Lord, she really was an impossible woman to hate.

"I always went back to you, Bernie. Because I love you. And about the baby."

Here Bernie caught her breath. More than anything else, she'd wanted another child. So had Chad at first.

As the years went by, though, he'd slowly given up on the dream. She hadn't. She'd demanded her doctor run tests to find out what was wrong. Once she'd been given a clear bill of health, she'd pleaded with Chad to make an appointment with his own physician.

But he'd refused. She supposed he was embarrassed. As if a man's sperm count truly did have anything to do with his *manliness.*

"I'll go see my doctor." Chad's complexion reddened.

"I'll take those damn tests. I do want to have another baby with you. I'm not sure why I fought the idea for so long."

She burst out crying. She just couldn't help it. Chad sat beside her on the sofa and wrapped his arms around her.

"I'm sorry, Bern, so sorry. About everything. I've been so bloody stubborn. Everything you asked for was reasonable. You even figured out my feelings for Miranda were getting out of hand before I did."

"Oh, Chad." She kissed his cheeks, his mouth. "I never expected to feel this happy again in my life. I was sure you were going to ask for a divorce."

"I came damn close to it," he admitted. "And it would have been the worst mistake of my life."

MIRANDA DIDN'T WANT TO attend church on Christmas morning, but her mother was going and it didn't seem right to stay home without her. She dressed somberly in black; the only color to her outfit were red mittens and a matching wool scarf.

She and her mother ate boiled eggs, toast and sectioned grapefruits, listening to a Christmas special on the radio.

"Should we open presents before church?" her mother asked.

"No. Later." Normally Miranda loved presents— the giving more than the receiving, and she'd been waiting a long time to see her mother's reaction to the beautiful blouse she'd bought months ago on Bloor Street in downtown Toronto.

But she was uncharacteristically despondent. This was, perhaps, the unhappiest she'd ever been at Christmas. Never had it bothered her more that she wasn't part of a couple, that she'd woken up alone, that no special gift from a man who loved her awaited her under the tree.

The ache in her heart only grew worse as she and her mother walked into the church vestibule together. So many families here, so many couples. Engulfed in her misery, she didn't notice at first that many of these people she'd known for most of her life were averting their gazes as she passed by.

Her mother paused to say hello to a lady from the bridge club. The woman responded warmly to Annie, but totally froze out Miranda's attempt to wish her merry Christmas.

The same happened when Annie stopped to greet other friends, other neighbors. Eventually Miranda grew tired of the rebuffs and told her mother, "I'll save us a seat. You come when you're ready."

The man already seated in the pew she chose—Stanley from the garage—drew his eyebrows together in a frown and scooted over several feet when she sat down.

Miranda sighed. So she was the local pariah today. Well, didn't that figure. Undoubtedly news of her scandalous dancing with a married man had traveled beyond those who had witnessed the event to the entire town.

Miranda supposed she should feel mortified. But she truly didn't care what anyone in this town thought of her. Only one man's opinion counted now and last night he'd made it clear he didn't want to see her. Was Warren, like everyone else in Chatsworth, outraged by her behavior at the dance?

To be so judgmental didn't seem like Warren. There had to be some other reason he hadn't wanted to see her. Maybe he'd grown tired of the video project. Maybe he'd grown tired of her.

Well, wasn't that a happy thought? Miranda drew her scarf close around her neck. It was cool in the church, although with this many people present—most of the pews were already full—it would soon warm up.

The murmuring of voices hushed. Miranda checked her watch. It was still ten minutes to ten. Why was everyone suddenly so quiet? Several people around her had turned to look toward the back of the church. She swiveled, as well.

The English family had arrived. Chad and Bernie holding hands, Vicky beside her father, grinning. Actually, they *all* had beaming smiles. Chad's mother waved from a pew on the other side of the church from Miranda.

Miranda swung back to face the front of the church. She pulled off her mittens and stuffed them into the pockets of her black pea coat.

Cautiously, the way a surgery patient might explore a fresh incision, she gauged her own reaction to seeing Chad reunited with his wife.

Strange.

She didn't feel particularly sad or jealous. Maybe a little wistful, but she'd felt that when she'd seen the Brownings come in with their troop of kids. Libby and Gibson had been the only two people to smile at her, although they hadn't stopped to talk.

The whispering started again. Louder than before, it seemed to Miranda. As if she'd suddenly developed radar, she felt glances coming at her from all directions. She kept her own gaze fixed to the front of the church, to the little boards where the morning hymns were posted.

She was reaching for the hymn book in the pocket of the pew in front of her, when her mother finally joined her.

Annie, back rigid, head angled forward proudly,

took her daughter's hand and pressed tightly. Miranda smiled.

"Thanks, Mom." From the corner of her eye, she saw someone else enter the church. A man, on his own. Warren Addison.

Something exploded inside her. Delight? No, joy! She couldn't stop smiling, even though he barely nodded at her before sitting in one of the pews at the back.

Maybe later, after the service, she'd have a chance to speak with him. If he was annoyed over some misunderstanding, she'd clear it up. Or if her behavior with Chad the other night had upset him, surely seeing the Englishes together would set his mind at rest on that score.

Either way, they'd talk and she'd persuade him—somehow—to see her again.

Miranda smiled through the entire service, despite the frowns and scowls leveled in her direction. During the slow procession after the service, which began with the front pews, she searched for signs of Warren at the back.

But he'd gone. Had slipped out without her noticing.

CHAPTER TWENTY

MIRANDA'S MOTHER LOVED the blouse. She tried it on immediately. The color suited her perfectly.

"Miranda, dear, it's lovely. Thank you so much." She gave her daughter a kiss, then went into the kitchen to check the turkey. Two of the women who belonged to the bridge club were coming for dinner, as was a widower who lived down the block.

Miranda was going to be celebrating Christmas with a bunch of geriatrics.

No less than she deserved. She'd been stupid about Chad. Not just at the dance, but earlier, forever. She'd thought she loved him, but the truth was, she didn't.

As Warren had tried to point out to her, they had few interests in common and totally incompatible lifestyles.

Thinking back, the only explanation that made sense to her was that she'd fixated on Chad because he was the one boy who hadn't chased her.

Then, when he'd married Bernie, he'd become even more unattainable. And her so-called passion for him had escalated.

What Miranda wanted to know now was why.

Why had she set herself up to be alone and loveless? Why had she longed for a married man she could never have?

Except two days ago, she'd discovered she *could* have him.

And she hadn't wanted him. Oh, she'd thought she was being noble, doing the right thing, saving his family. But the truth was, letting go of Chad had barely hurt at all.

What did hurt was Warren. Why was he avoiding her?

Maybe because you've spurned his every advance. Not to mention ignored his very perceptive advice about Chad.

Oh, she'd been a fool. Warren had been right when he'd accused her of using her feelings for Chad as an emotional shield. But she'd refused to listen. Worst of all she'd allowed herself to get so wrapped up in the fantasy of her and Chad that she hadn't even realized that something *real* was happening to her.

That she had fallen in love. With the most amazing man.

She had to find him, to tell him. She couldn't return to Toronto leaving so much unsaid between them.

What if his feelings for her had changed, or weren't as deep as she hoped? Remembering the blank expression on his face when his eyes had met hers at church this morning, she knew it was possible. That he'd just given up on her.

But she had to try.

So, after dinner dishes were done, she made an excuse to her mother. "You've got four for bridge, Mom. I'd just be in the way. I'm going for a drive."

Then, because her mother had been so super lately—not nagging her about the dance, standing by her when all the town was obviously against her—she told her the truth.

"I'm driving out to the Addisons'. I need to see Warren one more time before I leave."

"Be careful, darling" was all her mother said. Annie was already at the drawer where she kept her cards and her score pads.

One mile from Warren's family farm, Miranda remembered that he'd been invited to Christmas dinner at the Brownings'. Oh, well. If he wasn't home, she'd wait. Surely he wouldn't be too late.

Turned out, he wasn't. Pulling her Volkswagen into his lane, she saw his truck parked out front in the usual space. After retrieving the present she'd purchased during a spare moment in New York, she went to the back door and prayed he'd let her in.

On her second knock, he opened the door. He wore the sweater she'd bought him. And a scowl.

Her heart faltered, but she stepped inside, anyway. Stamped the snow off her boots and unbuttoned her coat.

"You're mad at me about something." She held out her present.

For an instant he paused, perplexed at her simultaneous offering and accusation. Finally, he took the gift and placed it on the table.

"Miranda, our work together is finished. Why are you here?"

"I'm going back to Toronto tomorrow."

"I know." He stood by the burning stove, arms crossed at his chest.

She removed her red mittens, surprised to feel wetness gathering in her eyes. "I guess I hoped that we'd developed a friendship, Warren." She took a deep breath for courage and met his gaze frankly, despite the tears that continued to accumulate. *Actually, something more than friendship. Much more.*

"Miranda, I'm sorry. But friendship is the last thing I have to offer you."

She gripped the back of one of his chairs, wishing he would sit down, instead of standing by the door as though he was waiting for her to leave.

Which he probably was.

"I know I deserve that. But I just want you to know that only one person matters anymore. You know I only care—"

"Stop." Warren's expression grew more distant, more disapproving. "If that person is Chad, then I'd rather not hear anything else you have to say. Seeing the Englishes together today must have been difficult for you. But you'll have to find another shoulder to cry on.''

''Warren—''

''I'm sure you noticed how happy they looked,'' Warren went on. ''If you can't care about that, then care about Vicky. She's just a kid. Do you really want to break up her home? Could you be happy, knowing the suffering you'd cause?''

Warren's speech almost floored her. But then she realized that of course he couldn't know what had happened since he'd left her and Chad at the Christmas dance. She'd seen him once, when Chad was holding her tight. And then the next time she'd looked for him, he'd been gone.

''I don't want Chad.''

''I saw the two of you dancing.''

''That was poor judgment.'' She sighed and moved to the opposite side of the table from Warren, by the window. One coffee mug, rinsed clean, sat in the sink.

''Warren, I guess I went a little crazy that night. I was pretending to be eighteen again, living out my favorite fantasy. And Chad—he was being stupid, forgetting that the woman he loved, the woman he'd *always* loved, was the woman he already had.''

''It almost killed Bernie, seeing you two together like that.''

She lowered her head. She had some real regrets here. This was the biggest. ''I'm sorry, Warren. I really am sorry about that.''

Emotions shifted in Warren's dark-gray eyes. He took a step toward her, then stopped. "For a long time I thought your feelings for Chad were mostly illusions. Lately, though, I'd started to wonder if I was deceiving myself. That you might love him after all."

"I thought I did. But I realize now that I don't. He isn't the man for me."

In the silence, she heard logs crackling as they burned, a chair scrape against the floor as he moved it aside so that it no longer stood between them.

"Do you care?" she asked. He stood in front of her now, not touching her, but close, very close.

"Tell me that you care, Warren. That I'm not making a total fool of myself right now."

She put her hands on his chest, leaned in toward him. Gently she smoothed hair back from his face, then caressed the curved line of his jaw. "I've been so mixed-up. But now everything is clear. I love you, Warren."

On his face she saw disbelief, pain, then finally, faintly...hope.

"You're so beautiful."

She flinched.

"I'm talking about on the inside. How could I not adore you? Every day I spend with you I become even more hopelessly ensnared."

"Oh, Warren—I worried I was too late. That I'd destroyed my chances with you."

"I've been patient," he agreed. "But no more."

She shivered in front of his gaze, knowing that he was mentally undressing her, knowing that soon he wouldn't have to.

"I have to warn you," she said. "I have this thing about your hands. I need them to touch me—everywhere."

"That will be my pleasure." He brushed a finger against the soft curve above her earlobe. "These earrings. I always wondered who gave them to you. Was it a man?"

She nodded.

"You don't know how jealous that makes me. You wear them all the time."

"They were from my father, for my sixteenth birthday. Usually Mom picked out all my gifts. It was his first real present to me, and the last. He left us a few weeks after that."

She'd never forget her father standing stiffly in the doorway to her bedroom, handing her the box at arm's length. "You're a lady now, Miranda."

With hindsight, Miranda realized that he'd considered her grown. Finished. That he could leave with a clear conscience.

"You ever hear from him?"

"No."

He brushed the hair off her forehead, ran his hands along the side of her face. "I'm never going to leave you. Or stop loving you."

Part of her believed him, totally. And yet, this was a world where marriages were strained, many to the breaking point, every single day. A world where fathers deserted daughters, where even mothers held out conditions for their love.

"How can you sound so sure?"

"Because I've always loved you, Miranda. And I always will. I wrote my first book for you. And I'll write every book that follows for you, too."

Finally, he pressed his mouth to hers, and Miranda felt her entire being dissolve under his kiss. Oh, if they'd only done this sooner. Then she would have known where she belonged.

"Oh, Warren..." Once again, she felt the strange sensation of melting—only it wasn't just happening to her legs this time, but to her heart, as well. Glancing at the clock above the stove, she saw that it wasn't yet midnight, it was still December 25.

Just as she'd promised, it had happened. Bernie and Chad were reunited. As for her and Warren, they were together by Christmas, too.

The way they were always meant to be.

The wait is over!

New York Times bestselling author

HEATHER GRAHAM'S

Civil War trilogy featuring the indomitable Slater brothers is back by popular demand!

It began with DARK STRANGER and continues in November 2002 with

RIDES A HERO

The war was over but, embittered by the conflict, Shannon McCahy and Malachi Slater still fought a raging battle of wills all their own. A Yankee whose only solace was the land she had struggled to save, Shannon hated the hot-tempered soldier, a rebel on the run who stood for all she had come to despise.

Don't miss the opportunity to revisit these classic tales of brothers who rediscover the importance of loyalty, family ties…and love!

HARLEQUIN®
Makes any time special ®

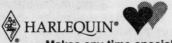

HARLEQUIN *Super*ROMANCE®

presents a compelling family drama—
an exciting new trilogy
by popular author Debra Salonen

THOSE
SULLIVAN
SISTERS

Jenny, Andrea and Kristin Sullivan are much more
than sisters—*they're triplets!* Growing up as one of
a threesome meant life was never lonely...or dull.

Now they're adults—with separate lives, loves,
dreams and secrets. But underneath everything that
keeps them apart is the bond that holds them together.

MY HUSBAND, MY BABIES
(Jenny's story)
available December 2002

WITHOUT A PAST
(Andi's story)
available January 2003

THE COMEBACK GIRL
(Kristin's story)
available February 2003

HARLEQUIN®
*M*akes any time special ®

Visit us at www.eHarlequin.com

HSRTSS